'An amazing acc ...nages emerge through ... self-loathing. There ... ...e at work behind this ...

'An honest, harro... ...iald [Glasgow]

'Eye-opening . . . a Hollywood script waiting to happen' *Scotsman*

'Close under the skin of Wang's narrative lies adroit political analysis' *Daily Telegraph*

'An engaging insight into two opposing cultures' *Big Issue*

'Lili is a coming-of-age novel, not just of a woman but also of a country' *Washington Post Book World*

'A love story with an edge' *Company*

'By turns political and personal, moving and outraged . . . highly recommended to anyone who enjoyed Amy Tan and Jung Chan, but wanted a touch of Sid Vicious as well' *Ham & High*

'Wang's triumph is in her vigorous portrayal of alienated young people and dignified older people . . . this is the stuff of great literature' *Seattle Times*

'Beautifully honest . . . a forceful and compelling story by a remarkable young woman hailed as a striking new voice in the literary world' *Cambridge Evening News*

'Compelling . . . it is disconcerting to realise that life is still going on around you . . . a powerful evocation of modern China' *Marie Claire* [Book of the Month]

Lili

Annie Wang was born in 1972 and grew up in Beijing. She moved to the United States in 1993 and graduated from the University of California, Berkeley, in 1996. She worked in the *Washington Post*'s Beijing bureau before becoming a contract interpreter for the US State Department. She has published several books in China; this is her first book written in English.

A NOVEL OF TIANANMEN

ANNIE WANG

PICADOR

First published 2001 by Pantheon Books,
a division of Random House, Inc., New York

First published in Great Britain 2001 by Macmillan

This paperback edition published 2001 by Picador
an imprint of Pan Macmillan Ltd
Pan Macmillan, 20 New Wharf Road, London N1 9RR
Basingstoke and Oxford
Associated companies throughout the world
www.panmacmillan.com

ISBN 0 330 41151 9

A CIP catalogue record for this book is available from
the British Library.

Printed and bound in Great Britain by
Mackays of Chatham plc, Chatham, Kent

FOR MY FAMILY,
WITH MUCH LOVE

Lili

ONE

Beijing always launches a crackdown on crime just before the annual convention of the national Communist Party.

Before my buddies and I can get wind of it, we are busted at Chou-Chou's. Chou-Chou is the son of two diplomats who work in Sydney; their house has become our hangout. We are thrown in jail. Eight of us. I am booked on charges of having a corrupt lifestyle and hooliganism, and sentenced to three months of rehabilitation through labor. There is no trial.

Each morning we learn revolutionary songs while marching in the jail's courtyard. During the day we make matchboxes. We have to work ten or twelve hours a day. But that's better than attending political study sessions: at least we don't have to confess or lie.

There is a guard named Erniu. She is in her late forties or early fifties, a short-tempered spinster who has probably just reached menopause. Her job is to conduct "thought reform" on female inmates. Liu Hulan will be our role model. Liu Hulan was beheaded during the Civil War because she refused to disclose Communist Party secrets.

"Look at Liu Hulan, she was so young, yet she had the courage to die for her beliefs. What revolutionary consciousness she has at only fifteen! Don't you feel ashamed of yourselves? Look at yourselves, a bunch of female hooligans, a pack of scumbags! Our party gives you enough to eat and keep you warm, but you still can't keep your pants on!"

Erniu's words don't bother me. Mama says that my skin is thicker than the city wall.

Erniu wants us to write reports about one another's behavior. Those who want to buy her favor report every small thing to her.

"I suppose you all know why you're here behind bars, right?" She looks at us seated in a circle around her.

"Yes," we all answer at the top of our lungs.

"That's good." She walks among us, points at one of us, Ding Ding, and asks, "Tell me, why are you here?"

Ding Ding recites, "I'm here to absolve myself of and atone for my past misbehavior, get rid of my dirty and unhealthy thoughts, and become a new woman for the new age."

Erniu nods with satisfaction and then raises her voice, saying, "You're here because you are wanton. Time spent here doing labor should clear your minds of filth. Yet I hear that one of you just cannot get rid of her wanton thoughts. I am told she likes to play with herself almost every night.

4

She even uses corncobs." Erniu is staring at the country girl, Chunni. Chunni is in jail because she was caught fucking the master of the house where she worked as a nanny. His wife reported them to the police. The man was sentenced to ten years in prison.

Chunni doesn't wash, and she smells. Her feet smell like soy sauce. She steals little things like hairpins or key chains from others. Once she even used her cellmate's toothbrush to brush her teeth.

Chunni lowers her head, her whole body trembling. I see bean-size drops of water on the floor. It's a hot day. I can't tell whether they're tears or sweat. All of us have this naive look in our eyes, as if none of *us* had ever played with herself.

"Shall we punish her?" Erniu asks.

"Yes," we yell.

"Suggestions are welcome." Erniu sits back and sips tea from her old enamel mug. There's an illustration of a scene from an erotic novel, *A Dream of Red Mansions,* on the side of the mug.

Inmates raise their hands.

"Since she has such excessive energy, she should have a higher matchbox quota."

"She should carry thermoses of hot water for the guards."

"She should sweep the floors as well as making matchboxes."

I keep silent. I can't help Chunni, nor do I want to. She's doomed. But I can't throw stones at someone who's drowning in a well. I don't want my conscience to be eaten by dogs.

Chunni is transferred; nothing more is heard of her. She

isn't the only one Erniu picks on. Erniu always looks for targets on whom to vent her sexual frustration. She makes sure that our hair is short enough and that we wear plain uniforms all the time.

New girls are also unlucky. The day Xiu Xiu arrives, Erniu slaps her face at lunchtime in front of everyone and snarls, "Do you know where you are, you whore? How dare you wear lipstick? Do you intend to poison more revolutionary comrades even in jail? You cheap, evil slut!"

Xiu Xiu blushes, bites her lower lip, opens her mouth, and musters, "The color of my lips is natural. I've never used lipstick."

Erniu slaps the girl's face again, on the same side. Xiu Xiu's cheek turns puffy, like a red bean pancake.

"Talking back to me, are you? Just ask everyone here, who dares do this to me?" Erniu turns to the rest of us. "There is no way out unless you wash off your old faces and become new women."

Erniu is killing chickens to intimidate monkeys. We listen with heads lowered and finish our lunch quickly and in silence.

The red-lipped girl is sent to a solitary cell, forced to work sixteen hours a day, and not allowed to go out to exercise.

By keeping my distance, I avoid trouble. I am released from jail on my twenty-fourth birthday. Standing outside in the noonday sun, I stare at my dwarfed shadow as if it were a distant relative. My eyes hurt from the dizzying sunlight that I had forgotten while locked up in a small cell.

My parents don't come to pick me up. They have never visited me during my incarceration, for I have dishonored our ancestors.

The bus ride home takes an entire day. I have nothing to eat. I have no money. My one possession is a small, worn military bag stuffed with underwear. I am not sure if I can call my parents' place home. They will not welcome me there, but it is the only place I can go. I am dying to have a real meal and wash myself. In the last ninety days I have taken only one shower, with forty-nine other women, all of us fighting for three showerheads. I stink to myself.

On the bus, a middle-aged woman and a clean-cut, pale man argue endlessly. The woman fiercely accuses the man of bothering her by constantly touching her rear end. She shouts at him, "What do you think you're doing, you little son of a whore? Don't even think about it. Save your stinking hands for your mother."

The man blushes and retorts, "Can't you see how crowded this bus is? Let me tell you, you fat old smelly cunt, I wouldn't give a shit if you dropped dead." Their feuding breaks up the trip's monotony. No one stops them.

Walking from the bus stop near my parents' home, I am greeted by no neighbors, except retarded Little Yue. She eagerly calls my name, her mouth drooling. Everyone else acts as if I didn't exist. I knock, and Papa opens the door and says, "Lili, here you are." He doesn't say anything more because my mother is staring at him, silently restraining him. Papa prepares an unusually delicious dinner later, but I eat it in silence. My parents watch TV in their bedroom.

In ancient China a husband was free to abandon his wife on their wedding night if he found out she wasn't a virgin. Widows were glorified for committing suicide to follow their dead husbands. There were three obediences and four virtues that women had to practice. I don't remember what the four virtues were, but the three obediences stated that before marriage the woman was to obey her father; after marriage she was to obey her husband; and finally, after the death of her husband, she was to obey her son.

The Communist Party is very proud of its role in liberating Chinese women from such ancient customs. But a woman's private life is still not her own. Those who lose their virginity before marriage are still spat upon. The only difference between feudal times and our own is that back then "bad women" were seen as amoral fox spirits, whereas now they are labeled corrupt bourgeois.

My mother likes to lecture me: "*Ren huo lian, shu huo pi*—'A man lives for his face, and a tree lives for its bark.' The most important thing for a girl is her reputation."

I am not a virgin. No decent family will accept me as a daughter-in-law. Nor does the Communist Party pin its hopes for the next generation of revolutionaries on women like me. With no foothold in the old world and none in the new, I am an object of contempt.

My father collects job postings and piles them neatly on my desk.

"Lili, if you have time, take a look at those job announcements," he says, almost begging.

His efforts are useless. It's simple: the government assigns all the jobs, and if one doesn't have the right connections, it is almost impossible to get a job. How can my father be so naive about the system after living under the red flag for thirty years? The Red Guard must have beaten his senses as well as his head.

The job postings solicit girls who are between eighteen

and twenty-eight and have "acceptable facial features" and well-proportioned legs. A bribe is expected, and that isn't all. I bet old Mao would have been surprised by the sexual appetites of his revolutionary disciples; or maybe he wouldn't. My friend Yuan says Mao was hungry himself.

Before the Cultural Revolution, people feared having overseas relatives; now everyone wants to have them, along with one or two American- or Japanese-made products at home.

City girls look for jobs as flight attendants or as desk clerks or waitresses at expensive hotels. These positions provide clean bathrooms with soft toilet paper and flush toilets, as well as air conditioning in the summer, equal to getting minister-level treatment.

Clerks in foreign hotels and flight attendants on foreign airlines are paid double or triple the salaries of my college-professor parents. Service workers in foreign-related jobs have access to both enviable imported commodities and rich foreigners—potential husbands. From time to time I hear rumors that someone who used to live at the poorer end of our alley has married some stinking-rich "foreign devil" whom she served in a hotel or on an airplane.

My parents have never flown in their lives. They can't buy airplane tickets because they are not Communist Party members. During the Cultural Revolution there were many classes of enemies, including landlords, rightists, traitors, and counterrevolutionaries. The intellectuals were ranked ninth among these enemies. Being "stinky number 9s," my parents were politically mistrusted.

My mother wants me to be a flight attendant. She tells

9

me, "Lili, you're not bad-looking, but you always use your good looks to do stupid things. This time, take advantage of your appearance and apply for this job. Look, it says here"—she points to the newspaper—"that the applicants should have Beijing residency and should be taller than five-four, with long legs and big eyes. You're taller than five-four. Not many Chinese girls can meet that requirement. Your legs aren't short, your eyes aren't small . . . you can serve the people and at the same time buy air tickets for us at a discount, or even let us fly for free."

My mother knows nothing about what girls without connections have to do to get jobs. She is stupid enough to believe everything she reads in the newspaper.

"Will people want to be served by a woman who has a police record? Won't they be afraid that someone like me would hijack them to Taiwan?" I taunt her.

My attitude upsets her, but she will not give up. She is Chinese; she doesn't give up easily.

I grew up in a culture where our folks' favorite pastime was to get together and show off their children. Every day after dinner, neighbors would sit around in the courtyard and parade their sons and daughters.

"My little Ming has been admitted to the best college."

"My big Hong is the first Communist Party member in his school."

My parents taught me to play the violin when I was three. My mother pinned her ambition on me. She fantasized that I would become a female Chinese Mozart. She used to sit with the neighbors almost every evening, asking about the progress of their kids' music lessons. She always made sure I was ahead of the others. Yet now I, her only child, her only hope, have become an unemployable good-for-nothing with a police record, a disgrace, a single woman without a decent boyfriend.

Mama no longer joins the after-dinner contest. She avoids talking about me; even my name is an embarrassment for her. The youngest schoolboy knows that it is a synonym for "fox spirit."

The neighbors never forget to gloat over my pushy mother's shame. It's their new pastime. They detest me because I already enjoy their marital privilege. I love to upset those old Confucians.

Two obstacles prevent my parents from joining the Party. The first is my mother's mother. Papa has told me pieces of stories about her when Mama wasn't around. Grandma comes from a wealthy and educated family in old Shanghai and can play the piano and the flute, speak English and French, and recite excerpts of Shakespeare's plays. As a young woman, Grandma led a luxurious life and was very *fengliu* before marriage. Papa has never elaborated on the *fengliu* part, but I guess it means she had many boyfriends, or affairs.

Grandma fell in love with a married man and ran away with him. But the man later abandoned her. She returned to her parents and soon got married. She married three times and was widowed three times. Her husbands were all rich and died young, including my own grandpa. During the Cultural Revolution, Grandma's early private life in Shanghai was dug up by thought reformers and Red Guards. Grandma was labeled a "smelly, corrupt, capitalist fox spirit" and became an enemy of the people and a target of the Proletariat Dictatorship. Her background killed her daughter's "red" future.

The second obstacle was my mother's half brother, Yin, Grandma's child with her first husband. Uncle Yin was sent to missionary schools as a boy and later married an American missionary's daughter. They fled to the United States in 1949. During the Cultural Revolution, because of her half brother's background, my mother was branded an "American spy." My parents were sent off to be reeducated in a rural community called Monkey Village. There my mother suffered a nervous breakdown and vowed that she would never join the Party.

After the Cultural Revolution, intellectuals like my parents were admitted to the revolutionary class again. Although they earn low salaries, they are respected for being professors. Knowledge is no longer poison.

Uncle Yin was allowed to return. In exchange for helping with the central government's new open-door policy, he has been elevated to the status of honored guest. The government calls him a "patriotic overseas Chinese."

Yin's son, my cousin "Johnny Cardiac," is a star in China, a pop singer. Johnny sings off-key, but his exotic European look and the cute way he speaks Chinese with an American accent thrill millions of schoolgirls. A ticket to one of his concerts costs an average worker a full month's salary.

Chinese film studios, TV stations, and advertising companies all want him. He is an actor, a model, a TV program host, and a DJ, but above all he is a teenage idol, outshining all the native pop stars.

Uncle Yin is my mother's only connection.

"One of my students tells me that I'm outdated. He says

connection is the most important thing nowadays. I almost forgot about my brother, Yin—he has lots of networks," Mama says to Papa excitedly.

My parents invite Uncle Yin's family out for dinner at a five-star hotel. It costs them two months' salary.

As college teachers, my parents are at the bottom of the financial pyramid. They are so frugal that for them, buying a watch is as painful as trying to have a shit is for my constipated grandma. Yet they are willing to pay for dinner at a fancy restaurant that ordinary citizens wouldn't even dare enter. Will Mama ever give up the hope that I can achieve something and become somebody, somebody that others can envy?

I decide to go along because I want to use the restroom in the hotel. I have heard that bathrooms in five-star hotels smell better than family kitchens.

Uncle Yin comes to dinner with his Caucasian wife, Sara, his celebrity son, Johnny, and a government VIP named Dong.

"Brother Yin, we haven't seen each other for so long! I almost didn't recognize you. You've become so fashionable! This must be my sister-in-law, Sao-Rao. Sao-Rao, how do you do!" My mother says "how do you do" in English.

Uncle Yin shakes hands with my parents and says to my mother, "Sister, you must have suffered a lot for having a U.S.-citizen brother like me. I hope we can do something to make it up to you. I have brought along Dong. He is the director of the personnel department for Xinan Airlines."

Dong looks at me and smiles. "This must be Lili! Yin, look at your niece, isn't she pretty? Johnny is handsome and Lili is pretty—your family has good blood!"

I try to avoid looking at his puffy, pockmarked face.

My parents grovel in front of Dong as if they were his grandchildren.

"Mr. Dong, please be seated here. This chair is for the most important person." My mother calls Dong "Mr. Dong" rather than the more commonly used "Comrade Dong" to show that she is up-to-date.

Uncle Yin shakes hands with me and says to my mother, "Lili is really tall. I remember she was born in the Great Famine. Am I wrong?"

"No. You have a good memory. She was born in nineteen sixty."

"It's amazing that she could grow so tall without enough food to eat," Uncle Yin comments.

"We have you to thank for this," Mama says eagerly. "During the famine, you asked a friend of yours in Singapore to send us powdered milk. Remember that? It saved our Lili."

"Oh, I had almost forgotten that." Uncle Yin waves his hand.

Mama presents Aunt Sara with a pair of carved ivory fans as the first-meeting gift. Aunt Sara thanks Mama in Chinese, polite and distant at the same time. Watching her relaxed, assured, and graceful manner, I feel as if *we* are the timid foreign guests in *her* country.

Uncle Yin introduces my cousin Johnny. "Here is my son, the rebel. We wanted him to study business in school, but he insisted that he was an artist. What does an artist know how to do except starve to death? I asked. But he has proved to us that he can make money as a musical artist in China. What can we say?"

Has Uncle Yin forgotten that we are a family of musicians? Maybe not. Is he telling us we're poor?

Johnny shakes hands with my parents and me. "Sister Lili, I've never dated any Asians back in the States. I hope I'm lucky enough to go out with a beautiful Asian woman like you here in China."

At the table Mama sits on one side, next to Aunt Sara and then Uncle Yin. I sit on the other, next to Johnny and Papa. Dong sits between Mama and Papa.

Aunt Sara is thirteen years older than my mother, but she looks half her age. In the States she must go to beauty salons all the time and use Western cosmetics; here they are locked up in Friendship Stores' show windows, reserved exclusively for customers from Hong Kong, Macao, and Taiwan. It is hard to imagine that Mama used to be the most beautiful "flower" of her college. She is wearing a cheap blouse that is half transparent, a scarf that is poorly dyed and doesn't match the color of her clothes. Her hair is as dry as hay.

Aunt Sara smokes a thin cigar, and the mixed smells of the smoke and her perfume enchant me; they represent America. She doesn't speak much Chinese, so most of the time she just smiles at us.

I notice two things about Cousin Johnny: his pierced nose and his ponytail. Chinese men don't have this "advanced" fashion sense. Some radical Chinese artists wear military boots to distinguish themselves from their more conventional counterparts, but Cardiac is Made-in-the-USA from top to bottom.

Although he never takes off his sunglasses during the whole meal—a security precaution, according to him—waitresses in the restaurant still recognize him.

"I remember on your CD cover, your hair was blond. How come it's black now?" one asks.

"I dyed it blond."

"So not all Americans are blond?" another girl says.

"Of course not. Hispanic Americans, Asian Americans, African Americans, and even some white Americans, like Italians, have black hair. Don't you know that the United States is a melting pot?" Johnny explains while autographing a white handkerchief belonging to one of the girls. His signature looks like a flying dragon.

"Wow, you wear earrings!" a tall teenage waitress exclaims. "Do many American guys wear earrings?"

"Some do."

"Are they all homosexual? I've heard that American men who wear earrings are 'rabbits,' " the middle-aged woman asks boldly.

"What? You mean only gay men are supposed to wear earrings?" Johnny laughs. "No, no, no, no, no . . . I don't know what your government says about our United States. It's ridiculous." Then he translates the woman's question into English for his mother. Aunt Sara laughs, her teeth glistening white.

"Hey, look at the hair on his arms—it's so long and curly."

"His voice is so beautiful."

"His nose is so straight and thin."

"His legs are so long."

He turns to us and shrugs. "Sorry about this," he says. I cannot tell if he is being genuine.

"No problem at all. We're lucky to be able to watch the news live!" I reply. Johnny doesn't catch my cynicism.

"Sometimes one has to pay for being a celebrity. I wish people could just treat me like an ordinary guy."

After signing autographs, Johnny stands up and stretches.

He turns to my parents and says, "I'm sorry, but I'd better be going now—I've got another appointment this evening. Nowdays everyone wants a piece of me. It's been so nice to meet you and your daughter." He extends his hand to my mother.

We haven't begun dinner because we've been waiting for him to finish signing his stupid autographs, and now he's leaving!

"Nice to meet *you*. We're proud of you, Johnny. Our Lili should take you as her model!" Mama says.

Johnny turns to me. "Lili, so nice to have met you, too! I'd like your family to come visit us in California someday. I'll show you my horses, and we can go riding together."

"Thank you for the invitation," I reply. I am not in the least interested. When my parents were sent off to work in Monkey Village, horses were the only means of transportation available. As a child, I rode ponies to fairs and watched horses screw each other in the spring. Horses only remind me of poverty and peasant life.

Once Johnny leaves, the conversation turns into a hard-nosed negotiation. Each party has its agenda: Mama wants Dong to offer me a job at the airline, while Dong needs Uncle Yin to sponsor his kid, who recently graduated from college and now hopes to study in America. Uncle Yin and Aunt Sara don't mind doing us this favor, since then they won't owe us anything more.

"What do you think of our Lili?" my mother keeps asking Dong.

"She has good qualities, but you must realize that the competition for such jobs is stiff. Of course, I want to be of help. She reminds me of my own daughter. My daughter is called Lala; she's about Lili's age. She graduated from college last year and wants me to help her study abroad. But I keep telling her I don't know anyone except old Yin here."

Uncle Yin asks Dong, "Has Lala taken the TOEFL and GRE tests yet?"

"Yes, and her scores were not bad, I'm told."

"Give me her documents. I'll be happy to help her apply to Stanford and Berkeley."

No sooner has Uncle Yin agreed to Dong's terms than Dong promises to comply with Mama's request. My mother's face lights up; she says to me excitedly, "You're so lucky that Mr. Dong likes you. You should tell him how grateful you are."

What makes her so sure I am? Yes, I want a job, any job, so that I can get out of this dead-end life. Perhaps I can even fulfill a small piece of my dreams—say, moving away from my parents' home and living by myself. But getting a job means nothing to me if it costs my parents their dignity. I thank Dong and Uncle Yin and tell them I have a headache. I leave. I forget to use the hotel bathroom.

On my way home I imagine how my upset my mother will be at having to deal with Uncle Yin, Aunt Sara, Dong, and all those unfinished gourmet dishes. This is the first time my mother and her brother have seen each other in thirty-five years. It is the perfect opportunity for my parents to vomit out their bitter waters of suffering. Will my mother tell about how my father was beaten up just because she was related to Uncle Yin? Will they blurt out how in their one-room shanty they quietly had sex in the middle of the night, trying not to wake up their young daughter, who was sleeping only a meter away? Will their sad stories make Uncle Yin feel more sympathetic, make him give them money? Overseas relatives like to give out things to Chinese relatives. They know we are poor and have lived like rats.

Yes, we are poor and have lived like rats, but can Uncle Yin play Bach and Paganini as well as my parents? I don't need pity! As I walk along the street by myself, I feel the soft wind blowing through my hair. A tear rolls down my face. I am surprised at myself. What's wrong with you, Lili? I think. Maybe it's just PMS.

My mother thinks that her inviting Uncle Yin and his family to dinner will prove her unconditional love for her daughter, her martyrdom for me, and that it will somehow compel me to take responsibility for and correct my past "misbehavior." None of her educational strategies—beating, begging, or domestic cold wars—has worked on me. Will she never give up?

I don't care what my parents think of me.

TWO

The highest stage of Taoism is the "Great Void," which basically means not doing anything. I regard being unemployed as a way of practicing the Great Void.

I get up each morning after my parents have left and take a long bath. I love to lock myself in the small, steamy bathroom; hiding behind its door makes me feel free and daring. It was in the bathroom that I first examined my most intimate parts, explored who I wanted to be, studied my menstrual blood, read handwritten copies of *Mona's Memoir* and other forbidden books, including *Anna Karenina,* and gave myself to a teenage thug. Its small space allows me to face myself: nude, vulnerable, and primitive. The hot, damp air somehow turns me on in ways that I have anticipated but don't understand.

After my bath I walk all around the apartment naked, with a cucumber facial mask that I have made covering my face and neck. Still naked, I prepare lunch and dinner, just like any ordinary housewife. While I cook, I hum revolutionary songs that I learned in jail.

In the late afternoon I put on some clothes and cheap makeup and go out, carrying a women's magazine under my arm. I read in a small park, sitting with the old, retired workers and their bird cages; I loiter in front of newspaper stands, killing time by reading tabloid news and gossip; sometimes I go to see a movie. But most often I visit my girlfriend Amei.

Amei works the night shift in a hospital. Her husband, Jun, is a representative for a big Chinese company in Europe. He has been working abroad for years. The company allows him to come home for forty days out of every year. People envy Amei because Jun can buy her French perfume and Swiss watches. She teasingly calls herself a widow, but she is a faithful wife.

We met five years ago in a public bathhouse. Amei and I were lying next to each other, each having a back rub. Amei has a husky, low-pitched voice that I admire. It sounds sexy and sophisticated compared to my soft, high-pitched, girly voice.

We became best friends. One day she told me that she was going to marry Jun, the son of a high-ranking official. Jun was once my boyfriend. Amei knows about my past with him but holds no grudges.

Jun is a meek, introverted, well-mannered man. He's a good husband, and Amei deserves him.

Jun's mother is a *guan taitai,* the wife of an important official. She likes to show her authority over others all the time. When Jun and I dated, she did not know how to deal with me at first. I had a bad reputation for hanging out with gang members. Jun's mother was scared to death that I would marry into her noble family. It never occurred to her that I might not want to be her daughter-in-law.

She ordered her husband's secretary to send a letter to my parents' work unit. In the letter she stated that I was a street hooligan and could only be a bad influence on her son. To maintain the purity of the Communist Party, I must leave her family alone. In a political study meeting, the dean of my parents' department read the letter aloud. My parents' colleagues heard it and laughed behind their backs. My mother screamed at me for a month and then didn't talk to me for three more months.

I broke up with Jun, but not because of the pressure; I just lost interest.

As the only son of an important official, and a college student, Jun was not lacking in female admirers. But he was obsessed with me for some reason. I remember his saying, "I like you because you're different." After we broke up, he twice tried to kill himself.

I am a quiet woman. Amei isn't talkative, either. That is why I feel so close to her. Words are unnecessary. We share feelings of peace and relaxation while we sip tea like two old sages.

I seldom care strongly about anyone or anything, but I feel a deep love for Amei. We shop together, share food and clothing, and work together on dresses we have bought. With her I am natural and simple because she does not ask nosy, stupid questions. There is time to dream because she does not bother trying to engage me in long talks. There is no past and no future because she cares only about living in the present.

Some of my old pals visit me after learning that I am out of jail. My pals are long-haired punks without legal Beijing residency; workers between jobs whose personnel files will not record their political backgrounds; and *getihu,* street traders without "an iron rice bowl" (that is, the security of a job in a state-run factory, which would probably reject them because of their criminal records). Newspapers like to call people like them *shehui zhazi,* meaning the scrapings from the bottom of the social barrel.

But I am tired of my empty life. At night I can't fall asleep. I use the *People's Daily* as a sleeping pill. I dream, but I can hardly remember my dreams. I wish I could remember them so that I could experience two totally different worlds without having to fantasize. I need something more in my life, though I am not sure what it may be.

I don't know what to do. I fumble through my closet and pick up my old erhu, the Chinese violin that I stopped playing years ago. After wiping off the dust, I try to pluck a sound out of it with my finger. The sound is the cry of an ancient concubine, abandoned by her king for ages. I am the king who has dumped my erhu concubine. But she has waited patiently for my return.

That night in the moonlight, I swear to Old Grandpa Heaven that I will get a job.

Two weeks later I begin to play the erhu at the Rose Café in the Great Wall Hotel. This job requires no background check, no connections. Rich customers eat, drink, talk, and read here, while I play background music to entertain them. My mother doesn't like the idea of my playing music in a hotel café. Serious musicians like her are stubborn: they think music is an art form, not a service, and believe that "it is a small thing for an intellectual to die from hunger, but a big thing for him to lose his pride."

"Your papa and I taught you music when you were young because we wanted you to be a professional soloist, not to play in a restaurant," Mother scolds. I'm insulting the holiness of the ancient tradition of music.

In ancient times musicians played music to entertain emperors; it's nothing new. But I'm glad that serious musicians will not take this kind of job. It is an undesirable job, and I am an undesirable musician. It is a suitable position.

I love my job. The pay is decent, and the environment is pleasant. I enjoy seeing the harmony and pleasure in customers' faces when they listen to my music. It feels as if they were listening to me in a concert hall.

There is a new fashionable social class in Beijing called White-Collar Young Ladies. These ladies are professional, chic, and well trained; they work in air-conditioned offices. Although my neighbors still think I am trash, I fantasize that I am a White-Collar Young Lady. I have a skill, and I do something that people find useful.

Foreign tourists try to tip me. I repeat with pride what my manager has told me: "Thank you, but our socialist country doesn't accept tips." That's the only English I know.

THREE

My childhood friend Yuan is a poet, a freelance writer. Since 1981 he hasn't been allowed to publish articles in China. Two years ago he started a travel company. Now he is a *wan-yuan-hu,* a ten-thousand-yuan-a-year fat cat.

One day he drops by my parents' apartment. We haven't seen each other in almost a year. In a small restaurant nearby we have some fried peanuts and beer. He asks me how I survived my imprisonment. I warn him, "If you keep saying things the government doesn't like, you'll end up there sooner or later. Remember to bring enough toilet paper with you!"

He laughs. "Don't worry about me. Money is my priority. Karl Marx said, 'Economy is the foundation of super-structure.' Poverty and a free society don't go hand in hand.

We cannot expect a bunch of starving peasants to build a civilized political system."

After several drinks we start to indulge in the Beijinger's favorite pastime, *kan-da-shan,* "shooting the breeze." He babbles on and on, talking about everything from the days when we were toddlers wearing split-seat pants to the current situations in the Middle East and Africa.

Like many Beijingers, Yuan never tires of analyzing the world situation, as if he were Henry Kissinger. He calls America "Old America" and Japan "Little Japan" as if the two countries were his brothers.

"The United States will get stronger and stronger, but the Soviet Union will get weaker and weaker. Old America might get involved in some kind of warfare, either with the Arabs or with some country in the Balkans, since the Balkans are the tinderbox of the world. You know why? When a country gets strong, it needs to expand. How to expand? Through warfare. China and the United States might have frictions over the Taiwan Strait or Tibet or both. The Soviet Union, Western Europe, and Israel will be friendlier to China, and North Korea and Little Japan will be less friendly. Africa is a sleeping lion. . . ."

Toward the end of the conversation, Yuan asks me if I am content with my life.

"The question of a poet," I say, and laugh.

"I want you to join a tour going through Inner Mongolia, and play the erhu for foreign tourists."

I don't hesitate. "Yes."

I have seen many pictures of Inner Mongolia: it seems a fairyland, where nomadic people spend all their time on horseback and live in tents.

Two days later I leave a note for my parents, quoting the

ancient Buddhist aphorism, "The drifter will roam like a cloud for a while." I carry my erhu, and the same military bag I brought home from jail, and join Yuan's culture tour.

An air-conditioned tour bus takes us to the steppes. There are two colors that strike out to me, blue sky and green pasture. White-domed yurts, fat white sheep, and horses are scattered about, a broken pearl necklace lying on a giant piece of green velvet. Flowers are blossoming everywhere. There is space enough for me to crawl like a baby and howl like a beast.

There is no electricity, no factories, karaoke bars, TV. People hunt or raise cattle, horses, and sheep, wear leather clothes, and burn cowshit for heat.

The tourists relax in the grassland. They drink wine from hollow ox horns. Drunk, they sing and dance with friendly Mongolian women. During the day they watch the Mongolian men do archery and wrestle. At night Mongolian families invite the tourists into their yurts to taste their fresh sheep's-milk tea and cheese. Although we are total strangers to the Mongolians, they treat us like family. They provide us with the best lamb, beef, and wine made from fermented mare's milk. The men invite the honored guests to sleep beside their wives to show their hospitality. Twenty years ago, I am told, sleeping *with* the hostess was an optional gift for a guest.

One night after playing the erhu for some of the tourists at a party, I drink like a sailor. The corn spirit makes me ecstatic. My untamed soul dances and roams with the wind. I join the crowd around the bonfire, swing my hips to the music. I am so drunk that I don't notice all the people have left and the fire has died out.

I can't fall asleep. I lie outside on the grass, looking up at the stars. The clear sky can't even be imagined in crowded, polluted Beijing. The stars remind me of a picture in a calendar on the wall of the dining room in my parents' Beijing apartment. It is a painting called *Starry Night*. The night turns and spins.

I feel like a lonely beast. Probably I *am* a beast. I have the impulse to howl, to chase, to mate. I wander in a green field. A camel follows me. Its eyes look like dark wells in the moonlight. A sad camel, I think to myself. The wind carries the rich scent of the grass. I can't believe that not so long ago I was locked up, working in a small, damp cell, making fucking matchboxes! I can't believe I can be so free.

I take in the moist air and give myself to the silent caress of the starry night.

Memories begin to flood my mind: memories of a good little girl admired by her friends, classmates, and relatives. Memories of a popular and accomplished student who could play many musical instruments and was skilled at basketball. Parents saw her as their children's role model, and teachers said she would be a great revolutionary for socialism. She was the pride of her parents.

When she was twelve, the government sent her parents to Monkey Village for reeducation. She had to follow. There wasn't any school, or electricity, and the peasants had never even seen a bike. Her parents worked so hard that they didn't have time to take care of her. During the day she fed the pigs like the peasants and cooked her own food. She was often bullied by the local kids and had no friends of her own. When her parents were home, her mother whined bitterly about their life, ignoring her. She dreamed of her old school and her home in Beijing every day.

At night, while her mother and father guarded a warehouse far away, the Party secretary often came to the shack where they all lived. He was there to reform children from families of the five black types. He asked her to spy on her parents and report to him everything they said and did. "That will be your way of showing loyalty to our great Chairman Mao," he said.

To conserve kerosene oil in the lanterns, the inhabitants of Monkey Village spoke together in the darkness after the sun went down. Her reports to the Party secretary were delivered in the dark, as she whispered to him all her parents' words and actions since their last meeting. The Party secretary smoked a pipe while he listened. She could see his hideous old evil face across the room, in the glow of the pipe. When all the tobacco had burned up, it meant the old farthead would leave.

One night the glow of his pipe went out, but the Party secretary didn't leave. He approached her slowly, his breath stinking in the darkness. He gagged her with a piece of towel and raped her. Three times in one night. When he was done, he sat on the edge of the *kang* and spat on the ground. "Isn't city girls' skin delicious!" He had finished a gourmet meal.

As the dirty old peasant left, he threatened her: "If you even *think* about telling anyone about this, you and your parents will never go back to Beijing." Lit by the moonlight, her body glistened with cold, sticky sweat—her body, still flat-chested and young but now bruised and stained. Aching and nauseous, she threw up.

She ran to the small river that flowed through the village and tried to clean herself in the freezing water. In the early morning, before her parents came home, she ran away from Monkey Village, taking with her five yuan she had stolen from them, some Chairman Mao badges, and her shame.

When she was able at last to make her way back to Beijing, she discovered that her official Beijing residency there had been withdrawn. She had no place to live, no money for food. She began hanging out with young thugs and roughnecks who, like her, were not old enough to be Red Guards. The parents of these roughnecks had been sent to the countryside for reeducation or to cadre schools to be reformed through labor.

Every roughneck wanted her to be his *quanzi*, his girl. Two thugs fought over her. One was stabbed to death by the other, which made her the most famous female hooligan in Beijing. She was given the nickname Big Trumpet.

The more I think of that young girl, the farther I walk away from the tents. I no longer know where I've come from or where I'm headed.

"Miss, excuse me, but please don't go too far away. You might get lost, and I've heard wolves here at night."

I turn around; a foreigner is looking at me. A foreigner who speaks Chinese. He calls me "Miss" instead of "Comrade." I have seen this man once or twice before, painting or reading in his hammock. I noticed him because I have never seen a left-handed person before. Mama once told me that I was born left-handed. But in China everyone is forced to be right-handed.

I have never seen this left-handed foreigner close up. He is tall and thin. His hair and eyebrows are thick and brown. He looks scholarly, but I can't tell his age.

"Oh, thanks for telling me," I say.

"If you like, I can walk you back. I know the way," he says softly.

I nod.

"My name is Roy Goldstein. You can call me Roy, or Luo-Yi." He speaks almost perfect Chinese. "I'm an American journalist and a friend of Yuan's."

"My name is Lili Lin."

"Yuan told me that already."

"If you know there are wolves around, why are *you* way out here?"

He laughs and says, "I couldn't sleep because I was so enchanted by your music. That was such a soul-stirring piece you played earlier."

"Yes?"

"It's beautiful and meditative. Can you tell me its title?"

" 'Autumn Moon over Han Palace.' "

"Your 'Autumn Moon' makes me feel like crying. It's a feeling of catharsis, like the feeling one gets after watching an ancient Greek play."

"Yes?" I don't know anything about Greek plays, but "Autumn Moon" is a real tear-jerker, telling the tragic story of an aging concubine who has been kicked to the curb.

"I've found that there are many monophonic tunes in Asian traditional music, which is so different from the polyphonic music of the West. Your performance reminds me of the Chinese saying *Yiyin chengfo*—'One note makes you a Buddha.' "

"Yes?"

"But of course, as a musician, you know that much better than I do."

I think to myself, Oh, Old Heaven Grandpa! He begins

by talking about catharsis and Greek plays, monophonic and polyphonic tunes. He must be a serious stinky number 9, more serious than my parents! With him, in contrast to conversations with other Chinese, there are no polite greetings like "Have you eaten?" or "How is your parents' health?" He gets to the point directly.

"I believe everyone has his Eastern and Western sides, just like yin and yang. That's how the universe becomes one. I'm here to find my Eastern side," Roy continues.

The language this foreigner, this stranger, speaks is Chinese. If I were to close my eyes, I would think it was a Chinese man talking to me. But in front of me is this American. Chinese are not eager to talk about serious matters right away. Did Uncle Yin and Aunt Sara find their other halves in each other? Is Johnny the fruit of the yinyang tree?

"What is your Eastern side?" I ask to keep the conversation going.

"I'm not sure, really. Maybe it's something about achieving peace in my consciousness by emptying my mind and weakening my ambition."

"Huh? Is that your impression of the East?" His answer has surprised me. In China I see everything but peace. People are wearing greed and impatience on their faces. Only on the steppes of Inner Mongolia have I started to feel a sense of peace and emptiness. Maybe his East exists only in ancient China, I think.

"Pretty much," he goes on, "but I admit that I'm still trying to understand the cultures and the peoples of Asia. I studied Mandarin for three years in Taiwan. It's too modern and polluted. Then I worked in Hong Kong for a year. It's adventurous, but too small and hectic. I visited Singapore. You know, the majority of people there are ethnic Chinese. But it's too restrictive and quiet. It reminded me of the Midwest of the United States. But I haven't found any place more exciting than Mainland China. It's always changing; you can never predict what's going to happen next."

I don't want to get into politics. The frequent changes make Chinese paranoid.

"To me, Chinese civilization forms the foundation of all East Asian cultures. There are just too many things to take in." He is captivated by his Chinese explorations. His frequent hand gestures and facial expressions remind me of the smells of Aunt Sara's perfume and cigar: they are all American imports.

"Lili?" Roy's call brings me back to our dialogue. "I feel I can be totally free and speak my mind with you. I hope you feel comfortable enough to do the same."

I am more than comfortable. Usually I love to play the role of a listener so I don't have to think; this time, instead, I watch him. His eyes are grayish blue. I have never seen an ocean before, but I imagine that on a cloudy, windy day, a deep ocean must turn this color. In the moonlight his nose casts a vivid, handsome shadow on his face. I like watching him.

"Why don't you tell me what *you* think? I'd like to learn more about China from you."

Oh, Old Heaven Grandpa! I think, but then I search for a reply and say, "You know too much to learn anything from me."

"Why do you say that? Confucius says that everyone is a teacher."

I don't have much of a clue as to what he is talking about. My later school years were spent mostly on the streets.

"Lili." Roy pauses. "Why do you look so gloomy?"

"Do I?"

I am not a sentimental type of woman. I have no goals, no sorrows, no complaints, no worries—why can't people believe I am carefree? "I guess I'm tired," I say.

"Do you want to go back to the yurt?"

"Yeah, sure."

That night in the yurt I have a dream, but it has nothing to do with Roy. For once, the next day, I remember my dream.

Roy and I take camel rides together every morning and talk. He tells me that the Mongolian lifestyle echoes that of Native Americans. He talks about his travels and adventures around the world: trekking in Nepal, boating on the Amazon, hanging out at morning fairs in North Africa. Roy visits me in the dome-shaped, rounded tent where I am staying. I play the erhu every night outside the tent. The notes of the erhu sound natural on this open, rural plateau. They penetrate the open air, flying boundless, like nightingales. Roy is fascinated by the erhu's crying.

"Music is about nature, the song of nature," he says. "I like to hear music played in an open place rather than indoors. I had a good friend who used to play Japanese music in a forest for me."

His comments make me think of my parents. They always perform in concert halls. If my mother sees a kid my age playing solo in a big concert hall, she says something like "When will you bring honor to our family as he has to his?" Roy's attention makes me feel like an accomplished musician.

After I finish playing, Roy has an endless list of questions.

"What do your parents do?"

"They're teachers."

"How many brothers and sisters do you have?"

"None."

"You're the only child?"

"Yes, the only child."

"Do you travel often?"

"No. I don't have any money."

"What's your favorite food?"

"*Mapo* tofu."

"Hot and spicy. It's my favorite, too."

"You like Chinese food?" I ask him.

"Of course I do. What's your favorite color?"

"Blue."

"Why?"

"It's the color of the ocean. I've never seen an ocean in my life," I say, looking at his eyes.

"What's your favorite book?"

When I was young, many books were banned. The only things available were collections of Mao's thoughts and Leninist-Marxist tracts and picture books called *xiao ren shu*. I developed the habit of reading picture books; at least they contained colors other than red.

I don't want to speak my heart to anyone, especially an American journalist. Girls like me can be sent to prison for getting too close to foreigners.

"I don't have a favorite book," I reply.

One night Roy asks me if I have any questions for him.

I think for a little while and then say, "Yes. I do. Everyone says the United States is the richest country in the world. Everybody in China wants to go there. So why are you here in China?"

"It's a long story. I love your music because it reminds me of Yoshiko. She was my college sweetheart. She was Japanese American. She played the Japanese musical instrument called the koto beautifully. Her music was very much like yours, filled with simple, plain tones. I lived with Yoshiko in the early seventies, and she often played her koto in the nearby woods.

"We were both in the movement protesting the Vietnam war. We were at Berkeley and decided to travel from California to Asia. But just before we were to leave, Yoshiko was killed in a car accident. Now here I am, finally in Asia, by myself. There is a part of me that's forever gone with her."

Roy begins to cry as he tells me about Yoshiko's death. His voice softens. What type of woman could have such an effect on a man? As I listen to Roy, the word *wu chang* constantly jumps back and forth in my mind. It's a word my Buddhist grandma uses. It means "transience." After Grandma's three husbands died, one after another, she became a Buddhist. Once, when my parents and I went to see her, she admonished us, "Everything is *wu chang* in this world. Life, love, beauty, youth, possession—all are clouds passing by. *Om mani padme hum.*"

I don't know how to comfort Roy. I don't have heartbreaking love stories to share; I cannot even imagine what such love feels like. I don't tell strangers about my private life. No matter how painful and bitter it may be, I swallow it alone. "Troubles come from a loose tongue"—that's what we Chinese learn from one political movement after another; that is what Chinese parents teach their children year after year.

Roy says he and his fellow activists in the antiwar movement were fighting for peace and love. Peace and love? Chinese are taught that as long as there are class differences between oppressed and oppressing, there can be no real peace or love in the world. While Roy was seeking love, people here were betraying their neighbors, their friends, even their parents and spouses.

And so Roy's love story fascinates me, especially the pain in his eyes when he mentions Yoshiko. I have seen hatred, when Red Guards beat my parents and criticized my grandma, but I haven't seen this kind of pain. Is the loss of love more painful than hatred?

Some of Yuan's friends want to explore the Gobi Desert. They're searching for the legendary Holy Lake. Yuan's writer friend Old Wood pulls out a worn map of China and points to an area with yellow-brown patches and dots. "It's high here, but it's miraculous," he says. "Just imagine roaming over seas and mountains of sand, discovering some dinosaur bones, ancient mummies, or lost dynasties, and then finally standing by the Holy Lake."

According to legend, the Holy Lake was formed from the tears of an ancient princess. She was married off to a tribal leader for political purposes. She missed her home and parents so much that she often wept at the spot where the lake is now located. After she died, her tears turned into its crystal-clear waters. The lake has saved many desert travelers.

I want to go. For me the word *holy* is magnetic. Roy can't come along because he has to go back to Beijing.

I am surprised at my own disappointment. I stand in front of him feeling numb, as if a cold winter rain had soaked me.

Roy gives me his business card and his leather jacket. "Lili, when you feel cold on the trip, wear this, OK?"

I thank him and then he tries to hug me. I step back.

"This is a small world, isn't it? And technology has made it even smaller. Perhaps it was fate that sent me here to meet you, and if so, maybe it will lead us to see each other again."

I nod, holding on tight to his jacket. I avoid his eyes because I am afraid he will see through my cool exterior. I can't say anything; fate never speaks.

Old Wood's father is a high-ranking officer in the Chinese army. With his help we get three jeeps for our trip to find the Holy Lake. It takes us seven days to cross the desert. We pass rosy willow woods, golden parasol trees, and sand dunes, feeling the beauty and wildness of these uninhabited lands. We see herds of deer and wild cattle grazing, goats loping, and geese in lazy flight.

One evening we stop at the ruins of an ancient castle. Tired, we sit and lie on the ruins. The moonlight covers us with a film of silver haze, and Yuan reads poems he's written about the ancient Greek god Dionysus, the spirit of wine.

I don't know which of the group it is who starts to mimic the actions from rock star Cui Jian's video "A Piece of Red Cloth." But some people cover their eyes with pieces of the red scarves that young Communist Pioneers wear around their necks to show their loyalty to the Communist Party. Yuan announces, "Here, on these ruins, is where our Dionysus begins." We pass wine bottles to one another and begin to chant softly "Originality, originality," a line from one of Yuan's poems. Somebody gives me a piece of red scarf and I cover my eyes, too. I hear giggles, and people start touching one another and asking others to touch them. It's certainly "hooligan behavior." But we're in the middle of desert, with no police, no restriction, and everyone grows wild. Men touch women, women touch men. They laugh and scream.

I hear Yuan ask everyone who is blindfolded by red scarves, "What have you seen?"

Everybody answers back with a lyric from "A Piece of Red Cloth": "Happiness."

"Does it feel good?" Yuan asks, meaning the feeling of being touched.

"It feels so good it makes me forget I don't have a place to live." All keep touching one another as they recite the lyric.

We never find the Holy Lake.

Happiness.

Happiness.

Happiness.

FOUR

I return to Beijing, that crazy, distracted city which is so familiar to me. Fancy hotels, supermarkets, discos, Kentucky Fried Chicken, construction sites, open-door policies, "socialism with Chinese characteristics," "spiritual pollution," export permits, handicapped role models, learning from the soldier Lei Feng, t'ai chi, Sigmund Freud, existentialism, "the Four Basic Principles of China's socialism," the one-child policy, foreign-exchange currency, Japanese soap operas, pest-extermination campaigns, nepotism, young nannies, kung fu novels, the new rage for studying abroad, breakdancing and the "moonwalk," Wham and George Michael, getting rich quick, the notion that foreign moons are bigger and rounder, color TV sets, dishwashers,

refrigerators, sewing machines, ESP, New Tide literature—
Beijing is chaotic, overwhelming, waiting impatiently to
change itself again and again.

I return to breathing foul, dirty air and watching millions
of people pedal back and forth, always rushing. The simplicity and freedom of life in Mongolia once again become
a fairy tale.

My parents don't ask where I have been. They refuse
to talk to me. We communicate through notes left on
the dining table. "Tonight we'll lock the door from the
inside at 10:00 P.M." "We are having a political meeting
and are not coming back for dinner." "I've watered the
plants and fed the goldfish." "Aunt Ma borrowed our scis-
sors this morning." "Tomorrow the Committee of the
Pest-Extinguishing Campaign is coming to check the pre-
mises. We need one person to stay at home." "Don't eat all
the chocolate."

I am in the middle of a domestic cold war, even as China
has started to woo its old enemy. But it doesn't bother me.
I am a hooligan. It is too late for me to be the Chinese
Mozart now, and too late to outdo the neighbors' kids. It is
too late for all of it.

My music playing at the hotel brings in enough money.
The rest of the time I sit around chewing gum, listening to
my Walkman. When neighbors speak to me on the streets,
I see only the movement of lips, hear nothing but the lyrics
of the Beatles' "All You Need Is Love." I nod and smile.

One hot summer afternoon, as I am painting my toenails
at home, I catch a glimpse through the window of Roy
walking toward our building. The neighborhood kids have
surrounded him, fascinated by his American jeep. I can see

them pointing to where I live. I know his visit will be a topic of discussion for the Neighborhood Committee.

Roy is dressed in a suit and tie, but his appearance brings back memories of the blue and green of Inner Mongolia.

"Lili, you haven't called me, so I came to see you," he say

My family can't afford a telephone. The only way we can reach each other is for me to call him. His business card is in my pocket every day, stained by my sweat. Yet I've felt little desire or curiosity with regard to him, and what little I *have* felt, I've ignored. He is polite and friendly. But my life is too different, too removed from his—he is as far away as a patch of drifting cloud.

"How've you been?" I greet him politely.

"Pretty good, thank you. And what about you?"

"Not bad."

We don't know what to say ncxt. We look at each other till I cast my eyes down. The silence makes me feel awkward. "What, uh, what can I do for you?" I feel like an inexperienced desk clerk.

"Lili, just seeing you is enough," he answers, his gaze never leaving my eyes for a second. I blush a little bit and look away, lowering my head.

"Do you know that the Philadelphia Symphony Orchestra is in Beijing?" Roy asks.

"Yes, there are ads for it everywhere." My parents have talked about the concert endlessly, but they can't afford to buy tickets.

"I've got two tickets for the concert tonight. I wonder if you'd like to go with me."

The concert doesn't particularly interest me, but I have nothing else to do, and I am curious to know why he wants to take me out. But instead of saying yes immediately, which might make him think I give a damn, I pause, staring at his leather shoes.

"Give me a few minutes. I'll need to change my clothes," I say without looking at him.

In the bedroom I spread all my dresses on the floor. My mind seems blank. I automatically choose a long black velvet skirt and a pair of red sandals. I drape a scarlet shawl over my shoulders. I look at myself in the mirror. I paint my lips crimson. I look at myself carefully in the mirror: my face is like that of a mannequin in a shop window, pale, dry, and expressionless, without warmth or animation. I become self-conscious.

I write a brief note to my parents: "Concert tonight. May be back late."

As we drive through Beijing's crowded, zigzag streets in an open jeep with a black license plate, eyes—from packed old buses, rusty bikes, sidewalks, and steaming food stands—stare at us.

Before the concert Roy takes me to dinner at a plush hotel. This hotel sits in an illuminating glow of soft green and yellowish lights. It towers over the ugly Russian-style buildings nearby, which look like matchboxes. Most of the people in the dining room are Americans—the only ones who can afford to eat here. There are some Asians, but they either don't speak Chinese or come from Taiwan or Hong Kong. Aside from the waiters and waitresses, I am the only native.

Roy introduces me to some of his friends, who are already seated at our table. "This is Richard. He works for Edelman Public Relations. That's Lisa from *The Washington Post*. And over there is Jack from Exxon." I nod.

The woman named Lisa asks Roy something in English.

Roy answers her, also in English. Then everybody looks at me and laughs. Roy doesn't translate, but I know the exchange was about me. I feel more self-conscious.

Roy and his friends enjoy the French food and listen to the tuxedo-clad musicians playing Brahms. Smiling flatteringly, Chinese busboys quietly replace the used silverware and plates. Two waiters in stiff, starched uniforms serve our table, speaking only in English. They assume that I am not a native but instead belong to this little American town within Beijing. Years ago, people used to call places like this concessions.

Unlike the others, who have full meals, I eat only some dessert and fruit. I don't know how to use a fork and knife.

I glance at Roy again. French food, candlelight, chandeliers—this well-mannered, well-dressed, well-educated foreign world is completely different from mine. I hate myself for being so uneasy in it.

The concert program is printed only in English and French, so Roy translates it into Chinese for me. I have been familiar with the tones, the rhythms, and the fingerings of these Western masterpieces since I was a child. I recall my parents' hand-copied musical scores synchronized to the melody, down to the ink stains on the coarse, brownish papers from the notes' being copied by hand.

With much excitement, Roy informs me in a low voice, "And guess what? They're going to play 'Autumn Moon over Han Palace' with violins."

"Autumn Moon" is the last piece, the only non-Western one they play. As it starts, Roy closes his eyes and slowly moves his head back and forth to the complex, Westernized version of the original simple tune. He says the music brings him back to our "idyllic" time in Mongolia.

The melody *is* beautiful, but I suspect Roy doesn't realize what "Autumn Moon" is intended to convey: the sorrow and sexual frustration suffered by an ancient Chinese concubine on a lonely night when the moon was full.

When the Philadelphia Symphony Orchestra plays "Autumn Moon," it puts an extra beat into it, making it powerful and masculine. It becomes a song about an independent American woman rather than a Chinese concubine with bound feet. I prefer this version to the crying notes produced on my erhu, though the delicacy and subtlety of the piece are lost. Still, Chinese women need this voice. Roy proclaims it an interesting experiment but—like eating pot stickers with a fork—not quite an authentic one.

On the way home Roy tells me he never could have imagined that a Chinese woman would feel so uncomfortable being wined and dined in a fancy restaurant. Most young Chinese women would have given anything to be in my place.

As we pass by Tiananmen Square, Roy points his forefinger at Mao's portrait.

"I can't understand how one person can so dominate this vast nation." Ever the journalist! He is digging for news even on a date. Is he interested in me as a woman or as a source of information?

"Does his appearing in one picture necessarily mean that he dominates the nation?" I play around with his question.

"Well, it's certainly true that he's thought of as a god, and that isn't right."

"What about the Washington Monument and the Lincoln Memorial? You treat your leaders like gods, too. You even put their portraits on your money. We Chinese have pictures of workers, peasants, students, and simple soldiers on our money."

"The difference is that we dare to *question* our leaders. We don't get in trouble if we criticize our president. How about here? Mao's policies have harmed so many innocent Chinese citizens, yet you still sing eulogies to him. Cabdrivers dangle his picture on their rearview mirrors, as if it were some sort of good-luck charm!"

I grow suspicious. I have heard that Western journalists often interview Chinese by treating them to lavish dinners and shows and then prying information out of them. Such Chinese "sources" usually get into big trouble afterward and are punished for "breaching national security."

I don't want to get into trouble for talking about politics with a Western journalist. Only crazy Yuan would do a dumb thing like that. I don't want to meet any more prison guards.

Getting no response from me, Roy continues, "Yes, Lili, you're right. I admit that we Americans still idolize our leaders—John F. Kennedy, for example. But God is God, and Satan is Satan."

"So . . ." I try to figure out what he's going to say next.

"The Chinese don't need to worship bad emperors anymore."

"What else do you think the Chinese need or don't need?"

"Well, you need a political system similar to ours so the people can rule. You need to have the courage to face the lessons history has taught you. You need to have freedom of the press like we have in the United States so the citizens can be told about it if their leaders are abusing their power. You need—"

"Roy, maybe you *are* smarter than the Chinese, and maybe it's true that yours is the greatest country in the world, but we Chinese don't like Westerners' giving us orders." I am quoting clichés from the *People's Daily*.

"What you say is true, but I think that should change. The Chinese can't always think of China as the best; they should let their nationalism and national pride cool down a bit. I think nationalism can be a dangerous thing. It isn't necessarily a bad thing to listen to what others have to say. Think of the Chinese idiom 'Xu hui ruo gu'—'A modest heart, as accommodating as a valley.'"

National pride is nowadays a favorite topic in classrooms and newspaper headlines, though certainly not in my circle. But I am not going to let Roy enjoy his own life of privilege on the one hand and tell us Chinese we are stupid and should listen to him on the other.

"Chinese people can think independently," I insist.

"Whatever you say." Roy shrugs.

I argue not because I wish to defend China; I am not a government lackey. I argue because Roy already has everything: money, education, respect from others, freedom to travel. And now he also wants to be right all the time. This is called *deli bu raogren*—meaning that once you have truth and justice on your side, you always want to have the upper hand. He would make a good Party member. I talk because it is the only way I know to save face.

When we get back to my parents' apartment, Roy says good-bye to me as if we had never argued at all. If the argument had been between two Chinese, we probably would have gotten very personal and stopped speaking to each other. But for Roy, political views seem to be one thing, and the relationship between us something else entirely.

Three days later I get a terrible sudden pain in my side. I am diagnosed with appendicitis and must stay in the hospital for several days. In the bare-walled ward, wearing only a flimsy gown, I can't move or even get out of bed by myself. I have to depend on my parents. I hate to be so weak, sick, and dependent on them.

I have three female wardmates. Their husbands visit them every day. They bring food they have cooked for their wives, carry them gently out to the hospital's open court-yard, and carefully wash their faces. So there isn't much left for the women's nurses to do.

The nurses flatter my wardmates, telling them how great their men are. My wardmates love to compete and show off their husbands, hinting that a husband's quality is the mea-sure of a wife's attractiveness.

I am the only one here being taken care of by her par-ents. Papa comes to visit me every day with his freshly cooked food.

"Lili, here I am," he always greets me in his soft-spoken way.

"You can go back to work now. I can take care of my-self." I don't want him coming to see me. I would prefer to stare at the ceiling all day. His presence reminds me of what I want to run away from. Years ago, in Monkey Village, when the Party secretary gagged me with a piece of towel, how much I wished then that Papa would appear and protect me! How much I wished he would say, "Lili, here I am!"

48

"Are you sure you'll be OK by yourself?" Papa asks.

"Yes, I'm sure."

"I'll leave, then. I'll be back at the same time tomorrow."

" 'Bye."

"By the way, what do you want to eat tomorrow? Pork? Chicken? Tofu?"

"You don't have to come. I can eat here in the hospital's cafeteria."

"How about chicken soup? I'll come back tomorrow. You take care. Your mother can't come, but I want you to know she's thinking of you, OK?"

"Yes," I answer impatiently.

Papa leaves. Within two minutes Roy shows up on my ward. He and Papa may have passed in the hall, but they don't know each other. I haven't told Roy or any of my other friends that I'm here. He doesn't explain how he found me.

Roy brings some sandwiches he has made and Chinese books he has bought for me. He helps me move about. He tells jokes as I lie in bed. My wardmates grow fond of him. When he's not around, they ask me, "Is your friend with the big nose coming today?"

They want to know how I met this handsome American. "Through a mutual friend"—that's all I tell them. A friendship with a Westerner can draw too much attention. People envy you because Westerners are rich. People look down on you because they think that Westerners are sex animals and that only sluts befriend them. I don't care what my wardmates think of me, but I don't want to be the center of attention.

I don't know whether my wardmates have told Papa about Roy. But in any case I tell Papa not to pick me up the day I'm to leave the hospital, explaining, "A friend of mine is coming."

"A new friend?"

"A new friend."

The day I'm released, Roy brings me a bunch of sweet-smelling red roses. He hugs me, and this time I don't resist; I embrace him in the sunlight. Wrapped in his big arms, I can't see his face, but I sense his body temperature and his heartbeat.

Roy works, eats, shops, and lives in an area called Jian-guomenwai, Beijing's "global village." Multinational companies, foreign embassies, expensive stores, and elite hotels are all located here. It is cleaner and has many more trees and flowers than other neighborhoods. Here the living standard is Western: air conditioning, nightclubs, twenty-four-hour hot water. It even has more janitors and security guards.

Teenagers love hanging around here, where they can practice their English on native-speaking passersby or watch the Cadillacs and Lincolns cruise past. Those who dream of getting out of the country come to this neighborhood because the American embassy is here. Every day at East Xiu Water Street, near the embassy, crowds share rumors about how to get visas. Some people wait outside the embassy compound for days; they are addicted to the prospect of going abroad.

"The consul at window number two is a bald man with a big belly. He's nice and not very difficult," someone says.

"The consul at window number five doesn't like to give visas to young women," according to another.

"The consul at window number one likes to ask what your plans are after you graduate from an American college. Just be sure to say you want to come back and serve the Chinese people," advises a third.

Roy and his foreign colleagues and friends can get imported products like Scotch tape and New York bagels in local stores, and conversely can enjoy exotic things unavailable to them at home—the *renli che,* or rickshaw, for example. Although Chinese still call it a rickshaw, today's version is no longer pulled by a barefoot Chinese man. After 1949, some Communist leader said, "We can't let American devils see men pulling other men in the new China." So rickshaws turned into pedicabs. Drivers now equip their pedicabs with copper bells; with each pedal, the bell rings. A rider can thus judge the speed of the pedaling by listening to the rhythm of the bell.

In Jianguomenwai, herds of pedicabs wait outside hotels and stores for customers with FEC, or foreign-exchange currency. One day Roy hails a pedicab to take me to the movies. It's my first time in a rickshaw. The driver is an old man, toothless, with a worn and sagging brown face and salt-and-pepper hair. He looks to be at least sixty years old, but he greets us warmly with a young man's voice.

It is a hot, drowsy afternoon, yet this old man pedals quickly. He wears a straw hat and constantly swings a towel from one of his shoulders to wipe the sweat from his face. His sweaty T-shirt sticks to his back. Drops of sweat roll off him, leaving a trail of salty drops on the ground. I feel like a member of the exploiting class.

Despite the physical effort he's expending pedaling the rickshaw, this old man still has the energy to talk with us as we travel down the road. He tells us that he is a retired factory worker and that his current income as a driver is triple what his salary was at the state-run factory where he worked for forty years. He is content with his life.

"Our leader, Deng Xiaoping, says that regardless of whether it's a black or a white cat, so long as it catches rats, it is a good cat. So whether I work in the public or the private sector, as long as I make money and serve the people, I'm OK. Deng Xiaoping also says it is OK for some people to get rich first. So I don't feel too guilty for making so much more money than my retired friends."

After learning that Roy is an American journalist, the man can't stop expressing his admiration for Deng Xiaoping.

"Tell your fellow Americans that Deng's great. In my opinion, though he's shorter than Mao and not as handsome, he's the greater leader." The old man makes a thumbs-up gesture as he pedals.

"I think you're a great guy, too," Roy says, complimenting the driver sincerely. "You work hard and make money in an honest way."

The old man laughs. "No kidding. I'm just one of the toiling masses, an ordinary citizen. I'm only a drop in the ocean. I'm uneducated, so I contribute to the people with my sweat."

"Do you like the current leader, Hu Yaobang?" Roy asks.

"Deng chose him as his successor. Hu is a liberal man. He likes things Western and wants to conduct political reforms. But I was told that the conservatives hate him. People say his family members don't have expensive overseas bank accounts. It is good to hear that. He has done some great thing for the intellectuals. It's wonderful because educated people can do more for the country than useless people like me who can't read or write." The man informs us that his grandson has been admitted to Beijing University, making him the first person in his family ever to attend college.

"But I don't like Hu Yaobang for inviting three thousand Japanese students to China," he continues. "Why should we pay for the Japs to come and have fun? They killed so many Chinese in the rape of Nanking and still refuse to apologize. I think Hu is a good man, but too honest and hot-blooded as a leader. Look at Deng Xiaoping—he's stern and crafty, always behind the curtain. He's smarter. People who are as hot-blooded and direct as Hu can get themselves into trouble sometimes."

"You sound like a political analyst!"

"Every Beijinger is into politics. Guangdong people love food; Shanghai people love clothes; and Beijing people love politics."

Roy offers him a generous tip. The old man doesn't accept it, saying, "I get what I deserve."

Jianguomenwai also attracts beggars, many of whom are not really poor at all; they're swindlers who make a fortune off foreign visitors.

One afternoon Roy and I are walking together in Jianguomenwai. A dirty, middle-aged woman with three little children, all wearing torn clothes, approaches us and asks for spare change.

"We haven't eaten for three days. For the past three nights we've slept in front of the train station. I'm from the countryside and have no relatives or friends here. Please, soften your hearts and take pity on me," the woman mumbles woefully in a southern dialect.

Roy immediately pulls out ten yuan from his pocket.

"Oh, thank you, thank you so much. You two are our reborn parents, and Avalokitesvara will bless kindhearted people like you. May you have many sons." The lady bows low before us. Before wandering off again, she gives me a special slick look. Her glance suddenly revives an old memory. Wait a minute: *I know her!*

I met this woman and her boyfriend at a wild party several years ago. I remember that she looked like a fashionable movie star that night, wearing a chic short black dress. After we were introduced to each other, she offered me some pot. I explained to her that I was already high enough. She told me that she was thinking of purchasing citizenship in a South American country for herself and her boyfriend.

Then she said, "It's no fun being Chinese. You know that, don't you? This place is doomed. It's dirty, poor, corrupted, and crammed with uneducated people. Nowadays everything is for sale, and everyone has green eyes out to get everyone else and is jealous of everyone else's wealth. Did you see on the news the other day where thugs from Henan killed seventeen people driving fancy cars in Shenzhen, using knives to cut their throats and genitals? It's crazy! To tell you the truth, I've had enough of this fucking place."

"But you can't speak any foreign languages. How are you going to get by in another country?" I asked her.

"No language skills, so what? Chinese are all over the world. What kind of life can't we Mainland Chinese survive?"

"Uh, maybe you're right."

"You're damn straight, I'm right. My boyfriend always praises me for being visionary. After we get our citizenship in Panama or Colombia or wherever, I plan to open a Chinese restaurant there. After saving up enough money, we'll travel to the U.S. as tourists and try to have a baby. If the baby is born in the territory of the U.S., it'll be an American citizen. Then we can immigrate as the parents of an American baby. Once we arrive in the U.S., we won't have to worry about life anymore. See, I've got it all planned out. You need a master plan, too."

I didn't reply.

She asked slyly, "Do you want to go abroad? Tell me, and maybe I can help you."

"You're asking the wrong person. I'm a loyal Beijing citizen." I didn't tell her the truth. I didn't like my life in Beijing and had no sense of loyalty to this place whatsoever, but I was used to it. I couldn't function elsewhere.

She grinned and said, "Don't shit me, girl. We're undesirable scum, with no diplomas, no high-ranking fathers, no good reputations or good jobs. The only chance we have is to get out. I bet you don't have enough money to do that, do you?"

"What do you guys do?"

"You'd never guess—I'm a beggar!" she told me proudly.

"Why are you so proud of being a panhandler? Being the real proletariat may have been a source of pride during the Cultural Revolution, but not anymore!" I teased her.

"I'm not a *real* beggar," she objected. She told me how she paid country kids and retarded people to beg with her in different areas of Beijing. "My boyfriend is the head of our crew. Every bum in his area has to pay him one third of what he or she makes. He has many connections in the city police."

I asked her if they made much money; I thought most people didn't have anything to spare for charity. I remembered that Papa had once contributed five yuan for street kids when Grandma Liu was raising funds to help them. Even that was considered a large donation.

The phony beggar laughed at me, then winked and lowered her voice to say, "Silly girl, don't you understand what the government's open–door policy is?"

"No."

"You should go to political studies more often! It means to open the door for foreign investors to come in. Our business complies with the new policy; we do business with old foreigners! They are our targets."

"That's why you've chosen Jianguomenwai as your main place of business?"

"Exactly! You can't imagine how much money we make. We don't even have any overhead."

I don't tell Roy her story. But when we meet the next group of bums, an old man and his retarded "son," I warn him so that his compassion will be used against him by these street hustlers.

"You'd better stop your charity," I say. "These people are fakes. They make big money by begging. Underground gangs control all of their hustling."

"Lili, maybe what you say is true. But look at these two, don't they need help? Not doing anything for them would go against my personal philosophy."

"Your 'personal philosophy'? Oh, I see what it is: you love to show off your superiority, don't you? It makes you feel good when these people beg from you, right? I guess you're the savior of the world here."

"You can think of me any way you want. But I need to do what I feel is right. It's my choice." And Roy proceeds to give the old man another ten-yuan bill.

The man bows to him and forces the retarded son to kowtow.

"Roy, you want to believe they're real bums. They're your next story: 'More Beggars in Communist China Now Than Thirty Years Ago.' "

"It has nothing to do with politics. When I see these poor people, I see them as individuals who need help."

"But they don't see *you* as an individual. To them you're a foreign investor as well as a foreign devil."

"Why do you like to differentiate me from the Chinese? Yes, I'm a Westerner, but so what? I don't judge people by 'ism' or nationality."

"The Chinese Communist Party says that individualism is all about egotism. Chinese can't afford egotism."

"That's bullshit! Anyway, *I* don't do something because my government tells me to. I'm an adult who does whatever I believe in my heart. Lili, let me tell you, I'm a citizen of the world. That's why I'm here with you." He's raising his voice now, obviously annoyed.

A citizen of the world. But the world isn't filled with equals, is it?

"You think you can save China," I tell him. "But you can't save China any more than your country can."

"I think you Chinese are too concerned with your national pride. Maybe it's a legacy of Western invasion and Western imperialism. But as I said before, nationalism is a dangerous thing."

57

I can't believe I'm defending China to him. Is it because of the insecurity and inferiority I feel? Am I protecting China's pride, or my own?

Roy takes me to the International Trade Mall. I try on the most expensive dresses while he stands beside me smiling and waiting to pay for whichever one I choose. The teenage clerks start acting lazy. To them I'm a Chinese woman with a "white devil"; I can feel their subtle, unfriendly, nosy stares. It is their animal instinct. Female monkeys do the same to one another. Are their feelings sour grapes, resentment, contempt, or all three? I blush and can't help feeling like a beggar accepting handouts from this rich Western man. But actually I'm worse than a beggar—I am like a concubine.

FIVE

Roy doesn't need to find stories to write about; they come to him. He doesn't have to approach people, because they approach him, too. The cultural elite—so-called avant-garde artists, musicians, prizewinning filmmakers, Taoist and Buddhist monks—are all eager to tell him what he wants to hear. The Chinese seem even more curious about him than he is about China. For example, after Roy hears about a place called Republican Village, he is invited to visit by the head of that village, nicknamed Old Fish.

Republican Village is a suburb of Beijing where many artists and eccentrics live. No one knows exactly how it came into being, but it has become a Mecca for artists, many of whom quit the jobs assigned to them and leave their hometowns to settle here, surrounded by white poplar woods, wild sunflowers, and wheat fields. The artists live in shacks rented from local peasants and share what little they have in equal poverty. The peasants have little sympathy for them; to them the artists are wasters.

One dry, windy night Roy and I head over to the Republican Village by taxi. The driver is a slick young guy, cool and clever, with a quick wit and a fast tongue.

Roy notices a baby picture hanging from the rearview mirror.

"Why do you hang a picture of your baby there, rather than Mao's portrait?" Roy asks the driver.

The driver laughs. "My buddies all hang Mao's picture from their mirrors and say old Mao can protect them from under the earth. Some of them even try to tell me that Mao has kept them from being killed or injured in car accidents. But I say to myself, Hell, so many people died when Mao was above earth. In my teenage years I fought with gang members almost every day. If I were going to die, I would have died then."

"You mean you were a hoodlum during the Cultural Revolution?" Roy asks.

"You got it!"

Yeah, I think.

"Why did you join a gang?" Roy must be thinking of writing a story set during the Cultural Revolution.

"Every teenager did. That was how we survived." He is exaggerating a little, I know.

"What else did you guys do besides fight?"

"Well, we smoked cigarettes, read handwritten copies of porno books, and watched girls in public swimming pools. We used to sneak into the park by jumping the fence so we wouldn't have to pay the admission fee."

"How did your folks deal with it?"

"My parents were sent to cadre schools. Yankee, do you know what a damned cadre school is? A labor camp for revolutionary cadres, but little better than the countryside. Anyway, most of my friends' folks, like mine, worked either in cadre schools or in the countryside, so no one was left to restrict us or tell us what to do. We kids enjoyed a lot of freedom back then." The driver emphasizes the word *freedom*.

"Were you a Red Guard?"

"No, but I was a Red Guard's little brother."

The driver is about my age. Our generation just missed becoming Red Guards—and also missed the disgrace that came later. After our parents and older siblings were sent to the countryside, some of us were left alone, while others were looked after by relatives who often gave their young charges a hard time. We hung out on the streets, lived for kicks and sex.

I remember when Papa and Mama returned to Beijing from Monkey Village toward the end of the Cultural Revolution in 1975. I was with several of my friends—Chou-Chou, Spring Ocean, and Little China—all of us drinking beer and reading magazines smuggled from Hong Kong, when my parents got home.

Mama yelled at my friends, "Get out of my house, you ruffians!" Then she pointed her finger at me. "You ungrateful wolf, you've become nothing but a female hooligan."

I yelled back, "Chairman Mao says young people are the morning sun."

Mama slapped me across my shameless face.

She covered her own face with both of her hands and wailed about my running away from Monkey Village without letting Papa and her know. They had searched for me everywhere, she said, and she had almost gone mad. "I thought you had been abducted. I couldn't sleep at night. Your father and I wrote letters to every county government trying to find you, but our letters were like stones thrown into the ocean; we got no reply. Finally your uncle Hua wrote to us that you were in Beijing but had become bad and were living with gang members. I didn't believe it. I sent him money and asked him to help you. But he said he was beaten by a bunch of ruffians when he went to give the money to you in your ruffian friend's home. . . . I'd rather see you dead than know you were a hooligan."

I looked at her crying and sneered. All this woman cared about was the family's reputation. The more she wanted to save face, I thought, the more she would lose! Papa stood behind her, saying nothing. He passed me a cold towel with which to cool my face, hot and red after Mother's slapping. The towel was of the same color and design as the one that dirty peasant had used to gag me in Monkey Village. It was probably even the same towel! I threw it out the window and ran away. I didn't tell them that when I'd asked Uncle Hua for help, he'd turned me away because I was the daughter of "American spies." Neither Papa nor Mama could protect me as well as the gang members with whom I'd been living. I'd rather be a hooligan than a pathetic stinky number 9 with no guts!

"What do you guys want to see in Republican Village?" The driver's words bring me back to reality.

"Artists," Roy answers.

"Artists? Are you kidding?" The driver smirks and says,

"Did you read yesterday's evening paper? A guy there was arrested the other day for jerking off in public. That lousy bastard calls what he did performance art. Fuck him. If a hand job were art, every family's bedroom would be an art gallery. He sits on eggs and tells people he's hatching them. Those punks are full of shit. They're just bums trying to get Beijing residency. They should go back where they came from."

"Have you met any of them?" I ask, wondering why he detests the artists so much.

"You bet. They tried to fuck with me. Last Friday night a couple from the village flagged me down on the Zhongguan Cun Road. The man had hair down to his waist and was so freaky that he didn't look like a man *or* a woman. The woman had her head shaved, like a nun. They spoke in a heavy southern accent that I could barely understand. No sooner did they open their mouths than I realized they were country bumpkins. I didn't like them from the start. As soon as they got in the backseat they started making out, feeling each other, making loud and disgusting noises.

"I told them to stop because I didn't want to get caught by the cops—it's illegal to do that stuff in a taxi, you know. But they just ignored me. I got pissed off and stopped the car right in the middle of the road. I told them to pay me and get out. Then the guy said he didn't have any money. That made me *really* pissed. So I kicked them out of my cab and beat the shit out of him. There were some people around, but nobody even tried to stop me. They were all standing by me because I'm a Beijinger. When those two assholes started to run away, I yelled, 'Don't ever fuck with a Beijinger again.' "

Roy frowns at the driver's words. I think it's funny, the way the man tells his story. His rudeness and smooth Beijing dialect remind me of the young thugs I hung out with in the seventies, who always thought they were being heroic, just like this driver now.

When we get to Republican Village, the driver eagerly opens the door for us and asks Roy in a low voice, "Hey, old foreigner, do you exchange money?" He's so anxious to exchange some cash that he doesn't notice Roy's contempt for his provincial ignorance.

"Oh sure," Roy says, "we've got some foreign currency, but it's Russian rubles. How much do you want?"

The driver misses the point and asks more urgently, "Can you check your pocket one more time to see if you have any other currency? Say, U.S. dollars, Japanese yen, German marks, French francs—anything but those Russian rubles? Of course, green money is the best. I'll give you RMB at double the official rate."

He's kissing Roy's ass now; the pride he displayed in boasting about how he beat up those hicks has vanished. As a Westerner, Roy is referred to as a *yangren*, a "man of the ocean"; a country bumpkin is a *tulaomao*, a "man of the earth." An ocean man is rich, and an earth man poor. I don't say anything. Roy ignores the driver, who pulls away empty-handed.

As we walk toward the village in the dark, Roy asks me, "What do you think of those two artists and the incident in the cab?"

"Well, what do *you* think?" I ask in reply.

"It sounds like they certainly had style! I know that artists' behavior is often considered weird by ordinary people who value conformity. Avant-garde art is new here. I think that's probably why the driver didn't approve of them."

Roy's comments make me think. My parents are excellent musicians, but do their conformity and obedience somehow make them not real artists? My friend Yuan once claimed there were no artists in our fathers' generation. Are they just technicians whose creativity and boldness were cut down, castrated? Who should be considered an artist? Is my cousin Johnny a music artist? He looks cool, hip, and he tries hard to be different, but he always sings off-key!

Old Fish is waiting for us in his tiny, run-down old one-floor shack. From a distance his door seems to be halfway open, and I think I can see a stereo system and color TV inside. But when we come closer I see he has painted these on his front door.

Old Fish leads us into his shack. It is bare inside. Except for his paintings, which are lying around everywhere, his only possessions are a bed, a small rug, a Sony audio-cassette Walkman, and a tiny stove that he uses for both cooking and heating. There are no chairs, so we sit on a rug on which he has painted one of van Gogh's sunflowers. Although Old Fish is constantly adding charcoal to his stove, the room is still as cold as a freezer.

Old Fish seems as incommunicative as a mute. I can't understand why he has been elected head of the village. Even when he shows us his recent work, we can squeeze only two words out of him: "Look-see."

The faces of his subjects are horrifying, with wide, gaping mouths and eyes that drip blood. Their eyes don't have pupils, reminding me of the dull gaze of the inhabitants of Monkey Village. He must be very familiar with the life of northern peasants, I think. I glance at him. He is cooking dinner on the stove, his back to us. He avoids all eye contact.

Roy examines each painting. One, entitled *Mao and Women*, shows Marilyn Monroe in a Mao hat, standing in front of a microphone like she was going to sing "Happy Birthday." In the dark background, Mao is dressed in a bikini, his face effeminate. Old Fish has given him a pair of funky braids. To me Old Fish seems to be conveying the old Chinese belief that men who have women's faces must be crafty and evil. I am stunned by his political bravery. He's dared to make fun of China's Helmsman! I love the satirical tone of this painting.

I have read in the *People's Daily* that "some hooligan artists make fun of Mao's sacred image and superimpose it on consumer products like Coke-Cola or Marlboro cigarettes." This type of art has been dubbed by the newspaper critics cynical realism, political pop, and wounded romanticism.

"So Mao has become an entertainment star and a mascot in your market socialism, yes?" Roy asks Old Fish.

Old Fish answers slowly and indifferently: "Fifteen years ago my father was persecuted and thrown in jail because he used a piece of newspaper to wipe his ass, and Mao's picture was on that paper. He used it because there was no toilet paper in our village."

"Are you trying to break old Mao's continuing psychological hold over the Chinese by transforming the sacred into the profane?"

Old Fish quotes a proverb: " 'Thirty years on the west bank and another thirty years on the east bank.' "

Roy, sitting on the rug, doesn't understand. "Are you talking about the whims of Chinese history?' "

"Maybe."

Roy wants Old Fish to elaborate, but the artist dodges his visitor's questions, claiming, "I don't talk about myself."

"Why?" Roy persists.

Old Fish pauses. "I don't think about myself much, I guess."

"Why not?"

Old Fish lowers his eyes, clears his throat, and then answers impatiently, "I don't know. I really don't know." He suggests that Roy would do better to talk with some of the others.

But Roy presses on. "Don't you want your paintings to be publicized?" he asks.

Old Fish turns back to his cooking.

We eat a wild herb salad and barbecued quail and drink the Five Star beer we have brought. Old Fish tells us that yesterday he climbed into the nearby hills and dug up the edible wild herbs and shot ten quail. "This is all I can afford," he explains.

Roy and I thank him for the special treat.

After dinner Old Fish takes us to the house of another villager, named Old Wolf, who's throwing a party. As we pass by a rundown adobe, Old Fish slows his gait and fixes his eyes on the big lock on its door.

"Black Dream lives there," he says. "He's a poet. He's working on seven epics. He locks himself up for months while writing, and everyone in our village takes turns serving him food through that small hole over there." Old Fish points to a dog-eaten slot in the door. His expression softens.

"Is Black Dream a hermit?" Roy asks.

"Yes, but he's also the best poet in China. He never compromises." Old Fish's admiration for Black Dream is obvious; later I will learn that the two men are lovers. They are quite famous among the Beijing queers. Both born into poor peasant families, they were caught having sex in a public boathouse in their hometown and were kicked out by their parents.

Roy asks Old Fish if he knows of the American poet Emily Dickinson, saying, "She was a hermit, too. Some people say that she went into seclusion because of a failed love, but I think it's not that easy. Poets have their own realm."

Old Fish's eyes glisten.

Old Wolf's house is much bigger than Old Fish's. He's married to a German art agent, and his paintings sell well in Europe. He is the *dakun,* the "moneybag," of the village. Old Fish introduces us to him and then leaves. Old Wolf welcomes us warmly and offers us imported beer.

"We are avant-garde artists," he says. "We aren't part of the mainstream and don't want to be. People call us punks, hooligans, hoodlums, trash, but we don't really care. We're having fun here!"

His house is full of characters in wild costumes. One lady is dressed in a military uniform like a Red Guard's. Wearing a red armband and a military belt, she is singing old Party slogans to the tune of Michael Jackson's song "Beat It," which is blasting on the stereo. She's dancing with a guy who has painted his body in a zebra's stripes. Another woman has her face vividly colored, like a Beijing opera star's, and wears blood-red Bermuda shorts; her dancing partner has the national flag of China painted on his bottom. They dance as though struck by lightning. Behind them is a drag queen. In a pair of ancient triangular shoes of the sort once used to bind women's feet, he looks like an old matchmaker.

Posted all around the room are traffic signs reading U-Turns Prohibited.

Roy shakes his head. I can hardly believe I'm in Communist China.

Old Wolf laughs. "The Chinese can be just as wild as you Westerners—wilder, in fact, because we've got three thousand years of sexual repression to overcome."

I drink some beer and listen to Roy interview some of these eccentrics. The assumptions he makes annoy me. "How does your work unit restrict your creativity and persecute you?" he asks, or "In what ways do the local police harass you?" or "How do political policies suppress your freedom of expression?" His questions, of course, evoke precisely he answers he expects.

Some of the partygoers joke around, refusing to be serious. But others start to denounce the regime and its traditional art and music.

One man, who calls himself Domestic Love, is very outspoken. He stands outside the house smoking a cigarette. He tells Roy, "You ask me if I feel any anger. Of course I do. You want to know who pisses me off? Too many people piss me off. Let me tell you." Then Domestic Love starts to curse at the top of his lungs.

"Fuck those old farts! Fuck revolutionary heroism. Fuck revolutionary romanticism and revolutionary realism. Fuck the Beijing police. Fuck the Chinese Art Association.

Fuck the Anti–Spiritual Pollution Campaign. Fuck patriotism. Fuck cabdrivers. Fuck shop clerks. Fuck Beijing natives! Fuck Chinese passports! Life is the shits!"

People come out to listen to Domestic Love. They applaud and whistle.His passion rouses them. They all have the same anger simmering within them.

Domestic Love finishes his diatribe, spits on the ground, yawns, and walks back into the house as if he has just had a satisfying shit.

He makes me think of my father. Nothing can make Papa raise his voice, even though we live in an angry society. He doesn't vent his anger; instead, he swallows it. Or maybe he lost his anger somewhere along the way, just as a eunuch loses his balls. What would Papa think of Domestic Love's dirty swearing?

Roy's attention is drawn by a couple of non-Han Chinese, wearing their own colorful costumes. They are Miao Chinese from a small town called Phoenix, in Hunan Province.

The woman's name is Lan Lan; The man's is A-yi. They have been married for four years. Teachers in a remote elementary school for all of their adult lives, they have moved to Beijing to seek their fame and fortune.

Lan Lan is a rock-and-roll singer. She tells us that she and three friends formed Beijing's first all-girl rock band, the Wild Nuns, in the basement of one member's house.

"In 'eighty-four," she says to Roy, "I arrived in Beijing, totally overwhelmed. I couldn't find a job. One day a friend of my husband's who had just returned from a short trip to America invited us to his house. We all watched a videotape of Madonna. It was my first experience of pop music in the West. I was astonished. She sang, danced, and yelled on the stage, and dancers danced with her. 'Fuck,' I said to myself, 'you may have been a music teacher, but you don't know music. If you can combine Madonna with Miao music, you can be a hit!' I quit playing the accordion and bought a guitar. I soon found some sisters and we practiced Madonna's dances every day. We formed our own band."

I look at her short, mannish haircut, the big muscles on her shoulders, her shining purple lipstick and eye shadow, and her black leather gloves, all mixed together with the handmade costume, silver necklace, bracelets, and rings of a Miao Chinese.

"What type of songs do you sing?" Roy asks.

"At first we sang Madonna's 'Holiday' and 'Like a Virgin' in Chinese. But then we realized that the sound wasn't hard enough, so we started to write our own songs."

Lan Lan's husband, A-yi, is a painter and former art teacher. Funky Republican Village has inspired his artistic creativity; he's thrown himself into a style of painting that he terms obscure. According to him, it is very different from orthodox Chinese art, which always has a political theme.

"I was the founder of the school of obscure painting." A-yi says. "My works were all concerned with the human id, so I drank a lot before I painted. I liked to paint my nightmares and illusions because they made me high."

Roy will later tell me that A-yi, like many intellectuals in Beijing, has been heavily influenced by Freud. I don't know what or who Freud is, but I sense that it's cool among intellectuals and artists to talk about Freud and the id.

A-yi keeps using the past tense because he doesn't paint anymore. He never sold a single work. "I burned all my paintings. I felt nobody could understand my art. I can't depend on my *laopo*—my old woman—to support me in Beijing. I just can't," he murmurs.

Lan Lan shakes her head and comments, "Chinese husbands are just too proud."

A-yi continues to tell us their story. "Last month the city government forced Lan Lan's band to break up. They said Lan Lan's lyrics 'I'm a nun, monks are my fans/ I'm on the run, police are my men' were obscene and spiritually polluting. Now she sings in a bar called the Emperor, and I'm the bouncer there. We've saved some money, and soon we'll be able to afford a bigger place."

Although A-yi is soft-spoken, or even a little timid, he has a tough, macho look and a shaved head like a bandit. I think of Yuan's joke, "Hunan is the birthplace of bandits, and Mao is the biggest one of all."

"You've gone from being a 'people's teacher' to being a hippie painter and now a bouncer at a nightclub. What has motivated you?" Roy asks.

"Dreams, I guess. You Americans have your American dreams, and we Chinese have our Chinese dreams."

"What is *your* Chinese dream?"

"To live here in Beijing is our dream."

A-yi's words surprise me. It has never occurred to me that my fucked-up life could actually be someone else's dream. How can his ambitions be so simple? What's so good about this city?

"I know life is difficult in Beijing for migrants," says Roy. "Because you're still officially residents of your hometown, you aren't eligible for ration coupons here, and if you have a kid, he or she can't go to Beijing public schools. Stuck-up

Beijingers look down on you if you have an accent. Isn't all of that true? Have you ever wanted to go back home?"

"All true, but we'll never go back!" Lan Lan puts in. "If we hadn't come to Beijing, I never would have seen those videos by Madonna, and they changed my life."

Lighting a cigarette and inhaling deeply, she continues, "You see, we call Beijing the heart of our Middle Kingdom, the heart of the Party. Historically, those who live here have been called imperial residents. So all the attention is on this place. And our backward and primitive hometown? It's the asshole of the country. The people who live there are referreed to as *manzi,* 'barbarians.'

"What can you do in the anus of China? Fart? Shit? Even if you pass a loud fart, nobody cares because it's still just a fart. Can you imagine the feeling? It takes a week, or sometimes even a month, for news from Beijing to travel to our town. I hadn't seen a telephone, bubble gum, or a foreigner until I came to Beijing two years ago. My entertainment was riding on pigs! We'd rather be bums in Beijing than have permanent jobs in our hometown."

Lan Lan sounds hard and masculine, her voice resounding and yet lyrical. I can imagine the power she must have onstage.

I can't understand such determination to leave home. I live with my parents and don't have a home of my own, but I can't picture myself migrating to another place. Beijing's dusty winds, gray skies, noises, and hassles, the fragrance of its August Chinese osmanthus, the taste of its sugar-coated chestnuts, the look of its zigzag alleys—all of these are in my blood. Where does this couple's desire to leave home come from? What has brought Roy here from a place so far away that it is hard for me to even conceive of? Has he never been homesick, or is he simply able to make a home for himself wherever he happens to be? Is it true that sometimes one has to leave home in order to find oneself?

Roy and I depart from Republican Village at around midnight. There are so many different worlds in Beijing that I never knew existed. The artists are as rebellious as gang members. On the one hand I feel they are my allies; on the other hand, they want attention, and I myself try to avoid attention.

As we stroll the streets near the ancient Summer Palace, Roy remarks, "The residents of Republican Village may be paupers in terms of material wealth, but spiritually, they're millionaires. It's so good to see that some people still have ideas, even though getting rich has become the most glorious dream in China."

"What's wrong with getting rich?" I ask. Yuan once told me, "The most painful thing for us Chinese is that when we awake from our ideals and spiritual dreams, we have nowhere to go. So we turn to money."

"Nothing's wrong with it; everybody should have the right to pursue his or her happiness. But getting rich shouldn't be *the* goal of our lives. We also need something more fulfilling. Our basic needs range from primitive to advanced, and to me, getting rich seems to belong to the primitive and middle stages. It satisfies our physical needs and makes us feel good about ourselves. Basically, when we get rich, we feel competent and get respect from others. However, the highest state of mind is to find and fulfill our own unique potential and set meaningful goals in life."

Roy's words pierce me like a pinprick. I've always drifted

around and have never felt the urge to aspire to any goal. Perhaps that's why my life seems so dull and empty.

Roy and I walk the quiet streets, which in daytime are filled with crowds of people. It's after midnight already, but he's wired and full of energy. He is always fascinated by those who stand out and create events and stories. He isn't much interested at all in common Chinese like my neighbors, even though their lives are more typical. With Roy I am able to see things that a normal Chinese woman would not otherwise see. I am learning about lives different from my own.

By the time I get back to the compound where my parents live, the gate is already locked. I have to find a dark corner and climb up the wall to get into the building without waking up the security guards.

Roy suggests, "Let me drive around to the outside of the compound wall so you can stand on top of the jeep and climb."

"That won't be necessary. I've been climbing up the wall for many years now." I show him my kung fu.

"So you've partied wildly and stayed out late at night before? Is that how you became an expert at climbing walls?" Roy teases me. He watches as I quickly scale the wall like an orangutan, bare-handed.

Standing atop the wall, I look back at him. His face looks soft in this light, his eyes glittering, his smile heartwarming. Such a beautiful human being, I think to myself. I jump down from the wall and walk back to him. "Actually, I did much more than that," I say. He hugs me. During all those years when I sought security and protection in the arms of gang members and thugs, I never feel completely safe.

Now, in the embrace of this American man, I do. I don't have to hide anything anymore.

Roy doesn't say anything, just presses his lips to mine. Even on this cold night, his lips are still as hot as the sun in midsummer. Oh, those talkative, expressive, soft, sexy lips. The moisture inside his mouth is like alcohol, making me drunk.

A week later I receive a letter from Old Fish, containing some of Black Dream's poems. The envelope is marked "urgent."

Dear Lili,

My name is Old Fish. I am the head of Republican Village. I hope you remember me. You and your American boyfriend Roy came to visit our village last Saturday. I'm writing to inform you of some bad news. A few hours after you and Roy left, the Haidian district police came to arrest some of the partygoers on charges of hooliganism. Almost all of those you met, including Old Wolf, Domestic Love, and the Miao couple, are being held in detention. I am OK. I was not at the party, and I didn't talk much with Roy. But as the head of the village, I have been warned that I can no longer invite foreign journalists to come here without first getting permission from the local authorities. The Haidian police say that local residents have filed complaints about our villagers' lifestyles. They don't like us. The police can shut down our village at any time. We live in peace and don't steal or rob. We don't commit any crimes. We express ourselves in peaceful ways. All we want is a place to do our creative work, but the local police always find excuses to harass us.

I know that if I were to write to Roy, the letter would be

confiscated by the Security Department. So I am writing to
you instead, to let you know about the situation.

Enclosed are some poems by Black Dream, the greatest poet
of modern-day China. I hope your boyfriend Roy can help
translate and publish Black Dream's work overseas. We all
believe that he will be China's first Nobel Prize–winner for
literature.

> *Peace,*
> *Old Fish*
> *At the end of the Year of the Tiger*

As Roy and I wandered around in the Summer Palace
area that early morning, talking about Western psychology,
the artists at Old Wolf's party were being arrested for indulging in "hooligan behavior." Things are tightening up
again. Then they will loosen. It is always like this.

I flip through some of Black Dream's poems. As I scan
them, I see lines like "The universe originated in a secret
dialogue" and "We lost our soil, so we became modern
souls, with burning desire, but homeless" and "Love me,
and drink me as you drink beer." I find these things difficult
to understand. But Roy will love the work, I'm sure.

SIX

Several days after our visit to Republican Village, Roy and I see an experimental drama called *Grandpa Doggie Obtaining Nirvana*. As we leave the dark theater, he whispers in my ear, "Do you want to come live with me?"

His hot breath tickles my ear. Later he tells me that he has been thinking of asking me this since the night I hugged him outside the compound where my parents live.

For seven months now we have been acting like two teenagers. Each time we return from a date, we kiss good-bye at the entrance to the alley where I live.

Before I can say anything, Roy speaks. "Lili, I don't want you to give me your answer now. Call me when you've made up your mind."

Although he acts as if it weren't a big deal, he is nervous,

I can tell. He doesn't realize that I know all the steps of this dance already.

"OK." I nod.

Roy smiles and hails a yellow cab for me. On the way home in the cab, I sink back in the seat. Buildings and trees whiz by. Children are playing and laughing in the streets. Suddenly bright red fireworks explode in the dark sky: Spring Festival.

Instead of going back to my parents' home, I go to Amei's. I tell her about Roy's request.

"Why are you asking me what you should do?" Amei says with a knowing look. "I bet you've already decided. You're always looking for crazy things to get involved in. It'll make a good piece of news for the *Beijing Daily;* the headline will be 'Ex–Gang Member Damages Chinese Women's New Image by Illegally Shacking Up with a Foreigner in the Heart of Our Glorious Motherland.' "

I'm not concerned about my reputation, because it can't get any worse than it is. I'm not afraid of being arrested by the police for illegally living with an American. So why am I hesitating about moving in with this man when I know I want to be with him?

"Lili," Amei says, "it's not a war between you and Roy. You don't have to use old Mao's military tactics. There's no winning or losing in a realtionship. If you've made up your mind, just do it. What are you waiting for?"

"I don't know," I answer honestly. Living with a man is nothing new for me; back in the Cultural Revolution, I had sex with young thugs in exchange for ration coupons or protection. But now something's stopping me from simply saying yes to Roy.

"Tell me, does he love you?" Amei looks intently at me.

"Love?" I'm surprised by her choice of words. "I'm not sure."

"Do you love him, then?"

"I don't know." I sigh and look back at Amei. "Why are you suddenly asking me that? Have you been watching too many Japanese soap operas?"

"Has it occurred to you that you and Roy want to be together because you love each other?"

My feelings for Roy are new to me. I almost never think about sex when I'm with him. Men usually get physical with me pretty quickly, but Roy isn't like that at all. I certainly find him good-looking, but there are other qualities in him that are more interesting to me than his looks. I always feel I need to keep my eyes wide open, my mind active, to catch up with him. Even when he kisses me, I dare not think any further ahead.

I remember that Amei said once I was a danger to men. She was joking, but her words, like a snakebite, left their mark.

"So do you still think I'm a danger to men?" I ask Amei.

Amei laughs, looks into my eyes, and strokes my hair tenderly. "Lili, you're a beautiful young woman, and you have your own unique style. You can be a blessing to a man. It's up to you."

"Thank you." I shake her hand. "I must go."

Amei hugs me good-bye. "Good luck!"

For three weeks Roy sends fresh red roses to me almost every day. I wonder whether we love each other. I try not to think of the past. But I keep asking myself, "Have you loved anyone, Lili? *Can* you be a blessing to a man?" I realize that I am trying to deny the past. And the memory of one man.

A man was once stabbed to death because of me. I don't know if I loved him before that; maybe not. But there was a time when he was closer to me than anyone else.

For years I have carefully and successfully buried all memories of him. But Roy's invitation has forced me to reopen that dark chapter of my life filled with blood and tears. The man's wolf eyes, the scars he had on his left cheek, and the smell of tobacco that always hovered around him all come rushing back.

His name was Little Rock.

I met him after I ran away from Monkey Village. At that time I was twelve and a half; he was sixteen. From Monkey Village I walked for five days and nights, alone. I didn't know where I was headed, exactly, but I knew I had to get away. The farther, the better. The food I'd brought along was gone by the third day. For two more days I ate fallen leaves and grass. The weather was chilly and stormy. I tried to walk fast so it wouldn't seem so cold, but a growing sensation of burning and pain between my legs slowed down my pace. I peed ten times or more a day. Every time I took off my pants to pee, the wind would blow so hard on my bottom, I felt I was going to freeze to death.

By the fifth night I was too tired to walk any farther and finally fell asleep on the dirt road. A strange yowling woke me: wolves, a pack of them, or maybe two or three packs, were gathering about ten meters behind me. The lead wolf was staring at me. Its stare was savage and unblinking. I was terrified. I wanted to scream, but I had no strength. I wanted to move, but I felt paralyzed. The night sky was clear, and thousands of stars were shining, just as they would years later in Inner Mongolia. Despite the cold, I couldn't stop sweating.

"Come on, come on and eat me, eat me into pieces, I'm waiting. I don't want to live anymore," I heard a small voice inside me say to the wolves. The voice got stronger and stronger. At last my fear disappeared entirely, the fear of death. The worst had already happened. What else could I be afraid of? I stared back at the lead wolf, silently waiting.

The wolves didn't move. I waited for some minutes more and then quietly stood up. I started to inch forward. I could sense that the wolves were following me. When I stopped, they stopped, too, always keeping ten meters away from me.

Strangely, I no longer felt any pain, exhaustion, cold, or hunger. I strode briskly. My mind concentrated on walking. One step, two steps—I heard nothing but my own footsteps. I even forgot the wolves. As I walked, the thick darkness faded, and the sun rose on the horizon. I don't remember when it was that I realized the wolves were gone. I fainted in the daylight, there under the winter sun.

When I regained consciousness, I saw a pair of eyes. At first I mistook them for a wolf's, long, slim, and savage. I screamed. My reaction must have frightened the apparition, because he shivered and then stepped back.

"Girl, how did you end up here?"

For days I had not heard a human voice—for days. It sounded funny.

I didn't say anything.

He offered me a piece of cold wheat bread, and I grabbed it and gobbled it up. Then I started to burp. He gave me some water and looked at me, smiling, his gaze almost exactly like a wolf's.

I gulped the water. As it ran down my throat, I thought to myself, Were there really wolves following me last night, or did I just have a nightmare?

"Why are you here in this wilderness?" This time I took a look at him. He was thin, of medium height, with a dark complexion. His nose was high and long. He had some scars on his right cheek. He was ugly.

I told him I'd been abducted in Beijing and sold to a peasant family in Monkey Village. I'd run away from there, having decided to beg my way back to the city.

"How—how old are you?" he asked, lighting up a cigarette.

"How old are *you*?" I asked in reply.

"I'm sixteen."

"I'm seventeen."

"Don't lie to me. You look at most fifteen."

I didn't say anything.

"If you want to get to Beijing, you're going in completely the wrong direction. This road will take you to the west," he said. "But if you really want to go to there, I can probably help you. In return, though, you'll have to pay me five yuan. Can you do that?"

I had stolen five yuan before I left, but I didn't want to give it to him. It was all I had.

"Why should I trust you?" I asked. Why should I trust a man with a pair of wolf eyes? I thought.

"If you don't trust me, you won't have *anybody* to trust. You won't find another soul out here. You can believe me or not, but I'm telling you, you'll get lost and starve to death and become a mummy in this wilderness!"

He was right.

"Who are you?" I softened my voice.

He started to tell me his story. He was an orphan who survived by stealing and begging. He had just offended a local bully in the township, and the bully had threatened to cut off both his hands. He was hiding out in this wilderness.

"How did you get the scars on your cheek?" I asked.

"I was busted once. The family had five sons. They said I deserved a souvenir," he said indifferently, as if the scars weren't right there on his face for all to see.

"Then why do you keep on doing it?"

"It's how I live."

After we used up the five yuan, we didn't have anything more to eat for two days. Every place we went, the local police harassed us because "beggars hurt the image of our great motherland." Sometimes we were beaten by ruffians as well as by the police.

One day Little Rock saw an old guy using a tricycle with a flatbed to move a lot of oranges. He offered his help, and the old man was grateful. But then toward the end Little Rock stole five oranges from the man and ran away. He gave four to me and ate only the smallest one himself.

I was deeply moved. I told him about my family. I told him I'd run away from Monkey Village because I'd been raped. I told him wolves had followed me and I'd wanted to die.

Little Rock clenched his teeth as he listened. After I finished, he asked me to stand on top of a rock at the side of the road. He looked up at me and raised his right hand. "Little sister, my little sister, your brother Little Rock will protect you from now on. If I fail, I deserve to die."

We became brother and sister. He was the only person I trusted in the world, and I was his only relative.

We begged our way to a city where we jumped a freight train. On the ride to Beijing, I promised to give Little Rock some of my comic books and my other treasures. I offered to give him a military belt made of leather, every teen's dream. But when we arrived at my parents' old home, the place filled with my earliest childhood memories, we saw two strips of paper making an X across the door, imprinted with the words "Sealed by the Revolutionary Committee of Beijing No. 4 High School."

I had not cried once during my long trek, even when the wolves were following me. But now I collapsed.

"I came from a long way away! I came from a long way away!" I shouted at the door hysterically, drumming it hard with my fists. My last hope was gone. I was homeless in my own hometown.

Little Rock hugged me close. I was shocked by this: he had never hugged me before. In those days hugging between a boy and a girl was taboo and considered hooligan behavior. That was why we had pretended to be brother and sister until now. But after all we'd been through, I hugged him back and cried on his shoulder. We two dirty kids just sat there in front of my old home, hugging each other, abandoned by the world.

Then he kissed me, on the cheek.

"What are you doing? I'm your little sister!" I became angry with him. The way he was looking at me made me uncomfortable.

"I, I, I'm sorry," Little Rock, embarrassed, stuttered.

"Let's go to Uncle Hua's to stay!" I said to him. Beijing was my hometown, and I had to act like a hostess.

Uncle Hua is my father's only brother and our only relative in Beijing. He is fifteen years younger than my father. My grandparents died when Papa and Uncle Hua were young, and Papa raised Uncle Hua like a son. Uncle Hua had married a difficult woman and became an obedient husband. After the Great Revolution started, they kept their distance from us. When my parents learned they were being sent to the countryside to be reeducated, they asked Uncle Hua to take care of me in Beijing. Uncle Hua refused because his wife didn't want any trouble. So my parents had to take me with them to Monkey Village.

Uncle Hua's was the only place I could go now. Little Rock knew it wouldn't be good for me to be seen with him, so he didn't come to the door with me. Aunt Bai answered my knock.

She recognized me but didn't greet me. She must have smelled my stink, because she used one hand to cover her nose. "So smelly! It's awful!"

She turned away and yelled to Uncle Hua, "Your counterrevolutionary brother's daughter is here. You have two minutes to get rid of her."

Uncle Hua came to the door.

"My poor Lili, what's happened to you? You look like a beggar. Where are your parents? You know what? Your uncle is now a clay Bodhisattva crossing the river—I cannot even save myself. I'm afraid I can't help you. You're the daughter of a reactionary family. I have two children and in-laws. You know what I mean." He gave me two yuan. "Find a place to take a shower and have a good meal," he said. "I'm sorry that's all Uncle Hua can do."

I didn't want to take the money. I wanted to throw it back into Uncle Hua's face. But then I thought, Why *not* take it? I had suffered enough from starvation and cold. At least I could use the two yuan to buy two bowls of hot noodles for Little Rock and me.

I turned and walked away from Uncle Hua's home. Little Rock emerged from the shrubs he'd been hiding in and said, "I heard everything, little sister. Do you want me to fix your uncle, that turtle's egg?"

I said, "The most important thing now is for us to get something to eat and then find a place to sleep."

At a small restaurant we had noodles with shredded pork. He had three bowls and I had two. After dinner I took Little Rock to see my classmate Sweet Grass, who had been my best friend in elementary school. Her parents were officers in the military. Before leaving Beijing, I had heard that her family was in trouble, too.

She was very happy to see me. "Come on in, Lili," she said. "No matter what's has happened to you, you don't have to worry anymore. It's safe here in my house. You can take a shower and change into my clothes. Who is this boy? Your bodyguard? We have plenty of rooms here in our house!"

Sweet Grass told me that her parents were locked in a cowshed. "Can you believe that? My brother Spring Ocean searched our house with his friends, and they threw our folks out. This house is run by him and me now! Bravo, Cultural Revolution! How's everything with your family?"

I told her.

"I'm glad you're back—we can have fun together! But go take a shower first," Sweet Grass said.

I took a long shower. I couldn't remember the last time I'd had one. I looked at my naked body. I saw two small lumps on my chest and a tuft of light, curly hair between my legs. I felt disgusted by those changes and wished I could be a little girl again. I started to rub my skin hard with a piece of towel. I wanted to rub off all the dirt, the dirtiness, the signs that I was becoming a woman. I was ashamed.

After my shower I dressed in Sweet Grass's new clothes. Little Rock stared at me.

Sweet Grass called from downstairs, "Lili, come down, there're some people here I'd like you to meet!"

Several boys and girls were sitting around, laughing, smoking, and drinking. One girl was even sitting on a boy's lap. The girls had short hair and were dressed in fashionable military uniforms. The boys likewise wore military uniforms and were acting cool.

This was hooligan behavior.

"They're my brother's friends," Sweet Grass said to me. All of them started to introduce themselves.

"East Wind. I'm from the People's Daily Compound in Wang Fu Jing. My parents are in cadre school now."

"Autumn Plum. I'm from the compound at the Academy of Social Science in Ritan Lu. My parents are in a cowshed somewhere in the suburbs."

"Big China. I'm from the military compound in San Li He. My parents are being reeducated in the countryside."

"Little China. Big China's brother."

"Chou-Chou. I'm from the compound of the Ministry of Foreign Affairs. My folks are in the Fifty-seventh Cadre School now."

"Spring Ocean. I'm Sweet Grass's big brother and the head of the household!"

I felt as if I'd found a long-lost clan to which I had once belonged. "Did you just get out of school?" I asked them.

"School? Are you kidding? Nobody goes to school anymore!" Spring Ocean laughed loudly. He was the leader of the group, tall and handsome.

"The more you know, the more counterrevolutionary you will become, just like my folks!" East Wind commented.

"Where are you from?" Autumn Plum asked Little Rock, who'd been ignored till now.

"I'm not from Beijing."

Some of the others started to snicker because Little Rock spoke in a heavy accent.

" 'I'm not from Beijing.' " Chou-Chou mimicked his inflection.

More laughs, laughs at the country hick. Little Rock's face reddened.

"Stop it! He's my brother," I said. I did not want them to make fun of him.

"Oh, sorry. We're just joking. Don't get angry. Relax!" Big China apologized.

Before I could say anything more, Spring Ocean hushed the group and announced, "Listen, everybody, I need your help. Lili can't go back to her home, and she doesn't have Beijing residency anymore; she's just run away from Monkey Village. She can't buy food because she doesn't have any coupons. Can we help her?"

"Yes. Count her in! Let her stay with us!" Everybody nodded.

At night the boys and girls all slept in the same house. We played cards and chess together till midnight. I felt so happy I thought I was dreaming. This was like the Communist society depicted in our textbooks. I had enough food to eat and nothing to worry about. I was with my peers, having fun.

I learned the girls' way of dressing. I cut my hair short

like a boy's. I wore black shoes and military pants. I learned the coolest swear words—for example, "cow's cunt" to refer to something good, "dull cunt" for something stupid, and "smelly cunt" for a whore.

Little Rock didn't get along with these Beijing kids; they were snobs, he said. Although he ran with them, he thought he knew more than they did and should be their leader. "They think I'm a country bumpkin and ugly and stupid. But sooner or later, I'll let them see who Little Rock really is!" He often said this to me. I thought he was oversensitive. I told him many times, "They just like to joke around. Don't take them seriously." But he remained unhappy.

Little Rock didn't like the change in me, either. He often mocked me bitterly, saying, "You look like a cheap whore!" or "Your bottom is getting bigger!" Little Rock was my savior, my big brother. No matter how harsh and sour his words, I never took offense. He especially didn't like my talking to the other boys. "*I* saved you, and *I'm* your big brother, not them! Remember!" he chided me.

I tried to keep my distance from them to make Little Rock happy, but he suspected that Sweet Grass's brother, Spring Ocean, wanted to seduce me. "Are you interested in him?" Little Rock must have asked me a thousand times. It annoyed me, but I didn't want to lose my temper.

Spring Ocean was the leader of the gang and took care of all of us. He brought food back for us. He knew all kinds of people. He was tall and thin, with big eyes and long legs. The other kids liked to say he looked European; at that time, anyone who looked European was considered handsome.

One day Spring Ocean told me that the paper sealing on the door of my parents' home had been removed, and I could return home. "Nobody's going to bother you," he promised me.

I was glad to be able to live in my old home again, but I missed the communal atmosphere at Spring Ocean's house. Besides, Little Rock still lived there, and I worried that he wouldn't get along with the others, so I visited often.

One evening the boys were playing poker, gambling. The losers had to drink spirits. The girls were watching and laughing. Little Rock always lost. He got quite upset and kept saying others were cheating. I suggested that he stop and go to bed since it was already very late. He replied drunkenly, "Kiss my mouth, and I'll stop."

Everyone laughed at us deliriously. Embarrassed, I got up to go home. Spring Ocean asked Little Rock to accompany me. "Behave yourself," Spring Ocean warned him. Little Rock left the house with me.

As we walked, he lit up a cigarette.

I asked him whether he liked Beijing, whether he was happy. He didn't answer. Instead, he blew smoke at me. The mixed odor of cigarettes and spirits in his mouth smelled awful.

"What are you doing?" I demanded. "I don't like that."

"Do you know that you've become uglier and uglier?" he asked.

"Whatever you say."

"Why do you always stick out your chest? It makes me want to throw up."

"You're drunk. You're talking nonsense."

"I'm not drunk. I know exactly what I'm talking about. I bet you really want to get fucked, don't you?"

"You're crazy."

"Everyone knows that if a woman gets fucked once, she

wants to get fucked again. You got fucked before, right? You told me the story. You must want it again!"

I had never expected that he would turn against me what I had told him in confidence. I said to him, "I can get home by myself. You must be tired. You can go back now."

He tossed away the cigarette he'd been smoking and sneered. "Somebody's waiting for you, right? I know it. You're no different from the other whores."

"I'm not a whore."

"You are."

"I'm not."

"You are."

"Go away!" I yelled angrily.

Seeing me this angry for the first time, he turned and walked away without another word.

I gazed at his receding figure, wondering how we'd gotten so estranged. Was he the same Little Rock who'd saved me in the wilderness? Why had everything changed between us since our arrival in Beijing?

As I walked homeward by myself, the road grew dark. I began to walk faster and then sensed that something was wrong. In the darkness, two hoodlums corned me, approached from different directions.

The shorter one grabbed my arms while the taller one started to fondle my breasts and pull my pants down. I tried to scream but felt something hard and cold pressed against my neck.

Suddenly Spring Ocean appeared with several of his buddies. "Spring Ocean is here. Who do you think you're fucking with?" he shouted.

Five or six tough guys carrying knives, rocks, bricks, and belts encircled the first two. They released me right away.

"Sorry. We thought she was somebody else," one of them said. They both knelt down and kowtowed to Spring Ocean.

"Slap yourself a hundred times!" someone ordered.

The two started to slap their faces and said, "Sorry, Great Aunt!" to me.

Someone else asked Spring Ocean, "What should we do with them?"

Spring Ocean looked at me, and I shook my head. I didn't want to see any bloodshed.

"Are you OK?" he asked me tenderly.

"I'm OK. You came just in time."

"If you ever again touch a hair on her head, you'll die like pigs in a slaughterhouse," he told my assailants. "Now get out of here before I change my mind."

The two ran.

When we got back to Spring Ocean's house, everyone sat down and waited for him to speak. Little Rock was off by himself in a corner.

"Little Rock came back too quickly, and I figured you might run into some trouble," Spring Ocean told me.

"It wasn't his fault. I asked him to go. It was my own fault," I said.

"Don't act like a heroine!" Little Rock shouted at me. "You think you're covering my ass? I don't need a favor from a whore!" Then he turned to Spring Ocean and said, "If you want to punish me, go ahead."

"We *should* punish you, because you put Lili in great danger. But since she has spoken up for you, we want to give you a chance." Spring Ocean's voice was calm and authoritarian.

"Who do you guys think you are? Just because you're

native Beijingers, do you think you can look down on me? I don't have any parents, brothers, or sisters, but I was earning a living wandering from place to place before you even started going to school. How dare you order me around? I'm leaving!" Little Rock raged.

"Don't go, Little Rock," I pleaded.

He looked at me coldly. "You're no longer my little sister. I don't know you anymore."

"Let him go. He's not happy here anyway," Spring Ocean said to me.

Why was it that Little Rock and I could share hardships but not comforts?

Spring Ocean assigned Little China to be my bodyguard. Wherever I went, he went with me.

One night, though, Little China was ill. After four or five of us had some drinks in a small tavern, Spring Ocean offered to take me home. I rode on the back of his Phoenix bike.

It was the first time I'd ever been alone with him. We didn't talk much on the way, but when we got back to my place, I asked if he'd like some tea. We looked at each other, not knowing what to say. I wanted to know what he did all day, for example, and where he found food, toilet paper, and soap for us, and why everybody was so loyal to him, but I waited for him to speak first.

"Can I see your photo album, if you have one?" he asked.

"Sure." I brought him the album that held all my childhood pictures. As he was flipping through it, I ran to the bathroom. Being alone with him made me nervous, and the bathroom seemed like a good hiding place. I stared at myself in the mirror, feeling my heart pound fast in my chest.

Then the bathroom door opened. Spring Ocean embraced me quietly from behind. He kissed my neck and started to take off my clothes. He didn't say a word, but he was very skillful. I didn't resist. I didn't know whether I felt happy or sad; nor did I know if I even liked him. All I felt was that his touch provided some consolation. That was how I gave myself to him in that stuffy bathroom.

From that night on I was known as Spring Ocean's girlfriend; others called me his *quanzi*. But however much he may have liked me, he was a gang leader first, and he loved his brotherhood better. He offered me to his buddies the same way he shared food and cigarettes with them. "Can you go with Big China today?" he'd ask me. "He really has a crush on you!"

I knew that if I wanted to survive, I had to listen to him. I became a trophy, a "comfort woman" in his gang. The other members became more loyal to him because their big brother was so generous that he didn't even get jealous when they slept with his woman.

Little Rock had formed a gang of his own on the East Side of the city; he had almost as many soldiers as Spring Ocean. Then I got pregnant and didn't even know who the father was; I had an abortion. Somehow Little Rock heard about all this. He also learned that Spring Ocean made me sleep with other men and that was how I'd gotten pregnant. Little Rock challenged Spring Ocean to a fight. He said he was going to disable Spring Ocean's manhood.

Nobody told me about the duel.

The abortion had left me very weak. Spring Ocean

came in to talk to me one day, his expression stern and frustrated, his shirt stained with blood. I had never seen him look so frightening.

"I'm sorry," he began. "I stabbed Little Rock. He said one of us had to die. He died on the way to the hospital. We're going to find a good place to bury him, don't worry. But right now I have to leave Beijing and hide out for a while."

"Where is he? I want to see his body!" I screamed and tried to get out of bed. I didn't know whom to hate more—Spring Ocean or myself.

"You'd better not, Lili. For what?" Spring Ocean held me back.

"He's my brother."

"Not anymore, he isn't."

"It's all my fault."

"It's *not* your fault. He wanted to be your man, but you treated him like a brother. He couldn't accept it. He went crazy!"

"He said that he'd protect me, that he'd rather die than fail in that. Now he's dead because of me! It's my fault. If he'd never met me, if he hadn't come to Beijing with me, if he hadn't cared about me at all, he'd still be alive . . . ," I wailed.

"Lili, from now on I'll protect you," Spring Ocean said. I laughed weakly. Did a woman like me need protecting? I had nothing left to lose.

Little Rock's scarred face haunted me. I thought of the wheat bread he'd given me when I almost died, the four oranges he'd stolen for me on the road: this man had saved my life, and I'd betrayed him. How could he die for someone who'd done that to me? I couldn't sleep at night.

Little Rock's death made me the most notorious female hooligan in the entire city. Big Trumpet became my nickname.

After the Great Revolution, Spring Ocean would be imprisoned for gang-related crimes, including the stabbing of Little Rock.

I've had other boyfriends since then, but I always run away when they start to get serious about me. Seriousness reminds me of a pair of wolf eyes. I'm just like my grandma, a woman who brings men nothing but bad luck.

I don't have the guts to talk to Roy. I remember vividly the softness in his voice when he spoke of his dead love, Yoshiko. His compassion is a part of his innocence. If we live together, if we become closer, will I endanger him, too?

SEVEN

The more I try to suppress my desire to see Roy, the more desirable he becomes to me. Each night before I fall asleep, I feel a pair of wolf eyes staring at me from the darkness. But the next morning, when I receive the flowers Roy has sent me, I want to throw myself into his arms under the sun.

This tug of war lasts for weeks, by the end of which time I can no longer remember Roy's face. The only thing I can recall about him is his smile. I have to see that smile once more. I need his healthiness to keep me sane.

I decide to drop by his apartment. Dropping by is the Chinese way. Before I go, I take an unusually thorough bath at a public bathhouse. I wear an old black skirt, put on only very light lipstick, and part my hair in the middle so it's long and flowing. I check myself in the mirror and am pleased to see how casual I look.

The army guard at the entrance to Roy's apartment compound stops me.

"Do you have a permit?"

"No."

"Why are you here?"

"To see a friend."

"Her name?"

"Roy."

"A male friend?" The guard raises an eyebrow. I am tempted to tell him that I'm not even wearing underwear.

"Is this your first time here?" he asks.

I nod.

He points to the reception room and says, "Go get a permit, then bring it back here."

An old man is sitting behind the glass reception window. He asks for my ID, then hands me a detailed guest form to fill out. The form asks for my name, sex, age, ethnic background, occupation, relationship to the person being visited, reason for coming, arrival time, and expected hour of departure. I have to fill in all of this information on two separate forms. When I finish, I wait for the man to return my ID. He tears apart the two forms and passes one back to me, saying, "Have our resident sign here before you leave so that you can get your ID back. Remember that you have to leave here before nine-thirty P.M. After that, we won't return your ID to you."

The compound is totally different from Beijing. In front of each tall building is a fresh-smelling lawn, one without hundreds of bikes parked all over it. There are cars and jeeps in the parking lot, many of them with diplomatic plates. Every apartment block has air conditioners sticking out of its windows. Unlike Chinese families' balconies, crammed with laundry and winter cabbage, the balconies here are adorned with flowers and hammocks.

As I enter Roy's building, I smell a fragrance, the scent of Aunt Sara, of expensive hotels.

As I stand in front of Roy's door, number 223, music that I recognize, from *Swan Lake,* filters through from inside. It stops me from knocking. Beyond the door is that smile of Roy's that I've been longing to see, but this is a foreign world, too elegant for a woman like me. I hold my breath and decide to leave. As I'm walking down the stairs, though, I hear the door open behind me.

"Why are you leaving?" Roy's voice isn't pleasant. He's standing at the door, staring at me with an angry expression on his face.

I don't respond. I walk back up slowly, casually, and silently go in past him. His apartment is twice as big as my parents' and decorated with tie-dyed wall hangings, silk fans, calligraphy, and Japanese *ukiyo-e* paintings. The rich hues dazzle my eyes. The furniture is in the ancient Chinese style, inlaid with seashells and jade. Roy pours me a glass of iced tea, and we sit surrounded by the music of *Swan Lake,* submerged in the almost psychedelic array of colors, watching each other.

An unfinished oil painting on his living room wall pictures a half-nude woman floating in the sky. I recognize her Asian face and the look in her eyes.

"Did you paint this?" I ask.

"Yes."

I walk over to the painting and make a dot with a black pen at the bottom of the figure's left breast. "She has a mole here," I say.

Roy's face lights up like a moon, and then, very naturally, we begin to kiss each other, slowly rolling around on the carpet. "Doll, my delicate doll," he whispers while kissing my bare legs. My body melts. There is a passionate force inside me, violent and unpredictable. I have tried so long to suppress it, but I can't any longer. Roy takes off my clothes, and I let him take his time. Then I stand before him, physically as well as emotionally naked. He gazes at me, then kisses my earlobes, my neck, and the soft valley between my bare breasts, my belly and my belly button. . . . He does it so wholeheartedly, as if worshiping his goddess. I am lying on the carpet running my fingers through his hair, with tears dripping down my face, but I can't explain what I'm feeling. No one has ever made me feel like this before. My whole body is trembling.

In the past I have had sex with men so that in return they would protect me. To me, sex hasn't been a pleasure; it has been a sacrifice, a powerful weapon. I have been not been a real woman.

In Monkey Village, parents wouldn't let their kids watch horses mate. "They're doing bad things," they would say. We have been taught that sex is dirty and bad. But with Roy I will find that sex can be as beautiful as a grand rite.

Roy decides to move out of the compound.

"I've found a flat near the Summer Palace for us," he says. "I think it'll be safer and nicer. We can have some privacy."

"Yes, we can have some privacy." I repeat what he says though I have no concept of what privacy is.

On the day I leave my parents to join him, I take only my erhu, two comic books, one pair of slippers, some underwear, and my diary.

My mother snarls, "Shacking up without marrying isn't only indecent, it's illegal. Even worse, you're going to live with a foreign devil. Do you know you can be arrested for that?"

"Yes. I know."

"Why do you always try to humiliate us?"

"Sorry, but I don't mean to. I just want to make my own decisions."

"How can children be so selfish! They don't think about their parents at all. All they think about is themselves."

"Did you ever think about Grandma?" I snap.

Mama is enraged. "Once you walk out, you'll never be permitted to come back here," she cries hysterically. "I wish you'd never been born, you ingrate, you Chinese sell-out."

Papa is by Mama's side, comforting her. He begs me, "Lili, how can you treat your mother like this? She's suffered too much already. She doesn't deserve this."

My father would never do anything to hurt anyone. I don't want to hear him begging me, his own daughter, for something. The thing I hate most is begging.

Everything I do shames Mama. I feel like crying, but I don't want to appear vulnerable. I have to escape.

I pretend not to care at all and leave their home without even looking back, like Precious Jade Jia abandoning his feudal family in the book *A Dream of Red Mansions*. Precious Jade Jia quits his parents' home to become a monk; I leave mine to live with a man. I even smile when I walk out. I can't escape this role that I am always performing, that of a Chinese daughter utterly lacking in "filial piety."

Roy names our new place the Forbidden Nest. It is a luxurious two-bedroom flat. The bedroom windows look out onto the Yang Qing Mountains. The bathroom has a marble floor.

I have never before bathed in a marble-floored bath. On our first night, Roy wants to take a bath with me, but I tell him I'd rather enjoy it by myself. In the steamy bathroom, I stretch out lying comfortably in the creamy-white bathtub filled with hot water. I realize that I am beginning to have a foreigner's lifestyle: hot water, marble floors, fragrant Zest soap, American-size towels. A life with privacy.

In elementary school we were often asked to write compositions about our happiest day. Typical themes were "The Day When I Became a Young Pioneer" and "The Day My Father Gave Me a Mao Badge."

Today, taking this bath, is my happiest day.

Roy wants to celebrate our union and our new home by throwing a party. In the living room he has hung up his abstract paintings and the photos he has taken all over the world. The Sony stereo plays a tape of an erhu solo I have recorded.

I invite only Old Fish, Yuan, and Amei to the party. Roy asks all his close American and European friends. There are more than a hundred invited guests, and still more who show up.

I open one wine bottle after another and empty the trash

cans while Roy mingles with the guests. His American friends Hugh, Frank, and Mike all have China-born Chinese wives. I recognize two of the women; they are former movie actresses who no longer appear on the screen. Roy tells me that marrying Asian women is very popular among foreigners in China. And "marrying out" is a new fad among Chinese female entertainers, I inform him.

The story of Hugh's wife, Joan, is this: "My husband knows enough Chinese only to say 'I want it' and 'I don't want it,' but the only thing he really ever says is 'I want it'; he's never said 'I don't want it.' Meanwhile, the only Chinese I say to him is 'I don't want it!' "

Another wife, Lucy, can't wait to toss out her husband's favorite line: "Once my husband went to a store and said to a female clerk, 'May I ask you something?' but he used the wrong tone for the word *ask,* so what he really said was, 'May I kiss you?' Can you imagine how embarrassed that teenage clerk was?"

The third woman, Mimi, whines to me, "Lili, you're lucky that Roy speaks perfect Chinese and understands it. You don't have to learn English. I have to speak English all the time—how unlucky I am! But I have no other choice."

It's funny to hear Mimi pretending to be unlucky when everyone knows that speaking English is a status symbol. It reminds me of how my mother used to pretend to complain to neighbors about my playing the violin when I was seven. "She plays the violin eight hours a day, and we don't know how to stop her. You're lucky that you don't have such a stubborn daughter."

Now I can't help but make fun of this woman. "Why say you have no choice? You could divorce your American husband and marry a Chinese man, and then you could speak only Chinese. There are half a billion Chinese men out there waiting for you."

Lucy jumps in and says, "Lili, you don't know what you're talking about. Mimi always wanted to marry a white man. She *never* dated Chinese."

Mimi protests, "No, that's not true."

Lucy exposes Mimi's old secrets. "I heard you chased after your husband in a disco and asked him to take you to America."

"That's ridiculous," Mimi insists, getting upset now. "My husband chased me first."

Old Fish seems a bit out of place. He knows no one here, nor does he like to initiate conversation. He is drinking by himself and playing with my puppy, Liu Ying. I greet him, and he tells me eagerly, "Black Dream is going to finish those epics of his." I introduce him to Amei so that he won't feel too lonely or awkward.

Later in the party, students from the Central Music Conservatory, the Drama Academy, and the Art Academy turn up uninvited to perform. The drama students dedicate their performance to Roy and me; the whole thing consists of nothing more than "I love you" spoken in different languages in different settings.

The music students chant in monotone, Buddhist-like, reciting a passage from the *Tao Tè Ching*.

Colors blind the eye
Sounds deafen the ear
Flavors numb the taste
Thoughts weaken the mind
Desires burn the heart

Success is as dangerous as failure
Hope is as empty as disappointment

No seeking, no expecting
Empty your mind
Feel at ease
Returning to the roots is serenity.

People are too busy talking to pay any attention to what the students are chanting.

Arts students often manage to show up at the most chic parties and clubs in Beijing. Besides seeing the chance to enjoy some free food and drink, they are eager to meet the city's elite. At the parties they make it their mission to get the phone number and autograph of anyone important or famous. They make the snobs feel more self-important.

A student from the Music Academy approaches me and says, "Lili, I've heard so much about you. Everyone says old Roy's girlfriend is an incredible woman. Very talented musically! I'm so glad to finally meet you."

I've never imagined that one day I'd hear a college student flatter me as if I were an important figure.

"Old Roy often mentions you to us," he adds.

"Really? He's never mentioned *you* to *me*."

My words don't embarrass the fellow. He keeps dropping big names and soon asks me to introduce him to some of the foreign ladies. I excuse myself and head into the kitchen to clean up.

Roy comes in after me and asks, "Are you having fun?"

"Of course, but it's like a zoo in there."

"Now you know what's happened to your compatriots under the open-door policy. They think coming to a party is like going to America. They arrive, with or without a visa."

At the end of the party, the student groupies demand that Roy and I kiss. Normally, women are expected to blush and play up a little affected bashfulness. But I kiss Roy in front of everyone without any shyness. Surrounded by this cultural elite, I want everyone to know that he lives with a Beijing street hooligan, not a privileged hostess. Amei watches me closely, and her gaze reveals that she knows what I am thinking.

Roy and I go to the North Sea Park in Beijing to have some tea in the Imperial Teahouse. Roy points to a vivid, child-like Chinese painting on one wall and says to me, "You see, that's the kind of lifestyle I'd like to have." The painting has a rich black outline, filled in with rosy pinks, vibrant reds, and bright oranges.

"A colorful life?"

"Yes." Roy is intoxicated by *renao*, the "fever of the crowd." He tries to explain it: "Lili, I told you that I'm Jewish, right? My father was a lawyer, but when he was in his thirties, he quit his job and became a farmer. I grew up on a ranch in northern California, near a very isolated town. We had to drive in our car, or ride on horseback, just to get to our closest neighbor's. My brother was my only playmate. We grew up with fields, woods, mountains, and pets, but we didn't have many friends. Later we moved to a city, and my brother and I both had difficulty dealing with urban people. My brother is still like that. He prefers nature and animals. What about you, Lili? I've noticed that you often seem disoriented in a group of people. It's as though you were in a trance sometimes."

I want to tell Roy that I take pride in my ability to dodge contact in crowds. My mind is able to drift around in another world even as I greet and talk to people. A crowd is a perfect place for me to rest my mind. But Roy won't understand this. He asks me what I *don't* like about parties.

"Too many people," I tell him.

"You don't like *renao*?"

"No." *Renao* reveals the excessive eagerness of Chinese to spend all their time at get-togethers just so they can pry into one another's business and envy one another.

Throughout my life I have had to share my space with others, fight against endless gossip, be constantly interrupted. I can't even find a nook or cranny in which to pass a good healthy fart.

"You must like peace and privacy," he says.

Privacy is a foreign word. In Chinese translation it refers to something evil that one doesn't want others to know about. For example, my grandma's three marriages and many affairs are "private."

"Tell me what *privacy* means in your language," I say to him.

"I think it means being secluded. You want to have your own, isolated space and don't want to be bothered."

He's describing the feelings I have when I'm locked up in a bathroom. I laugh.

"Lili, you know what?" Roy looks at me.

"What?"

"I know you don't like for me to ask you too many questions. So I'm sorry for my American curiosity. But I want to know your purpose in life."

"Well." I shrug, not knowing what to say. "Killing time, I guess."

"Come on, Lili; be serious." Roy combs his fingers through my hair and then cups my face with his hands, searching for answers in my eyes. "I know you want more than that. Why must you always be so guarded?"

"That's a question I ask myself," I murmur, turning my head to the side.

Roy lets his hands drop away from my face, but he keeps looking at me. "The more you try to protect yourself, you know, the more I want to unveil you. As Lao Tsu says, 'Those who know don't tell, and those who tell don't know.'"

"Actually, I'm pretty boring, Roy. You'll soon be disappointed."

"Lili, you'll never disappoint me." Roy's voice has a tremor of passion. He gently puts his fingers to my lips to make me shut up, then says slowly, "I've known from the first time I met you that you're a woman I'll never completely know."

EIGHT

Beijing's most beautiful time is before sunset. Morning is too chilly, and noon is too bright. Only before sunset is the city soft and golden. It becomes an old imperial city, the city in the novels of the Manchu author Lao She, with arches and teahouses, street performers and antique stores.

Behind Tiananmen Square is the Forbidden City, the palace of ancient emperors. The palace is surrounded by high old brick walls and a peaceful moat. Under the setting sun, dragonflies glide low above the surface of the moat, sparrows fly high under the eaves of tower gates, thin date trees grow between the cracks of ancient bricks, and flowers blossom in the shade cast by the gray city walls.

My parents used to bring me here as a child. They would each hold one of my hands. Papa would buy me a toy windmill or a yo-yo and some sugar-coated chestnuts or pumpkin seeds from the street peddlers. Sometimes he would take pictures of me and Mama. Each time I would feel so proud to have my picture taken in front of the grand Gate of Heavenly Peace, the symbol of China.

My childhood is long gone now, along with the happiness I felt then being with my parents, the pride I felt standing in front of Tiananmen. Only my love for the peaceful moat remains.

Ancient Chinese believed that the palace and its surroundings had a lucky *feng shui,* the arrangement of wind and water that could bring the residents good luck. It is said that an ancient emperor chose the location to build his home because his astrologer carefully read his horoscope and concluded that this was where the "genuine dragon," the emperor, should dwell.

Along the moat there are elegant houses with yards, big windows, and gates guarded by armed soldiers of the People's Liberation Army. I have heard that these are the residences of old high-ranking Communist officials.

As we wander along the moat, Roy becomes quiet and peaceful. Bathed in the setting sun, we stroll hand in hand, like a pair of lost schoolchildren. Only our shadows follow us, loyal, speechless.

Sometimes we stop and kiss tirelessly, as if we will never be able to meet again. I am engulfed by the pleasure that pours over my tongue and floods every nerve of my body. I love his tongue, his soft tongue that speaks both English and Chinese. As we walk along the city walls, I feel that our modern love story is being played out on an ancient stage, at once real and fantastic.

Roy says it's as if we're somehow communicating with

each other through our spirits. He quotes from the *Tao Te Ching:* " 'One may move so well that a footprint never shows, and speak so well that the tongue never slips.' "

I can't sense the spirits that he talks about, or understand the *Tao Te Ching*'s words. We walk around the moat again and again, as if we were on a carousel, with no beginning, no end, no destination. I am content. There is no push or shove or babbling or staring, just Roy and me and this ancient setting.

We discover a ruined amphitheater hidden in a bamboo grove outside Heaven's Temple. We sit on the abandoned stage where the Beijing Opera once played. The performers used to wear their colorful masks, singing, crying, and dancing here. The audience used to drink tea and cheer or boo from the seats. The rows upon rows of seats are still there in front of us, but they're rusted and empty now. Roy holds me in his great arms; I listen to the relaxed pounding of his heart. As I look up at the sky, a gaggle of geese fly over, honking. They fly in the shape of a V, the Chinese character for "human" turned upside down.

Sitting on a ruined stage in front of ranks of empty seats, in my foreign lover's embrace, and seeing "human" fly across the sunny blue sky, I wonder if my life isn't a Beijing opera. But what role am I playing? What mask am I wearing?

"Lili," Roy whispers into my ear, his voice husky and sweet, "I know we're very different. Not only do we have different cultures, but our attitudes toward life are different. We have a perfect yin and yang balance. Don't you agree?"

I nod, noticing that his heartbeat is accelerating. Mine is, too. I have no job, no pressures, no worries, no plans for tomorrow or next year, no goals. I have a lover who doesn't know about my past. He just wants to be with me, it's as simple as that.

"I want to ask a question," he says.

"Go ahead."

"What do you think is the most important thing in life?"

The Chinese character for "human" is still moving in the distant sky, so I answer without thinking much: "To live, I guess. What about you?"

"To love and to be loved," Roy says, kissing my hand. "I love you, Lili Lin."

I am stunned by his words. I am in an opera.

"We want to live because we want to love. Do you agree?"

"Yes."

"Tell me you love me, Lili." Roy looks into my eyes. I know I can't refuse him.

"I . . ." I clear my throat and look away. "I love you." I must sound awkward.

Roy's face turns rosy, and he smiles at me like a kid who has a piece of candy. "If I died now, I'd have no regrets," he says. "To die next to you would be like obtaining nirvana."

I didn't know the word *love* could have such a strong effect. When I say "I love you" to him, I don't really know what I'm talking about. I feel as if I were mimicking the sound of a foreign language; I'm not even sure my intonation is right.

Roy's naïveté intensifies my disgust with myself. I want to tell him about my past. I want to let him know that I am not worth his love. I want to tell him that when I was a teen, I was in gang fights and carried red bricks in my military bag every day. I threw the bricks at everyone I hated. I wouldn't stop hurting someone until I saw blood flowing. I know hatred but not love.

I want to scream at him that I'm no goddess, just a shallow, hollow, empty woman who can speak in the most vulgar manner without the slightest embarrassment.

"What have I done to make you feel this way?" I ask him very slowly, looking at the sky.

"You exist, Lili. Your existence is a blessing for me. When I'm happy, you're my catalyst. When I'm sad, you're my tranquilizer. You have this magic power over me. When I'm with you, I feel incredibly lucky and romantic," Roy says fervently, stroking my hair with his fingers.

I want to cry. I am not as he has just described me. That isn't me. I can't let him weave this unrealistic image of me, innocent of my past. It's unfair to him.

"Roy, you know what?" I bite my lower lip.

"What?" he asks airily.

I close my eyes. "I'm not what you think I am."

"What do you mean?"

"I'm a female hooligan; I was sent to jail for sexual misconduct." I thought it would be hard to say this, but I'm finding it easy. I just have to touch my upper lip to my lower, as if I were telling the story of a stranger.

Silence. Deafening silence. I hold my breath. I have just sentenced myself to death. I am about to observe my own execution.

Roy faces me. He looks at me seriously. "I know all that, Lili; I've known since the day you came to visit me at my apartment. The security people checked your background and called me."

I don't know whether I'm more astonished by his words or by the calmness in his voice. My mind turns completely blank, as if I'd been hit by a thunderbolt. I lose my voice. I hear myself murmuring, "You knew. You knew. You mean to say you learned about this before I—I moved—moved in with you?"

"Yes."

"Why didn't you change your mind?"

"As a matter of fact, I did. At first I wanted to live with you in my Jianguomenwai apartment. But as an unmarried woman with a previous police record, you can be harassed for living with a foreigner. And because that was more likely to happen in that compound, I decided to move."

"Why didn't you break it off with me then? You can still do it now, it's not too late."

"What are you talking about?"

"Who would want a woman like me?"

"Fuck reputation and records and all that bullshit. It's you I care about, Lili Lin," Roy says, raising his voice and holding me tightly and firmly.

It's unusual for him to use swear words. Cradled in his arms, I feel my tears rolling down my cheeks. How can this man possibly trust me so unconditionally?

"Do you know that people used to call me Big Trumpet? Do you know that no Chinese family wants its son to marry a woman like me? Do you know that men who don't care about their women's chastity are laughed at in my country and called turtles?"

Roy wipes my tears away with his thumbs. "That's what others think. I don't really care about any of it because it has nothing to do with *us* and what we think of each other."

I keep seeing myself being trapped by the opinions of others. After all, I do care about my reputation. I try to deny it and act as if I didn't care, but the fact is that I'm no different from other Chinese: we all live for reputation and are victims of it. Once we have lost face, we ourselves are lost.

"Can you tell me what you think of me?" I ask Roy.

"I think you're a wonderful woman, a rare treasure!"

"Do you really think so?"

"Of course. Why would I lie to you? But what *I* think of you isn't as important as what you think of yourself."

"And what if I tell you that I think I'm a bad woman?"

"Don't let the stupid old culture keep victimizing you. Let it go, Lili."

What makes Roy so steadfast? I shiver and feel a hot current rush quickly from my lower belly to spread throughout my body. I feel powerless, weak, and I surrender to his arms. It feels as if we are under a spell. It is beyond my understanding.

NINE

I don't have any particular religious beliefs. My generation was taught by the Communist Party that religion was poison. In spite of my education, though, I occasionally go to Taoist and Buddhist temples in the mountains. I enjoy secluded retreats where I am removed from the crowds and can listen to my own footsteps.

A few young men who learned to play the Chinese zither from my parents later became monks. We sometimes meet at the Great Wall Hotel and play traditional Chinese music together. Roy has long philosophical talks with my monk friends. They often discuss the essence of the Tao, religious art, and the mystery of the mysterious. They can babble on for hours about "eternal namelessness," "limitlessness," or "dawn breath," all of which I find incomprehensible.

On the birthday of the Grand Jade Emperor, my Taoist friend Monk Bright invites us to attend his religion's greatest rite, at the White Cloud Temple, in a Beijing suburb.

Even though we get there early in the morning, the temple is already crowded. The never-ending kowtowing of the worshipers reminds me of woodpeckers beating their beaks against the trees in the woods surrounding the temple.

Roy and I can barely see the Taoist master who stands in the center of the hall near the altar. He is dressed in a purple gown embroidered with golden edges, a white jade tablet in his hands.

Other monks, dressed in yellow gowns, stand behind him inside an eight-sided diagram symbolizing the cosmos. Each of them holds a musical instrument poised to play a birthday tribute to the Jade Emperor.

The ceremony starts with the master's burning a yellow paper box inscribed with esoteric religious symbols and ancient Chinese characters. The monks standing in the octagon begin to chant scriptures and to play music with their bells, drums, gongs, and wooden fish (an instrument tapped with a small wooden hammer, the playing of which is supposed to extinguish the flames of nuns' and monks' desires). The chanting rises in a resonant crescendo, like a surging ocean wave. Murmuring, the master spreads incense ashes over a number of small sacred statues sitting on the floor; these will later be given away to worshipers, to guide them on the spiritual pathway leading to higher consciousness. The monks believe that the ashes carry mysterious spirits that can enter the wooden or clay figures.

Right after the ceremony ends, people swarm forward to grab the free statues. Two middle-aged women pull each other's hair, fighting for a cute set of the Eight Immortals; nobody tries to stop them. These worshipers don't appear religious to me; for them the immediate availability of free gifts seems to be much more compelling than any abstract Taoist doctrine.

Seeing the commotion, my friend Monk Bright sighs and says, "Taoism nowadays has become a fad, and this temple has become a circus."

I agree: "There's no quiet place in China anymore, except for the cemeteries."

"But at least people can now enjoy freedom of religion to some extent," Roy says. "That's a good sign."

"You may not believe this, Mr. Roy, but I'm not here to practice freedom of religion," Monk Bright confides. "I'm here to save money."

"What?" Roy sounds shocked.

"As a monk I get free food, shelter, and schooling. I receive a stipend every month. It's much better than being a peasant. If I had stayed in my hometown, I never would have made so many connections or been invited to give speeches in foreign countries. I never would have been able to even imagine doing such things."

"But you *do* believe in Taoism, don't you?"

"For me Taoism has never been a religion. It's more an attitude toward life. I believe one learns it by traveling and experiencing life, rather than by staying in the temple and reading scriptures every day."

Before we leave, Monk Bright gives Roy and me a tape of Taoist chanting as a gift. "You probably won't see me here next time," he says.

"Where will you be?" Roy asks.

"Anywhere I happen to be."

Monk Bright isn't joking. Not long after this, he will leave the White Cloud Temple. Some will say he has converted to Mormonism and enrolled at Brigham Young University in Utah; others that he has married a young nun and started a real estate business in the special economic zone called Shenzhen, next to Hong Kong.

After Monk Bright disappears, the tape he gave us is the only connection I have to him. Listening to the hypnotic religious chanting, I think of transience again.

Everything changes so fast. People come and go; the life I have with Roy is like the swiftly changing collage shots on TV—colorful, distracting, hypnotic to look at, yet disconnected and temporary. Maybe this is the typical life of a journalist. Or maybe China is changing too fast.

After Monk Bright, Roy's focus shifts from Taoism to Buddhism. He becomes enchanted by the Buddhist mantra *"Om mani padme hum"* after watching a documentary about Tibet.

"In the documentary," he tells me, "the lamas chant this six-syllable mantra all the time. In this vast universe, which Buddhists refer to as 'three thousand grand worlds,' everything from the seven emotions and the six desires to reincarnation, nirvana, and karma seems to be condensed into this mantra. I know that it literally means 'Hail to the jewel in the lotus,' but I'm curious to learn more about the underlying concepts. What do the lotus and the jewel represent? I'd love to talk about it with a Buddhist and find out how he or she interprets this."

His mention of the mantra reminds me of my grandma. Almost every time my parents and I go to visit her, we hear her chanting *"Om mani padme hum"* in a low-pitched voice, as if her only purpose in life were to chant this mantra.

I tell Roy, "My grandma is a devout Buddhist. If you like, we can go and ask her."

"I'd love to meet a member of your family! Tell me more!"

"My father says she had many admirers when she was young. She married three times and became a widow three times."

"Your grandma sounds as wild as you! Tell me all about her."

I tell Roy what I have heard from Papa. "When Grandma was young, she was well known in the social circle of Shanghai. Her nickname was Party Queen. At eighteen she fell in love with a married military officer. Her family, rich and prestigious, was outraged and locked her up. She escaped and ran off with the officer. But after they'd been living together for a year, he left her and never returned. He went back to his wife.

"At that time there were almost no jobs for women. Grandma had to return to Shanghai and seek help from her parents. She was no longer a virgin and couldn't find a husband in Shanghai, so her parents married her off into a landlord's family in the countryside. The family was wealthy and had two sons. The first was named Heavenly Rain; the second was Summer Rain. Grandma married Heavenly Rain. He was an opium addict and always carried the smell of expensive cologne and opium. He discovered on their wedding night that Grandma wasn't a virgin, and almost immediately shut himself off from her. He went to brothels, opium houses, and casinos every day. My grandmother was very unhappy and lonely. Her mother-in-law didn't like her, either; she thought Grandma was too modern because her feet weren't bound.

"Summer Rain, the second son, was sympathetic toward Grandma and wanted to help her. When he found out that she was educated as well, he fell in love with her. A year after her marriage to Heavenly Rain, Grandma became pregnant. Some of my relatives say that her son, my uncle Yin, is Summer Rain's, not Heavenly Rain's. Nobody knows the truth. After she gave birth to Uncle Yin, Grandma thought her husband would become interested in their son, but Heavenly Rain still spent his nights in brothels. At that time China was in chaos."

"It was the warlord period, wasn't it?" Roy cuts in.

"Yes. One night their town was under a curfew, but Heavenly Rain didn't realize that. He left a brothel early in the morning and was accidentally killed by soldiers on his way back home. Grandma became a widow, and her parents-in-law grew ruder and ruder to her and allowed her to be with her son for only two hours a day. They thought she had brought bad luck to Heavenly Rain. Grandma had to wear a white linen mourning dress and stand in front of her husband's memorial tablet for one hundred days.

"After one hundred days of mourning, Summer Rain told his parents that he wanted to marry my grandma and be the father of the boy. His parents told him they would disown him if he married my grandma, the bad-luck widow. To separate them, the in-laws sent Summer Rain up north to Beijing.

"Summer Rain was admitted to Beijing University, but he couldn't stop thinking about my grandma. After his first semester there, he sent his classmate A-cheng to his home.

Supposedly A-cheng was carrying greetings on Summer Rain's behalf. But his secret mission was to bring Grandma and Uncle Yin back to Beijing with him."

"Did A-cheng succeed?"

"Yes."

"Wonderful. What happened then?"

"It was during wartime. They faced a dangerous journey to Beijing, but A-cheng took really good care of Grandma and her son. He was enchanted by her beauty and secretly fell in love with her himself.

"When they finally arrived safely in Beijing, they learned that Summer Rain had been put in prison for participating in a student movement. His parents sent their servants to the city to bribe jailers and catch Grandma.

"Grandma had to live in hiding at A-cheng's apartment and couldn't go to prison to visit Summer Rain. Later, rumors spread that Summer Rain had been executed."

"Were the rumors true?"

"No, but he had been badly beaten and was crippled. His family bribed the police department, and he was released. But it was too late; Grandma had married A-cheng. She thought Summer Rain was dead. When Summer Rain learned about the marriage, his heart was reduced to ashes. He quit school and became a Buddhist monk. Grandma was terribly upset, too."

"How was her married life?"

"A-cheng was good to her. He came from a wealthy family in Beijing."

"Was A-cheng your grandfather?"

"Yes, but that's another sad story. His mother hated Grandma. No mother at that time wanted her son to marry a widow. Besides, A-cheng was the only son in the family;

his mother got especially angry when she saw him treat Grandma like a queen and listen to her obediently. Grandma couldn't get along with her new mother-in-law. Seeing that his wife wasn't happy, A-cheng decided to take her to Japan. He wanted to get a master's degree there. His parents agreed to let him study abroad, but they insisted that he go first and that Grandma join him two months later. The ship that was to carry him to Japan sank in the sea. He drowned. His mother was heartbroken; she blamed Grandma, saying that she was a jinx and that her aura was too strong for a woman. She kicked Grandma out.

"Grandma wanted to end her life, but she discovered that she was pregnant with my mother. She sent a letter to her parents asking for help. They gave her some money but didn't want her to come back home; they said married daughters were no better than splashed water. Grandma searched for Summer Rain. She found his temple and traveled all the way there. But he said that he was no longer the Summer Rain she had once known, and that his only interest was in Buddhism."

"Did anyone offer to help your grandmother?"

"There was a military man who had been Grandma's admirer and follower in Old Shanghai. He became a general after winning several wars. He was married, but he still loved Grandma. He asked her to be his second wife. With Uncle Yin a young boy and my mother in her womb, Grandma consented.

"Although the general was fond of Grandma and nice to her two kids, she didn't like him because he was uneducated and rude. She had affairs with his assistants. Because the general was on the side of the nationalists, after the liberation of the Communists, he was thrown in prison.

"He was very stubborn and refused to be reeducated. In a public criticism meeting, he shouted, 'Long live the nationalists!' The masses were angry and beat him to death. Papa told me that Grandma was forced to watch the beating."

"So your grandma married three times and became a widow three times."

"Yes. Relatives on her husbands' sides say Grandma must've been an evil vampire who sucked out all of her men's energy by demanding too much sex from them. That was why they all died young."

"Obviously that's bullshit."

"Papa said that even though Grandma had three marriages, she wasn't able to marry the two men she really loved."

"The married man she first ran away with and Summer Rain?"

"Yes."

"Tragic."

Grandma doesn't care what others say about her. One just can't rub her the wrong way. Many old people like to live in big families and enjoy being served by their children and grandchildren and in-laws, but she lives by herself near the Fragrance Hill. She doesn't want my family to visit her.

"She doesn't eat meat, but she smokes a pipe—puffs on it like a chimney. My father says Grandma was a musical genius, but I've never heard her play. Every time I see her she's either puffing on her pipe or tapping the wooden fish and chanting the Buddhist mantra."

"When can I meet her?"

I haven't told Roy about Grandma and Mama's relationship. At the beginning of the Cultural Revolution, my mother was very enthusiastic about joining the Communist Party. But Grandma was labeled a corrupt capitalist by the city's Revolutionary Committee because her parents and husbands had all been rich. Red Guards made Grandma dangle a pair of worn shoes around her neck and walk around the neighborhood that way. "Worn shoes" is a term used of women who sleep around. Every day Grandma had to go out into the street with worn shoes hanging on her chest. Children and adults threw rocks at her. She had cuts and bruises all over her face.

Mama did nothing to protect Grandma. She felt only shame at being her daughter. I can remember the public criticism meeting at which she denounced Grandma. My parents and I were sitting together in the audience, and Grandma, her head half shaved, was standing in the center of the stage wearing the dangling worn shoes, enduring the taunts of the teenage Red Guards:

"Say you're an American spy who married off your son to an American ghost."

"Say your third husband deserves death a thousand times!"

"Say your parents were vampires who sucked out the blood of the poor."

But Grandma said nothing.

The Red Guards kicked her, and one yelled, "You're an old turd in a toilet, smelly and hard. Somebody's got to fix you!" Another of the Red Guards pointed to Mama and motioned for her to come up.

Mama got up and rushed to the stage, where she stuck her finger in Grandma's face and told her, "Listen carefully, you capitalistic rodent, you reactionary, you dirty old woman: I'm not your daughter, you're not my mother!"

Mama slapped Grandma. I followed Mama and spat on Grandma. I remember the round of applause we got from the audience for doing this. "Good class consciousness!" said the chairman of the Revolutionary Committee of our district. Then he praised both Mama and me and shook hands with us.

I stole a glance at Grandma and saw that her face was expressionless. I was seven in 1967. I couldn't understand then, and still don't quite understand, how she could show no emotion on witnessing her own flesh and blood betray and insult her in public. How could she possibly contain herself like that? Her face turned red and puffy but registered nothing. She raised her head high, stubbornly. It was the last time I saw her before she was sent to prison in 1968. She refused to admit that her third husband was a bad man or that her son was a spy.

Mama's denunciations of her own mother didn't help her. Her Party membership application was rejected because of Uncle Yin's American wife. Mama suffered throughout the entire Cultural Revolution.

Grandma was released from prison after the revolution ended in 1978. The house in which she and my grandfather had once lived was returned to her after being confiscated for twenty-six years. It's the eleven-bedroom house in Fragrance Hill.

I have never asked Mama whether, at the time of the meeting, she really hated Grandma for being a capitalistic rodent, whether she regretted slapping her. As for me, though I've learned a lot of bad tricks during the years, I've never spat in anyone's face again.

Mama, Papa, and I used to try to visit Grandma every other week. "It is our family duty," Mama insisted. But

Grandma would not pay us any notice. She would just sit on the side of her bed, tapping her wooden fish with her eyes half closed, murmuring, *"Om mani padme hum."*

My parents would wait for a while and then leave their gifts for her. The last time we went to see Grandma, probably two years ago, she wasn't home. She'd left a note on the door, which read: "To you who live in the mundane world and regard yourselves as my children: go back and work out your salvation with diligence."

Her neighbor told us that Grandma had gone by herself to the Buddhist Mountain, Ermei, in Sichuan Province, taking with her only a small bag and a stick. My parents eventually stopped trying to see her, muttering that perhaps she had become a saint. A saint needs no family.

Roy can't wait to visit her. We drive for three hours and finally arrive at the foot of Fragrance Hill. Hidden in a thick bamboo grove, her compound is an ancient-style *si-he-yuan,* with three connected buildings arranged around a courtyard. She lives in this big place all alone, a hermit.

As Roy and I walk through the bamboo grove, we hear the chirping of birds and the bubbling song of a running brook.

On the front gate is painted the Buddhist symbol of lotus blossoms. The gate is unlocked; the silence inside is deafening—no chanting, no sound of drumming on the wooden fish. We stand in the courtyard, and I call, "Grandma!" No one answers. I feel funny about this emptiness. Is she dead? Has she at least reached nirvana? I enter the living room.

The smell of tobacco relieves me—she's here.

"Grandma, where are you?" I call softly.

"I'm here, I'm awake." I hear her slow and calm response; her voice seems hoarser than I recall. Following the sound, I find her sitting in a rocking chair at the other end of the room, smoking a pipe, her constant companion. It is too dim for me to see her face.

"Grandma, I know you like quiet and don't want to be disturbed. But I have a boyfriend now. His name is Roy. He is interested in Buddhism and wants to learn the meaning of the mantra *'Om mani padme hum'* from a Buddhist. So we're here."

"Master, I need you to enlighten me," Roy says courteously, walking in past me and putting his palms together in front of his chest.

"One's enlightenment must come from oneself," Grandma replies, putting her palms together the same way. For the rest of our visit she remains as quiet as still water in a pond.

It reminds me of a visit my parents and I paid to her three years ago. Mama was talking about the return of Uncle Yin and how he was an honored guest of the Beijing government. Grandma didn't say anything. She was practicing calligraphy. Before we left, she wrote the character for "emptiness" on a piece of rice paper and gave it to us.

Roy and I thank her and leave the quiet house.

Grandma's silence only makes Roy more eager. His reaction reminds me of myself as a child, the way I tried to figure out the riddles written on red lanterns during Spring Festival. The more difficult the riddles were, the more urgently I was drawn to them. I still remember one of them: A three-legged monster with many black and white teeth likes to eat steel strings. I couldn't figure it out, and my life stopped. I didn't eat or sleep. I thought about the monster every day until Mama gave me a hint: "The monster can sing." I yelled happily and eagerly, "It's a piano!" I was six.

Roy is anxious to know the answer to his riddle. He says, "Yes, it's true that one's enlightenment should come from oneself. If I want to learn the meaning of the mantra, I should find out through books and research."

"Why do you care about this so much?" I ask.

"The Dalai Lama says that without the mantra, Buddhahood can't be attained."

"You want to become a Buddha?" I tease him.

"No, but I want to understand Buddhism. Why is the mantra considered a required element for spiritual advancement?"

He drags me to the Beijing library. While Roy reads the English books on the subject, he makes me read the Chinese ones. It's hard for me to sit still and do "research." I'm not curious about Buddhism, nor do I want to be a Buddhist.

I stroll through the stacks of books. A title catches my eye: *Buddha, the Awakened One.* Suddenly I realize why my grandma replied, "I'm here, I'm *awake*." She was not just telling me that she hadn't fallen asleep; she was talking about her state of awareness.

Maybe if I study the mantra, I'll understand Grandma, I think. I start to flip through the big old book. It says that very few people in the world are able to live an awakened life and reach enlightenment. Most human beings are not aware of the world they live in. Their minds are in hibernation without their ever realizing it. But through self-restraint, abandonment of ambition, and mental concentration, one can reach the final enlightenment. It doesn't make much sense to me. "Self-restraint"? Does that mean the life of a nun, with no meat, no men? This so-called enlightenment isn't for me.

Roy finds me and says he has discovered an explanation of the mantra in a book written by a Western scholar. *Mani* ("diamond") represents enlightenment, he tells me, and *padme* ("lotus") the human mind.

"So the mantra is talking about awakening, enlightenment. Maybe what your grandma meant was that by repeating the mantra, one can reach enlightenment?"

What does *enlightenment* mean, anyway? Does it mean that we will no longer have feelings of sadness, anger, doubt, resentment, or envy and will instead become happy forever? Will the world be different if we reach enlightenment? I don't tend to think much about the meaning of life. I lead a life with a past, without a future. Does this mean my mind is in hibernation? Thoughts of enlightenment are too intellectual and too vague for me.

I am frustrated by these questions. Being with Roy forces me to think. And the more I think, the more questions come up, and the more confused I feel. Is Roy trying to turn me into an intellectual? It seems to me that intellectuals like to confuse themselves with all kinds of questions that have no answers. But what's the point of that? To make their lives more complicated?

After several more days of research, Roy decides that the mantra's intent is to bring together mind and heart. When those are united, anything is possible.

"Let's go see your grandma again and tell her what we've found out," he suggests

We start our second trip to Grandma's on a cloudy day.

As we drive, it starts to rain. The weather in Beijing is as unpredictable as a naughty child. For Roy it's a trip undertaken to gain knowledge; for me it's a search for links that will connect my grandmother and me.

We arrive at around noon to find Grandma napping in her living room. We wait quietly for about forty minutes in the courtyard, studying and enjoying the bonsai she has planted. Then we hear her composing a short refrain, right after her nap:

> *I have just awakened from a dream,*
> *but perhaps I'm dreaming that I'm awake.*
> *I have a dream about clouds,*
> *But perhaps it is the clouds dreaming about me.*

She comes out holding a goose-feather fan in one hand and a cup of tea in the other. She sees us and shows no surprise. She nods at us.

Unable to contain his eagerness, Roy blurts out, "Grandma, I want to know what *'Om mani padme hum'* means to a Buddhist like you. Are the syllables energy-based sounds? When you chant the mantra, it produces an actual physical vibration. Does the vibration match the level of your energy? How about your mental intention when you chant? Are you very focused when chanting? Do the six syllables bring you peace and connect you with the deity?"

Grandma calmly continues fanning herself, then takes a sip of her tea and responds, "Truth, without words." Without saying another word or giving any further hint, she turns her back on us, returns to her room, and closes the door behind her.

Roy and I stand in the courtyard, stunned. We weren't expecting so simple an answer!

On our way back it starts to rain again. Roy has to drive slowly. He is silent, deep in thought, his thick brown eyebrows knotted. He wants to take in over one thousand years of Buddhist practice in a day.

"What do you think of my grandma?" I ask, breaking the silence.

"I see her genes in you."

"What does that mean?"

"She's uncommon, mysterious, like you."

"After what she's been through, I guess the world seems irrelevant to her."

"What do you think that means, 'truth, without words'?"

"Why do you want to know the truth so much?"

"Because I want to learn, and also because I'm uncomfortable with ambiguity. Aren't you troubled by that kind of vagueness?" Roy turns toward me and looks into my eyes while we wait at a traffic light.

"The vagueness doesn't bother me." I shrug. "Westerners always want logical answers and specific definitions for everything. But remember, we Chinese like to say it's harder to remain in confusion. Sometimes one question can have multiple answers."

Obviously frustrated, Roy says, "Yeah, I've found that Chinese culture likes to leave things ill defined. It's as though you Chinese actually *enjoy* ambiguity. That's the wisdom I can't understand." He sighs. "This cultural practice of leaving things unclear makes analytical logic useless. I don't feel comfortable with it."

"Don't think about it, then. Don't be so serious."

Roy doesn't answer me; probably he isn't listening. He looks puzzled and continues babbling: "Maybe you're right. There is no definite answer. Maybe that's why your grandma answered me the way she did: she was being *intentionally* vague. What do you think?"

"It's possible."

"Which is to say that I'm hammered by my linear thinking from the very beginning."

I have no clue what he means by "linear thinking." As he talks, I look out the car window. Everything is blurred and misty in the pouring rain, but it's beautiful. The beauty of vagueness.

When we get home, Roy says, "I think I should stay in a temple for a month or two."

His sudden idea doesn't surprise me. He can't let go of his search for answers. I wish him good luck and go into the kitchen to cook dinner for us. In the kitchen I think to myself, I hope he never decides to study *me* the way he's studying this Buddhist mantra. I don't want to be his research subject, not ever.

When dinner is ready, I wash my hands and go into to the living room to get Roy. He's fallen asleep on the sofa. His search has already become too arduous for him.

For the next two months Roy stays in a monastery in the mountains. I am bored without him; there is too much emptiness around me. I go back to playing the erhu in the Great Wall Hotel, but I miss the fun of being with Roy. I start to feel depressed and anxious, like an intellectual. Something intense gnaws at my body, bite by bite, like an infestation of fleas.

I can't understand Roy's passion for intellectual pursuit or his strong curiosity about the unknown. What can he possibly find in a dull monastery? I spend hour after hour lying in bed, trying to imagine what he's doing and why he's doing it.

I look at the English books on his bookshelf, wondering what linear thinking is and what analytical logic means. Maybe those strange alphabet letters will tell me what's inside Roy's brain. So I randomly pull out a volume entitled *The Birth of Tragedy* and start to read it with an English–Chinese dictionary in hand.

I find the meanings of the English words *birth* and *tragedy* in Chinese. But knowing little about English grammar, I can't tell whether the title means that giving birth is tragic or that a tragedy is being born.

The first sentence contains forty-three English words, of which I know four: *we, have, for,* and *sexes.* It takes me half an hour to find the meanings of the rest of the words. The translation that I put together doesn't make any sense; it's like Martian to me. According to the dictionary, *aesthetics* refers to the "science of beauty, which Kant used in his methodology." But who or what is Kant? How can beauty be a type of science? Finally I just give up, sigh, and think to myself that maybe I can never fully understand Roy's world.

After I put the book back on the shelf, I notice that it's pouring rain outside. The curtain of the mist reminds me of the second trip Roy and I took to Grandma's.

I rush out, jump onto a bus, and head in the direction of her house.

On the bus I fall asleep. The conductor wakes me up at

the last stop; the bus is empty, and we've reached Fragrance Hill. The bus station is at the foot of the hill, near a temple with a huge statue of a sleeping Buddha.

Still in a daze, only half awake, I walk slowly through the drizzle, up a mountain path, for about half an hour.

Wet from the rain, I stand numbly in the drizzle-soaked bamboo grove in front of Grandma's compound. The bamboo leaves shine with raindrops and smell fresh and sweet. I see her standing on a small, old-fashioned stone footbridge in the woods, practicing t'ai chi. Her movement is slow, almost like that of a crawling snail, but it flows naturally and rhythmically, in tune with her surroundings.

The overwhelming freshness of the bright green bamboo, the rustic old stone bridge in the drizzle, the tiny white-haired figure with face obscured—all of these remind me of a scene depicted in an ancient painting.

It seems impossible that such greenness, freshness, and spaciousness could seem to exist only in modern China. It's hard to connect this world with the busyness of Beijing, but here we are in the midst of the city. Grandma is head-strong. Feudal expectations of women didn't turn her into a chaste widow who would commit suicide to follow her dead husband; during the Cultural Revolution, violence and prison life failed to convert her from a Buddhist into a revolutionary. Neither has China's new open-door policy made her a capitalist. She lives in her own time. Nobody can change her.

I don't greet Grandma because I don't know why I've come here in the first place. I decide to leave. I give her a final glance. Surprisingly, she begins walking in my direction, carrying a vertical bamboo flute in her hand. She stops about twenty feet away and asks, "Since you're here, would you like to hear me play a piece?"

I can't remember when Grandma last talked to me. Maybe she asked me once or twice if I liked school when I was young. We're family, but I don't know how to react when she talks to me. It's all I can do to keep saying, "Yes, yes."

Grandma bows and starts playing her bamboo flute. It's the first time I've ever heard her play. She chooses an ancient piece called "Three Variations on Plum Blossoms." I've heard it played before, but not the way she does it, so free, so natural, and so mysterious. It's music from another realm. It breaks through this time and space and transports me somewhere immortal. I feel like I'm floating and spinning.

Plum blossoms bloom only in wintertime, showing off their beauty in the harsh, cold weather. Chinese love them because they symbolize beauty, strength, perseverance, and pride. I study Grandma as she plays, her eyes half closed and her eyebrows locking into each other, the drizzle wetting her white hair and face. Her facial expression is as calm as it was all those years ago when Mama slapped her face in public. What is Grandma trying to tell me? Is she playing the music of her whole life, using the plum blossom as a kind of image?

The music finally stops. Grandma bows slightly and tells me, "It's for the enlightenment of you and your friend whose presence is somewhere else today. *Om mani padme hum.*" Then, she walks away, leaving me to stand in the drizzle, speechless.

On my way home I get lost. I can't remember how to get back to the Forbidden Nest! With no idea of where to go, I board a bus, planning just to ride it to wherever it takes me. It's nearly empty at this time of day; the only other passengers are an old couple with a baby wrapped in a dirty white blanket, a wrinkled, toothless old man carrying a birdcage, and two fat middle-aged women. I am the only young person on the bus. While most people my age are advancing toward their goals and future, I'm getting lost on my way home. Where is home?

I can't stop thinking about Grandma. When I was young, if Mama was really mad at me, she'd point her finger at me and yell, "You're your grandma's child!" That was the worst thing she could say to me. When she was yelling at me like that, her face would often turn so sour that it would start to twist and distort. The last thing I wanted to be was like Grandma. When I spat in Grandma's face, I thought I was doing a good deed for my mother and for Chairman Mao. I was so proud of myself.

Mama thinks I became more and more like Grandma as I grew up. We're both tall and slim, with big, almond-shaped eyes and high cheekbones. People say women who have high cheekbones can bring their men bad luck. She and I share the same stubbornness, the same detached attitude toward life.

I wonder how she felt when Summer Rain, clothed in his monk's robe, told her he was no longer the man she'd known, or how she endured witnessing the death of her third husband and then the betrayal of her own daughter and granddaughter. What has she not seen in this world? Is that why she has lost interest in it? But still, how can life, for her, have turned into just six syllables—*Om mani padme hum*? Is life really so simple? What has Roy gone to search for?

138

Having learned that I am alone, Amei comes to the Forbidden Nest to visit me, bringing snacks and books.

After looking around, she praises me: "You keep the apartment so clean! You've done this room up nicely. I love your flowers—they're beautiful. You must have spent a lot of time decorating the place. It's neat and comfortable. You're a great hostess!"

Although the Forbidden Nest is only my temporary home, it feels like a real one to me.

Amei and I cook together in the kitchen. She doesn't ask me any questions, but I badly want to ask *her* some.

"Amei . . ."

"Yes, Lili. I know what you're going to ask. I've been waiting."

"How long have you been married?"

"Almost four years now."

"And Jun has been working in Paris for . . . ?"

"Three years."

"Do you miss him from time to time?"

"Of course I miss him, but you know the rules—I can't live with him in Paris. His company is afraid that if we both go overseas now, we'll want to stay there and not come back. So what else can I do? I'm not the only half widow in the city."

"So how do you kill time?"

"You know I'm a nurse. I have my patients to take care of at night. During the day I have different roles to play. I'm a daughter-in-law, and Jun is the only son in his family. So I visit my in-laws—take them gifts, cook for them, that sort of thing. You know Jun's mother, she's a difficult woman. A woman in her position has lots of social obligations. As her daughter-in-law, I am always expected to attend as well. And then I have my own folks to take care of. I'm also a big sister, and my brother, Gang, is quite spoiled and always makes trouble. He still thinks that because he has powerful parents, he can do anything and get away with it."

"No wonder everyone thinks you're a good woman."

"But I'm not myself. I live for others, not for me. I have to do things I hate, like going to see my mother-in-law. I'm tired, really. Lili, I admire you for being yourself. You're doing the most difficult thing: being your true self."

"It's not that hard if you want to pay the price, which is to be a bad girl."

"Lili, do you really think you're a bad girl?"

"Do you?"

"Of course not."

"Really?"

"Lili, let me ask *you,* why are you asking me so many questions today?"

"Because I'm bored."

"You're missing Roy, right?"

"Yes."

"You feel attached to him."

"Yes."

"Well, this is something new to me. I didn't know Lili could be attached to any man."

"Don't tease me. I'm confused myself."

"What part of Roy do you miss the most?"

"His eyes, probably."

"Why?"

"I've never seen the ocean, but in my imagination, the color of his eyes is the color of a deep ocean on a cloudy, overcast day. I like looking at his eyes. They make me puzzle, and . . ." I search for the right word.

"And they make you addicted."

"Amei, people say eyes are the windows of the self. His eyes tell me that his world is too far away from mine, just like the ocean."

"You live with him, and you still feel his world is far away from yours?"

"Yes."

"Why?"

"There're too many things I don't understand about him."

"Like what?"

"He's very intellectual. He likes reading books and doing research. He often cites this and that from so-and-so. He talks about many things I just don't understand. But at the same time he can be so naive. He speaks Chinese and hears Chinese, but he doesn't know how to listen or understand."

"He doesn't understand *you*."

"Probably not."

"But he trusts you."

"Yes. But I don't understand how he can trust somebody he doesn't really know."

"Because he loves you. Love is about trust. One doesn't have to know everything about a person to trust him or her. That's the feeling of love."

"That's how you feel toward Jun?"

"Yes."

"What about Jun's past, then? For example, his past with me?"

"Lili, I trust both of you. Your past doesn't lessen the trust."

"Amei, thank you."

"Have you talked about your past with Roy?"

"I've told him about my police record. And he wants to know more. How can I start? We're so different."

"What do you do when you're together?"

"He likes to go out, make friends, ask questions, learn about interesting things."

"He has a very active mind."

"He's trying hard to understand China."

"You can help him understand China by letting him understand you."

After Amei leaves, her words "Love is about trust" linger in my mind. But is love also about betrayal and hurt? I wonder to myself. *"Om mani padme hum"*: I murmur Grandma's mantra, willing it to bring me closer to the truth.

One day Roy shows up unexpectedly at the hotel where I am playing my erhu. He has grown a beard; he looks like a really sexy guru. It feels so wonderful to have him standing here in front of me. Life comes alive.

"Welcome back to the mundane world," I greet him, and throw myself into his arms. He kisses me in the lobby of the hotel, in front of everyone.

"It's been two months." Roy speaks under his breath, grabbing my hands. "I've missed you a lot."

We are facing each other, both of us smiling. Before we can even find a place to sit down, Roy starts to tell me excitedly about his adventure. "It's amazing—I mean the Spartan life that the monks live. During the time I was meditating in the monastery, incredible things happened to me. I didn't go there as a journalist; I went there to join the monks. I meditated for four or five hours a day, just like most of the others. We read Buddhist scriptures and beat the wooden fish. Sometimes we discussed various sacred writings.

"At first I was bored to death and didn't want to stay on. I didn't like the vegetarian food or the silence in the monastery. I decided to pack up and leave; I simply wasn't a monk and couldn't become one. Then I started to talk with an eight-year-old boy who had been in the temple for two years. Although he was only a little kid, he talked and acted like an adult—an adult monk. He meditated all day long and could recite many of the sacred writings. You see, he'd been *born* a monk. When I complained to him that I couldn't settle down, he suggested that I take off my watch. He said I had a 'hurry sickness.' He instructed me, 'Relax, then you can become healthy. Pay attention to the silence, and you can see the truth.' The boy was teaching me the words that his master had taught *him*.

"Later we meditated together. This child became completely immersed whenever he meditated. Sitting next to him, I began to really smell the air and feel the touch of the wind. Gradually I could sense my blood running through my veins and my heart beating. My whole body flowed with nature. I had a picture in mind of my body as the universe—my blood like rivers, my bones like trees, my flesh like the soil, and my hair like blades of grass.

"As your grandmother said, it is 'truth, without words.' It's hard for me to describe my feelings because they're in here." He points to his heart. "When I first went to see your grandma, I was curious about Chinese religious practices. I tried to study Buddhism as though it were an academic subject. I wanted to know exactly what the lotus and the diamond symbolized. But that was my American mentality. It just didn't work. Buddhism is about self-development and self-enlightenment. You can study its history, its doctrines, and all the rest, but you can't grasp its essence if you remain separate from it and try to observe it from the outside."

I can't understand why Roy is so excited. His enthusiasm reminds me of the books on his bookshelf—those Martian letters. He is playing the lute for a cow. But maybe it doesn't matter to him. All he wants is an ear.

Not knowing what to say, I ask him, "You haven't converted to Buddhism, have you?"

"No, I still consider myself Jewish," Roy replies quickly. "But Buddha is in my heart."

TEN

"Lili, I want to see the place where the Communists started before the liberation, and where your parents were forced to go during the Cultural Revolution," says Roy, half joking, half serious. "All my Chinese friends are journalists, professors, artists, and authors. It's time to overthrow the avant-garde. I need to meet the Chinese peasants."

He sounds like a guilty capitalist in the Cultural Revolution.

"Do you know what I think of peasant life?"

"What?" He squeezes my shoulder.

"It's backward, bitter, ignorant, filthy, superstitious, and empty," I say with sudden anger, gritting my teeth.

"Maybe you'll change your mind. Your impression is left over from Mao's day. Now it's Deng Xiaoping's time, and the countryside has changed a great deal." Roy's optimism is annoying. He doesn't have a clue.

"You don't even know what it smells like," I tell him.

"Why do you dislike the country so much? I know that many city people were forced to work in poor villages during the Cultural Revolution, and I know that your family was among them. But maybe if you can look at it from a distance, as an observer, you'll see it differently."

"Why should I? The countryside has nothing to do with my life!" I yell. I shiver, smelling the old stench of the Party secretary's pipe in Monkey Village all those years ago. I regret showing such emotion. How can Roy understand?

"You should care about rural China because you're a Chinese citizen, and it's your country and your people."

He believes the countryside will add flavor to his life, like tomato ketchup. But for me it's a heavy, sealed jar that pickled us in salt.

When we arrive at the Beijing railway station, Roy discovers that he can't get off the train in rural areas without first getting permission from the Ministry of Foreign Affairs. And I can't buy a ticket because I don't have a reference letter from my work unit. The only way either of us can go without having to get such permits is to visit some approved tourist area. Even though it's winter, we decide to go to Chengde, a town about two hundred kilometers from Beijing. Chengde was once the hiding place of the notorious Manchu dowager empress Cixi, one of the most powerful women in the history of China, who began as a concubine but moved up the ladder. She governed China from behind a bamboo screen set up at the back of her son's imperial throne.

When I was young, I liked to listen to stories about history on the radio. I learned many things about Cixi—for example, that she was served 150 different dishes at a single banquet; that she drank from a jade cup and ate with golden chopsticks; and that the recipes for the dishes served at her meals were top secret, and anyone who revealed them outside the imperial gates was executed.

Roy doesn't have to wait long on line at the foreigners' ticket window inside the heated station. But I have to stand for hours in a line outside the station, in the piercing-cold winter winds, to get my ticket from the window reserved for locals. My ticket is a lot cheaper.

We go inside to escape the cold and wait for the train. The railway station is packed with people. It reeks of the stink of too many travelers who haven't bathed for days or weeks, mixed with the stench of cigarettes—almost every man in sight is smoking. Peasants are lying on the floor, sleeping on bulky blankets wrapped around their belongings, bundles that hold all their hopes and dreams.

Some people are curious about Roy and say hello to him in heavily accented English. They ask him where he's from, and he tells them, "I'm from XinJiang Province." XinJiang is near China's western border; the natives there are mainly Muslim and have Caucasian features.

"So you are a *huihui*?" Someone asks if Roy is a Muslim.

"No, actually, I'm Jewish."

Overhearing this, a man wearing a pair of dark-framed glasses which make him look educated, approaches us. "We Chinese like Jews," he says. "Your culture is similar to ours. I know that you value education and family just as our Confucian culture does."

"This is the first I've heard of Chinese and Jews being similar. As far as I know, China has always backed the Muslims against the Israelis in world affairs."

"Yes, we support our Arab brothers, but it's a different issue." The man continues, "Historically, China has never excluded Jewish people. During World War Two, a lot of Jews escaped German persecution by emigrating to Shanghai, and the Chinese people treated them well."

"That's right." Roy nods. "My grandparents lived in Shanghai in the forties. They still cherish the memory of good days they spent there."

"So you know what I'm talking about," says the man. Then he looks at me for an instant, carefully, and turns back to Roy to ask, "Is she your wife?"

"She's my girlfriend."

The man speaks directly to me for the first time. "Are you from overseas?" he inquires.

"I'm a native Beijinger," I reply.

Raising one eyebrow slightly, he says with subtle surprise, "You don't look like a native."

"Why?"

"Your eyes, the way you look at us," the man remarks.

"What do you mean? What exactly are you trying to say?"

"It's hard to explain. It's just something about the way you carry yourself. You just don't seem to be as curious as we Chinese usually are, and you don't look as traditional as us, either."

"She's not a typical Chinese. She's a citizen of the world, as I am," Roy chimes in.

"Are you an Israeli?"

"I'm an American Jew."

"A Jewish man from America and a native Beijing woman together. So interesting," the man mutters thoughtfully.

"Why is it 'so interesting'?"

"The relationship between the Chinese and the Jews is interesting."

"Why are you so interested in the relationship between Jews and Chinese?" Roy asks.

"It's not surprising that you should ask." The man smiles at Roy and offers him his business card. "Artist FeiFei," it says.

"All right. But you still haven't answered my question."

"I've just come back from New York, where I sold all of my paintings to a rich Jewish businessman. Through him I met a number of people in the Jewish community. I was introduced to several interracial couples and a few Jewish men with Chinese wives. Thanks to my contacts there," Artist FeiFei continues, "I have applied to a Jewish foundation to underwrite a film about Jews' lives in Shanghai."

"Good for you!" Roy says.

FeiFei asks Roy where we're headed. No sooner does Roy tell him about our plan to see the countryside around Chengde than FeiFei volunteers to help. He tears a piece of paper from his notepad and scribbles some information in English. "Here are the name and address of Little Liu, one of my relatives. He's my cousin, my uncle's second son. He would be very happy to show you around. He has a high school education and speaks some English. I will send him a telegram and tell him to watch out for you."

Roy says, "That'd be great!" and carefully folds the note, then tucks it into his pocket. He thanks FeiFei with a slight bow like a monk, and cups his hands below his chin.

FeiFei waves his hands, saying, "Oh, I'm happy to help.

And do come visit me if you ever make it to Shanghai, where I live. The address and phone number are on my card. Shanghai is better than Beijing!" He leaves to catch his train, waving farewell to us.

Minutes later we board the train to Chengde. It leaves the station, passes through the Beijing suburbs, and finally enters the darkness of the countryside, where the rhythmic click-clack of its wheels on the rails and its hypnotic swaying lull me to sleep.

We arrive in the early morning. The cold air outside is dewy and fresh. I stretch, inhale deeply, and think to myself that the air is much cleaner here than it is in Beijing; maybe I'll like the countryside after all. I glance at Roy and give him a big, cheery smile.

As soon as we exit the Chengde train station, local hustlers surround us. "Need a tour guide?" "Need a taxi and place to stay?" they ask Roy in English. He shakes his head and holds up his hands, rejecting them. A young man whose face is tough, dry, and ashy, his cheeks red from the winter wind, follows us persistently. "Only fifty. I'll drive you around and show you everything! Come on. Let's be friends. Come on!"

"OK, OK." Roy finally surrenders.

The man grabs Roy's bag and directs us to his old, beat-up green jeep. As we walk, he holds out his other hand to Roy, saying, "My name is Yao. I'm a private tour guide. Nice meeting you."

"You're your own boss!" Roy says, shaking hands with Yao.

"Exactly. I'm a *getihu*. That's why I work so hard." Yao grins and volunteers his story after we're settled in his jeep. "I was a history major in college, but what do you do with that after you graduate? When I graduated, I was assigned to work as a secretary for the Birth Control Department's district chief. But I turned that down and decided to be my own boss, to work as an independent tour guide. After a while I made enough to buy this jeep, which helps me earn even more money. It's great."

Roy listens with interest and amusement. But to me the man seems slippery.

Yao changes his voice into that of a professional tour guide to announce, "We're going to see the Imperial Summer Villa. It was built by Emperor Kangxi during Manchu's Qing Dynasty, as a place where he could escape from the heat. But now," he adds with a laugh, "it's not only the heat but the traffic in Beijing that he'd want to get away from, I guess."

After a twenty-minute drive, we see some temples on our left—seven of them, in the Tibetan, Mongolian, and Manchurian styles, brightly colored and very ornate and detailed. They sit in the mountains, fortresslike, towering and mystical. Roy recognizes that one of them is a replica of the Potala Palace at Lhasa in Tibet. Yao casually parks his jeep at the gate.

"Beautiful, isn't it?" he says to us after we climb out.

"It's more than that," says Roy, starting to take photos. "Look at those colors! They're incredible."

The colors *are* dazzling. The roofs are of shining gold, with green edges. The gilded flying dragons on the roof ridges seem almost alive, glittering against their background of blue sky and white clouds. The walls are either bright white with crimson windows or dark red with white windows.

"They're known as the Eight Outer Temples, even though only seven of them are left. The Red Guards destroyed one during the Cultural Revolution. They were built in the seventeen-nineties, by Emperor Qianlong, in the Lama style, to cater to envoys from Tibet and Mongolia. They are also used to celebrate the birthdays of Manchurian emperors and their mothers. Go take a look. I'm going to stay here," he says, pulling out a cigarette.

Roy and I walk to the main entrance. The clerk at the ticket booth stares at us as though he is surprised to see us. Roy and I are the only visitors.

The dark red walls remind me of the Forbidden City, of the robes of Lama monks, and of my own lipstick. Why did the ancient Chinese like crimson so much?

Although it's a shiny, gilded compound, it gives me a feeling of desolation. Where are those wicked days of excess—the wasteful banquets, the endless orgies, the wild hunting? Damaged Buddhist statues stand abandoned or have been removed to dark corners. All I see are the weeds growing from the temple roofs, waving in the wind, and the sparrows roosting in the overhangs, fluffing up their feathers to keep warm.

"That's how China treats its history and its treasures." Roy points to the disfigured statues in disgust.

"They must have been destroyed during the Cultural Revolution, when anything old was considered bad and counterrevolutionary," I explain.

"Chinese revolutionaries like to destroy things, and the sad thing is that they believe they can rebuild better things. In contrast, we Americans like to keep things, the older the better. Maybe it's because China is so old, and America so young."

"Maybe," I echo.

By the time we return to Yao's old jeep, he's finishing his second cigarette. "How do you like it here?" he asks.

Roy answers, "It's fabulous."

Yao later shows us around the Imperial Summer Villa. Surrounded by a wall seven miles long, the city has nine courtyards, eleven small temples, beautiful gardens, numerous pavilions, and a large herd of deer.

Yao says, "When Emperor Kangxi toured this region in the early days of his reign, he loved the natural beauty of Chengde and its cool climate in the summer. The Qing Dynasty emperors who followed Kangxi lived here from May to October each year. In eighteen-sixty they retreated here when Anglo-French soldiers approached Beijing. An emperor died here a couple of years later."

"Since you mention foreign soldiers, let me ask you," Roy says, "is it true that at that time white people were thought to be devils instead of human beings?"

"Yes." Yao nods. "After the Boxer Rebellion, foreign troops came in. One of Dowager Empress Cixi's advisers told her that white people's knees didn't bend: you could hit one with a pole, it was said, and he would topple over, unable to stand up again. How stupid those Manchus were! After the allied foreign soldiers looted Beijing, the empress had to hide here.

"The emperors' Summer Villa is up there on that slope. From here you can see some of its eighteenth-century architecture and landscaped gardens." Sounding like a travel brochure, Yao adds, "Note that the courtyards are in the typical northern style, while the landscapes more closely follow the soft, misty southern manner."

We go up to the villa through a moon gate in the wall. I

stand in the middle of this royal palace that was built only for the old emperors and their chosen companions, and I feel like an ancient spirit myself.

Yao points to a small lake not far away, saying, "It's winter, so of course the lake is frozen. But in the spring, summer, and autumn, the water's surface is like a mirror, with water chestnuts and lilies floating on it." The frozen lake has a white stone bridge across it; the bare willow wickers at the two sides of the meandering path dance in the wind. On the tile roofs, frost glitters in the sunshine; the air has the smell of a delicate fragrance.

I have never liked winter. It always takes me back to Monkey Village, where I chewed at the calluses on my hands, shivering beside a charcoal stove, as I waited for the spring that took forever to come. But in this summer villa I fall in love with the season's beauty.

As we pass by a tower beside the lake, Yao explains, "This is called the Tower of Misty Rain. When the mountain rain comes, a veil of mist surrounds it. With the mountain in sight and the lake waters close by, it was a great place for the emperors to enjoy the mist of the rain."

Roy says, "Well, those ancient emperors really knew how to enjoy themselves."

Stereo speakers installed along the sides of the path start to play "Autumn Moon over Han Palace."

Roy and I give each other an "It's-our-song" look. The music's sad tone makes me imagine myself as an ancient concubine, living in the villa of the royal family. What would I think about when my majesty was with one of his other concubines, leaving me all alone and bored, staring at the lotus blossoms on a hot summer afternoon? Would I dare flirt with some young eunuch standing behind me, waving a fan to cool me off? Would I risk it even under the watchful eyes of my loudmouthed maids? It's beautiful here, but the beauty is caged.

Roy shakes my shoulder and says, "Lili, what are you thinking about?"

I come back from my fantasies, to reality, and answer, "Oh, just the past. What about you?"

"I'm thinking that on the way here, the area seems very desolate. It's hard to imagine that such a magnificent palace could be hiding behind these walls. It's so amazingly different inside from how it is outside. Did those Manchu leaders know about the suffering of the villagers who lived outside? They obviously isolated themselves from the people, behind these dark red walls. They probably didn't care about anything except their own pleasure, like Cixi!

"And," he continues, "why are there so many walls in China, anyway? I don't like walls; they block freedom and segregate people. Maybe it was better for the Chinese that the Western nations did invade. At least that helped break up the corrupt Manchu government."

Yao clearly doesn't like Roy's comment. "You mean you think it's good that China was invaded and colonized by Westerners?" he asks, seeming incredulous.

Roy answers, "For the majority of the Chinese, the Hans, the Manchu were every bit as much foreign invaders as the Westerners. At least the Westerners brought the opportunities of technology and science. Hong Kong is a good example. The only things the Manchus gave China were destitution and corruption. They signed those unequal treaties with foreign powers."

"No, you're wrong. To us the Manchus are as Chinese as the Tibetans. Many of them were corrupt, like Cixi, but they didn't bring imperialism, opium, gunboats, and colonialism." Yao gives me a look of disapproval, as if I were agreeing with Roy.

Roy sighs. "You're right about that. That part of history was horrible. Westerners should be ashamed of it."

"I know some Chinese love to have foreigners rule. They say that China should be colonized for three hundred years." Yao looks at me again, as if I were one of those Chinese. "But many others, including me, can't forget the way we were treated in the past."

"No one should forget about history."

"History has a strong impact on how we think of foreigners."

"Can you be more specific?"

"On the one hand, the past has taught us to hate Westerners; on the other, I personally have to love them because I get only Westerners as customers, never locals. That's why I follow you like a dog. I'm not shy; I want to get ahead. I know you've got money in your pocket. I use the money I earn from you guys to go to nightclubs that have blonde Russian waitresses."

Roy asks, while looking out at the mountains surrounding the villa, "Why the Russian blondes? Is it because you have more money than they do now?"

"Absolutely. We say that to screw white women is to get revenge on the intruders of the eight nations," Yao replies bluntly. "Sometimes I ask myself, 'Why should I always serve Westerners; why not the other way around? Why does the whole world have to listen to the United States?' Then I realize that it's very simple: I'm from a poor country, just like those Russian waitresses."

"So you think it's a universal truth that 'money talks'?"

"Hell yes, for better or worse."

When we get back to Yao's jeep, it is early afternoon. Yao asks if we'd like to have lunch with him. Roy says no, explaining that we need to get to Up Village before evening. He takes sixty yuan out of his pocket; I guess that the ten extra yuan are a tip. "Thank you so much for your company." Roy says. "We really enjoyed being with you."

Yao's face changes quickly, turning almost purple, when he sees the money in Roy's hand. He doesn't take it. Instead, he folds his arms. "So the ten extra are a tip, right?"

"Yes?" Roy is obviously confused at this sudden change in Yao's attitude.

Yao sneers at Roy's reply. "You Westerners are *really* clever. No wonder we were colonized and exploited."

"What do you mean, Yao? What are you upset about? Is the tip not enough for you? Let me add another ten yuan." Roy begins feeling in his pockets for more money.

"Are you an actor, or what? You must think I'm just an ignorant fool!" Yao yells at Roy.

"I'm sorry. I really don't know what you're talking about."

"Don't play games with me!"

"Be careful what you say. Just tell me, what do you want?"

"I want you to give me fifty U.S. dollars."

"Well, why didn't you tell me that in the first place? I think you're trying to scam me." Roy is angry now; he drops his arms to his sides as if ready for a fight.

"I'm trying to rip you off? Are you out of your fucking mind?" Yao shouts. "I drove you around the whole morning with my own jeep and consumed my own gasoline. From six A.M. to now. I never let my mouth rest for a second. You think you can get rid of me with nothing more than sixty yuan? You probably even expect me to be grateful for your lousy ten-yuan tip. You think that's all I deserve? Are we Chinese so worthless in your eyes that you're willing to spend more money on dog food than on a hardworking Chinese tour guide, a college graduate?"

I want to help Roy, but I know my participation would only add fuel to the fire: Yao would just ignore me or maybe even attack me for being a Chinese "sellout." Such a person is considered even worse than a Western intruder.

"Don't bark at me!" Roy stands his ground in the face of Yao's fury. "You want American dollars. If you had said so in the first place, then we wouldn't be having this argument now, because it just so happens that I don't carry around American money in China. OK, I'll give you four hundred yuan, and you get off my back. Take it or leave it!" Roy removes four one-hundred-yuan bills from his wallet and slips them under one of the jeep's windshield wipers.

Before Yao can comment, Roy removes me by the arm and says, "Lili, let's get the fuck out of here."

But I can't help stealing a glance back at Yao after several steps. He's shaking his head, his face dark with frustration and disgust. He chews his lower lip, staring at the money, lost in thought. As I watch, he takes the money from his windshield, wads it up, and stuffs it into his pocket.

ELEVEN

Before Roy and I can find a cab to take us to Up Village, where FeiFei's cousin Little Liu lives, a man driving a beat-up pickup truck stops on the road and offers us a lift.

In the back, I huddle against Roy in the cold wind as we're tossed from side to side with every bounce of the truck along this rugged, uneven road. With hair flying and clothes flapping in the wind, I feel like a fugitive in some Hollywood movie, fleeing with my partner to the Mexican border.

The hills on both sides of the road are bare, with no sign of green grass or vegetation. They look like gigantic idiots who forgot to get dressed and are standing out in the piercing winter winds, naked, shameless, and numb.

"No trees?" Roy remarks, as swirls of dust blow off the hills.

"No trees," I shout back above the wind and the noise of the truck. "Peasants don't plant trees here; they prefer to cut them down. They're used to breathing dusty air."

When we arrive in Up Village, Roy offers the knotty old driver some money, but he refuses to take it, saying, "Let us shake hands instead."

We are standing on a rough, narrow dirt road; a dozen peasants are leaning against a clay wall and staring at us with their mouths half open. There is a large slogan painted in red on the wall behind them which reads, "For the Sake of Yourself and the Glorious Motherland, Marry Late and Have Children Later."

The villagers—young and middle-aged, some squatting, others slouching lazily—are all wearing old blue-quilted Mao coats stained with dirt and grease. Many have their arms folded, each hand up the opposite sleeve, hidden against the cold. One of them wipes his runny nose on his coat sleeve. These yellow-toothed, glassy-eyed peasants look the same as the ones in Monkey Village, equally numb and emotionless. Years ago thousands of parents were sent to the country to learn from the peasants, but what did they learn? The same numbness and the same inability to get angry.

"What are they doing there?" Roy asks me under his breath.

"It's a slow season for farming but a busy time for gossip and sex."

"Be serious, Lili."

"I'm telling you the truth."

Roy waves to the peasants and greets them: "Hello, comrades!"

They stand with their mouths open wide now. They don't know what to say to a foreigner. Some modestly cover their mouths with their dry, rough, wrinkled hands.

"We're looking for Little Liu," I tell them, trying to sound local.

One of the men says, "We'll go get him," and three others quickly set off.

Ten minutes later the four men in their torn blue coats return with a tall, slim young man wearing a bright red tie and a crumpled yellow Westerner's suit. He seems a crane among roosters.

He greets us in English, but Roy replies in Chinese.

"You speak Chinese?" Little Liu is dumbfounded at Roy's perfect pronunciation.

"You speak English?" Roy jokes, mimicking Little Liu's tone.

Little Liu bashfully scratches his head and says, "I've learned a little bit from radio programs."

"Aren't you cold not wearing a coat?" Roy asks Little Liu. I don't know whether Roy is really that insensitive or just if he's indulging in a bit of black humor with Little Liu.

"Little Liu has dressed himself so formally, in such light clothes, just to meet you," I say.

Little Liu smiles shyly, like a new bride. "Two visitors, one from the U.S. and one from Beijing—what a great event for our village!"

"How did you know about our backgrounds?" Roy asks.

"I received the telegram yesterday from my uncle FeiFei and have been waiting for you ever since."

"What do you do?" I ask Little Liu.

"I work for the village's Youth League of the Communist Party. Every now and then I also try to teach illiterates how to read newspapers."

As we walk, a couple of big-mouthed kids follow us like a wagging tail. Three, four, ten, twenty, thirty—the tail grows larger and larger and finally turns into a parade. The kids scream at one another hilariously, as if it were a holiday.

"They're peasants who have never been outside this village. They've never seen foreigners in their lives. It's a big thing for them," Little Liu explains, wearing his forever-humble face.

Roy replies, "I completely understand. You'd see the same thing in really isolated rural areas of America."

As we wander along, we see run-down mud huts and footpaths strewn with garbage, leading up to more shacks.

Pointing to a hut at random, Roy asks Little Liu, "Can we see inside?"

"Yes, of course."

We enter without knocking—typical peasant behavior. Pasted on either side of the door is a pair of old scrolls, forming a *duilian,* or antithetical couplet. Made of red rice paper, the scrolls are rippled from years of weathering, but I can still read the black characters: "Mother is dear, and Father is dear, but nobody is as dear as Chairman Mao; the sky is great, the earth is great, but nothing is as great as our Communist Party."

A cluster of red peppers and a head of garlic dangle from one corner of the door, meant to drive out evil spirits. The octagonal mirror placed above the doorway is also used to keep bad spirits out.

The living room is dark and dusty, with no furniture. A small, hunched woman is sitting on a stool, hand-stitching soles for cotton padded shoes. Her two children are playing around her, their noses running. Her hands are ashen; the room is cold as a freezer. The family can't afford charcoal.

The woman is so preoccupied with her work that she doesn't see us come in. We startle her. Her children stop playing and huddle next to her. Roy seems to frighten them; when he raises his camera to snap a photo, the children and mother shriek at the camera's bright flash.

Roy holds up his hands and apologizes, saying, "I'm very sorry. I didn't mean to scare you. I want to be your friend."

"Want to make friends or become famous?" I mumble under my breath.

Roy ignores my comment, noting instead a shrine in one corner of the room. "You believe in Buddha?" he asks.

The woman looks at Little Liu in confusion. Little Liu explains to her, "He's a journalist from the United States of America. America, do you know it? And this lady is from Beijing," he continues. "So don't be afraid."

She nods several times, like a woodpecker, and then nervously turns back to Roy, answering hastily, "I'm so absentminded, I keep forgetting to take the Buddha down. We don't believe in those superstitions anymore. Now we believe only in our glorious Party." The woman sounds like a schoolchild reciting her lesson.

Little Liu pats the woman's shoulder and assures her, "It's all right to have religious beliefs now; the Cultural Revolution is long gone and over. You don't have to be afraid anymore."

"In America there are people who believe in Buddha," Roy adds.

The woman nods her head again but doesn't say anything. I can tell from her eyes that she's still nervous.

Her children watch me curiously; I smile at them and gesture for them to come to me. They come slowly. I squat and extend my arms to show my friendliness.

"Blood!" the kids yell upon seeing the red color of my polished fingernails, and they pull at their mom's sleeves to show her, as if they had discovered a monster. The mother softly says, "You silly kids, that's not blood. It's a fashion from Beijing."

After that the woman becomes a little bit less nervous and smiles at me, showing her yellowed teeth.

"How old are you?" she asks me.

"I'm twenty-eight." In the countryside, on the day you are born, you're already one year old. I calculate my age as the peasants do, adding a year to my real age. "And how about you?"

"Twenty-eight also," she says. The wrinkled woman's reply shocks me. She looks older than my mother. I know that by city standards she is only twenty-seven.

I stand up, not knowing what to say next. Here I am, towering over all of them, wearing a leather coat and high boots, coming into their home with my foreign boyfriend. Yes, I am a "fake foreign devil"!

I notice that one of her two skinny children is wearing a pair of sandals even though it's the middle of winter. I reach over and gently stroke his ankles to make them a little bit warmer.

"My sin," the woman explains to me in embarrassment. "I didn't do well in my previous life, and now I can't even afford another pair of cotton-padded shoes for my children. They take turns wearing the only pair they have."

"Are you making a second pair for them?" I point to the shoes she is stitching.

"No. I have to sell these to buy food." The woman sounds even more ashamed.

"Where is their father?" Roy asks.

"In prison," the woman answers, turning back to her sewing. Everyone is silent.

After we leave the house, Little Liu tells us about the woman's husband. "He left for the county's township four years ago, to seek his fortune. He worked as a waiter in a restaurant in the city of Shi Jia Zhuang. At first, he was treated badly by his coworkers. City people think we country folk are dirty and uncivilized. Finally, desperate and frustrated, he joined a local gang of hoodlums and worked for them."

"What was he convicted of?" Roy asks.

"Gang rape and murder." Little Liu shakes his head. He makes clear his impatience with the peasants' backwardness. "A college graduate came once to help them plant orchards. But when he trimmed off some branches so the trees would grow better, these stupid peasants thought he was killing the trees and drove him away. We're poor, but what can I say? I see these peasants' ingrained ignorance and bad traditions every day!"

"Aren't you a peasant yourself?" Roy asks Little Liu.

"Yes, but I don't feel bound to this village. Sooner or later I'll leave," Little Liu says. His words remind me of a conversation Roy had in Republican Village, with the Miao couple from Phoenix. They all feel repressed by life in the countryside now. The earth used to mean everything to Chinese peasants; I wonder when they began to feel they were no longer bound to the soil.

Roy taps Little Liu's shoulder and comforts him. "Don't be pessimistic. I sincerely believe that the spring breeze of the open-door policy will soon blow into your village." Roy uses the Chinese newspapers' phrase "the spring breeze." I can't tell whether he's honestly trying to reassure the man or if he's just joking about how the policy is propagandized.

Two sows follow us, their mud-caked tits quivering beneath them. Stinking, wet shit—from humans, pigs, cows, and chickens—is scattered everywhere. An old woman passes us, her face wrinkled like a dried prune; she is bent over under the weight of a bundle of hay twice as long as she is tall. It amazes me to see that she has tiny feet that were obviously bound when she was a child. She hobbles, moving as fast as her feet will allow.

Little Liu leads us to another shack. He tells us that this is where one of the poorest families in the village lives. The walls of the hut are blackened by smoke from many years of burning wood. Hay from the roof has begun to drop to the floor, and wind blasts in through a big gap up there. The windows have no glass; instead they are covered with pieces of plastic pierced through with holes.

The room is so dark I can barely see anything. In a corner an old man squats, his back to us. He is cooking some small potatoes on a stove on the floor. He glances briefly at us, his unexpected visitors, and then returns to his cooking. Dark, ugly, and shrunken, he looks at least a hundred years old. His ancient quilted coat is greasy and raggedy.

A young boy jumps out from an inner room. He is wearing a baggy uniform with patches on it, which I will later learn was a donation from the military. But his eyes are bright, and he looks at us with curiosity.

"What's your name?" Roy asks the boy.

"Math," the boy replies slowly, his eyes fixed on Roy's big hands.

"How old are you?"

"Twelve, and my dad is sixty-seven." He calls the old man his dad, even though he looks more like his grandfather.

"Do you go to school?"

Math shakes his head no.

Roy turns to the father and asks, "No money for sending him to school?"

The old man says nothing, just continues to distribute the potatoes among four wooden bowls. It feels as if ten thousand years had passed before he finally clears his throat and speaks: "Having money or not doesn't make any difference. I'm halfway into my tomb now—if he went to school, who would take care of my family?"

Roy has bought some bread and chocolate, and he offers them to Math, who takes them and wolfs down half. Finding the food sweet and good, he saves the other half and tells us, "That's for my mother and my little sister." He leads us into the inner room.

There is no furniture in here aside from a heated *kang,* a clay bed, which occupies two thirds of the entire space. The mat on top of the *kang* is worn out, with holes in it. A middle-aged woman is sitting on the warmer end of the *kang,* stuffing a sack with cotton pads. Seeing us, she smiles weirdly, exposing red, bleeding gums. Next to her a little girl is crawling around like a small cat, her legs crooked as crescent moons.

I have never imagined that such poverty could exist in a place so close to Beijing. The voices of these peasants are unheard, their image unseen in that neon city.

"Hello, Aunt," I greet the woman in traditional Chinese style, and I wave my hands to draw her attention.

But she makes no reply. Instead she sticks her fingers into her mouth and chews their ends, her eyes full of confusion. She looks through me, as if I didn't exist.

"My mother can't hear you," Math says.

Later Little Liu will tell us the story. Math's father was from a miserable, poor family. He had eight brothers. The nine of them all saved money in one piggy bank. When one brother got married, he would borrow all the money from the bank, and then the rest would start saving all over again for the next groom. Math's father was the youngest, and so he loaned all his money to his eight older brothers as each one married in turn.

There was no money for the ninth brother's marriage until he was in his late fifties. Then the matchmaker found him a woman who was thirty-six and not bad-looking, but deaf and mentally retarded. But that didn't bother Math's father. He badly needed a woman to have sex and children with, so he married her. They had two sons and a daughter. One son died of starvation; Math is the other.

There is no doubt that Math, too, is starving. At the age of twelve, he is no taller than most six-year-olds.

Math's mother pulls a comb out of her shabby coat and works it through her daughter's hair. She is so caring and gentle while doing it that tears well up in Roy's eyes.

I notice a big scar over the girl's scalp, like a spider. Little Liu says to me, "She's a poor girl, doesn't even have a name. After she was born, her father wanted to give her away because she was a girl and he couldn't afford to raise another child. But her mother, despite being retarded, has a mother's instincts. She cried and held her baby tight every day. Her husband beat her many times, but she never gave up. Finally the father let the girl stay, but he didn't even bother to give her a name, and her mother is too handicapped to name her.

"The girl got the scar at the age of five, when she accidentally fell into a pot of boiling water and burned her scalp. The family had no medicine. Her mother didn't know how to help her, and the father didn't care. The wound eventually healed, but that part of her scalp will never grow hair. She had polio, and no treatment was available for her; that's why her legs are crippled."

I look at the girl. Her big, bright, fearful eyes are dodging us. She is frightened of our presence. We walk out with Math.

"Tell us about your mom," Roy encourages the boy.

"My mom is the kindest person in the world. Whenever my sister and I get hungry, she goes out to look for food. If our old man has a hard time at work or something, he'll punch my mom hard when he gets home. He beats us, too.

"Yesterday our family's mule got lost. Our old man sent my crippled little sister out to find it. She looked all day but couldn't find anything at all, so he didn't let her back in the house or give her anything to eat. My mom thought he'd tried to give my sister away again, and she started to pound on him with her hands. But our old man just grabbed her by the hair and banged her head against the wall. Her head started bleeding, but she didn't cry. My mom never cries; she never makes a sound."

In Monkey Village, I remember, men used to call their women cows. Nothing changes.

"How often does your father hit you?" Roy pries deeper.

"For him, hitting us is like taking a piss. It happens every day," says Math.

"Do you hate him?" Little Liu jumps in. It's funny to hear him mimic Roy's journalistic tone.

"My old man? No." Math shakes his head. "His life isn't easy."

Before we leave, Math volunteers, "Do you want to see more? There's someone up the hill who's poorer than we are! I can take you there."

Little Liu shakes his head and sighs. "Achieving psychological balance by laughing at those who are worse off than you—that's the Spirit of Ah Q, described in Lu Xun's novel sixty years ago."

"I remember the character Ah Q," says Roy. "A cowardly, greedy, selfish, envious, shortsighted peasant living in a small village. He's a loser, but he can always muster a laugh about anyone who appears to be weaker than him!"

"That's the sad aspect of all Chinese peasants. They never change, because they always think they're better than others." Little Liu sighs again.

As he leads us up the hill, Math looks triumphant. He curses and throws rocks at everyone we pass who stares at us. It's his way of showing off that he's with us.

A narrow footpath winds its way up to an even smaller old hut on the hillside. It's leaning in the wind, as if about to fall at any moment.

"In the States, *rich* people live up in the hills," Roy jokes.

Math looks at him and points to the door of the shack. "Here it is," he says.

Understanding immediately that the boy expects a tip,

Roy gives him two cups of instant noodles. Math leaves us, happy and content.

Little Liu suggests that Roy and I wait outside while he goes in first by himself. After a time, he waves for us to come in. There is dead silence. I shiver.

The window openings have no glass or even plastic. The wind comes in through them like a swarm of hungry insects. No sheets cover the clay bed, another *kang*. Two people are sitting on its cold surface, huddled together against the freezing air: an old woman with tangled, matted hair and a middle-aged man who's drooling. They're holding a clay bowl with some heated rocks in it. The *kang* is filthy and smells awful.

The man is wearing Little Liu's coat. Apparently he doesn't have any clothes at all, and Little Liu has made an effort to cover him, at least partially, so we won't be embarrassed. But below the coat we can still see the man's penis, which is standing straight up like a transparent carrot. An erection in the frigid air.

The man seems happy to see us. He tries to talk to us, but we can't understand him; he drools every time he attempts to speak.

The old lady cries out when she sees us. She must not have seen any other humans for quite a while. She complains loudly, with pent-up anger: "Why should I live on in such a hell? Why does Buddha still keep me alive to suffer? I want to die, I want to die. Isn't it nice to die? Lie down forever, no more worries, no more troubles, no more pain. But I can't die. If I die, who's going to take care of my son here, this forty-year-old dummy? Who's going to change his diapers and get food for him?

"People say that having sons is parents' luck. I have three sons, and they bring me nothing but misery. My other two sons got married last year. But their wives look down on us because we're poor. They made my sons move out. After they left, the two bitches wouldn't even let them come to see me. They live down the hill, but they haven't come to see us once since they moved out.

"One day this dummy here disappeared. My old man and I searched all day and still couldn't find where the stupid boy had gone. In the evening my husband went to our other sons for help. But you know what? The two bitches drove him away! Later that night my poor old man was searching in the dark and fell down a ravine. He hit his head and broke ribs in his chest, but we couldn't afford to get a doctor for him. His broken ribs must have punctured his lung, because he died three days later. His eyes were wide open until his last breath. During his three days of pain he cursed those two toads he fathered. They're sinful, sinful. . . . Now I'm just waiting to starve to death with this idiot son of mine. For the sake of Buddha, I can't leave him alone."

That's how human beings live like animals.
That's how human beings live like animals.
That's how human beings live like animals.

I repeat this over and over to myself after the old woman finishes her bitter speech. Roy's eyes are teary. I feel sorry for the old woman, but I have no tears for her. Over the years, too many such stories have hardened my heart.

Little Liu tells us, "Being a peasant is becoming harder because the government is paying for our crops with IOU's that we can't collect on for a year or longer. But while we peasants are getting poorer, the sons of government officials are busy using government money to operate their own companies, developing fancy villas on public land and then selling them to rich overseas Chinese and foreigners."

No wonder the Party loves peasants: they don't question, and they don't complain! After educated city people like my parents were sent to the country to learn from the peasants, they also shut up and stopped questioning. They became peasants, too.

Roy turns to me. "The Communist revolution is supposed to be a revolution for the peasants. But look at these poor people—they've received almost no benefit at all from it."

He reaches into his pocket and hands Little Liu four hundred yuan. For Roy it's the admission fee to a single concert, but for a peasant it is half a year's income. In this destitute Chinese village, Roy wants to be a philanthropist, a savior. But he is not a savior. He can't save these people from their fate.

Little Liu understands what Roy wants; he gives the money to the old lady and explains, "This is some money for you from this kind American gentleman."

The old lady insists that she can't accept it. She clears her nose with a sniff and wipes it with the back of her hand, saying, "I don't want to bring troubles to our government, and I don't need money. Please give it to someone who needs it. I gave birth to two ingrates and one idiot, and now I must eat the bitter fruit of the tree I planted."

Roy searches in his bag, trying to find something other than money to give the old woman and her retarded, middle-aged son. All he has left is some Nestlé's instant coffee. The old woman has never seen instant coffee before. She says, "No. I don't need Chinese medicine. There is no cure for my sickness."

Roy, Little Liu, and I leave the shack. People often say, "No pain, no gain," but I wonder what pain really does to us. Enduring hardship has made me insensitive to the hardships suffered by others. It's too easy to say, "If I can survive this hell, so can you" or "Your suffering is nothing compared to mine."

And what is poverty, really? To me poverty is the absence of opportunities. Roy and I can come to this place, observe the nudity of a retarded man, and listen to his mother's sad story, but they can't get out of this dead end of their lives. This is what all poverty is about. That's why I would rather be a rich foreigner's mistress than live an honest life here.

When we arrive at Little Liu's for lunch, his entire family is waiting for us in the front yard. His folks are there, along with four of his brothers and two sisters. He jokes about the size of his family: "Life in the countryside is the same old thing day in and day out. So people go to bed early, and their only pleasure is having sex. That's why each family has so many children."

"But now your parents can't have any more, because of the one-child policy," Roy comments. Little Liu nods and adds in a low voice, "They're too old for that anyway."

Little Liu's family is well off compared to most others in the village, who live in clay houses and have no furniture at all. Little Liu's family has a two-story brick house and outdated red-lacquer furniture inlaid with portraits of old Mao.

In the living room a picture of a young man with a

shaved head, wearing a gray monk's robe, hangs on the wall. He appears detached and peaceful and has a look of wisdom that distinguishes him from the poor, ignorant peasants.

"Who is that?" I ask Little Liu's mother, Iron Beauty.

My nosiness brings tears to her eyes. "That's my oldest son," she says. "He went to a Taoist temple many years ago and never came back. He used to be the only high school graduate in our village. We thought that someday he would become a great person in the city, just like his uncle FeiFei, and bring glory and pride to his clan. But my son was cursed when he met an old monk named Jade Fox, who took him away, and we have never heard from him since. My eyes are blind from the tears I've shed for him."

Iron Beauty rises and fetches a basket filled with the things her son left behind. "This is all we have left of him. His papa and I worked so hard to pay the tuition to get him through high school, and this is all we got in return."

Inside the basket there are some sketches and calligraphy that her son did when he was young, as well as a worn pocket edition of Lao-tzu's *Tao Te Ching*. I open the old book, printed in 1951 in orthodox Chinese characters. On the first page there's an inscription in small, beautiful handwriting: "Practice not doing, and everything will fall into place. Peace Liu, 1979."

I feel sympathy for Iron Beauty and try to console her. "You still have Little Liu and your other sons," I offer. In the countryside it is considered a blessing to have many sons in one's household. Iron Beauty has five more, and all of the older ones have finished high school. She should be proud.

"Yes. I thank Buddha that they've been good and loyal to

their family." Iron Beauty wipes away her tears and turns her eyes to me with a sigh of relief. She makes me think of my mother. Mama has tears, too, but not this gentleness. Her gaze is always cold and critical.

Little Liu's sisters begin serving lunch. They put ten steaming dishes on a low rectangular table that has been placed on top of the *kang*. It isn't just the place where all the members of the family sleep together and the parents have quiet sex while their children sleep next to them; it is also where they eat, drink, smoke, play cards, and gossip. The *kang* is both their living room and their bedroom.

I am surprised to see that the top of the clay bed is covered with linoleum tiles, of the kind that city people use only as flooring in their bathrooms and kitchens.

When I ask Little Liu about this, he absent-mindedly scratches his head and explains, with a little embarrassment, "It has become fashionable to use linoleum tiles as bed liners in the countryside nowdays."

Old Liu, Little Liu's father, is our host. He orders his youngest son to go out and buy us something to drink: "Naonao, go get two bottles of sorghum spirit from the co-op." Roy frowns. Naonao looks to be only about ten years old.

Old Liu invites us to be seated around the table. We take off our shoes and sit cross-legged on the linoleum-covered *kang*. Aside from Roy and me, there are seven of Old Liu's friends gathered for the meal. Old Liu introduces his card-game friends, his wine-drinking friends, his meat-eating friends, and his mah-jongg friends to Roy and me. One guest is a Party member. I am the only woman present.

"Where are the hostesses, Iron Beauty and Little Liu's sisters?" Roy asks impatiently.

Taking a pinch of snuff from a jade snuffbox, Old Liu puts it to his nose and sniffs, his eyes cast downward. "They're in the kitchen, cooking."

"Can't we invite them to join us? We still have some space." Roy fails to sense Old Liu's hesitancy. He doesn't understand the rules: women don't eat with honored guests.

Without asking permission of his host, Roy stands up and enters the kitchen.

Old Liu looks embarrassed and displeased, but he holds his temper and manages a tense smile. Pretending to ignore Roy, he says, "Eat, let's eat."

Roy says, "Lili, come over here," gesturing for me to join him at the kitchen door. I glance at our host, who nods his head slightly, hinting that it is all right for me to leave the table. I join Roy.

Iron Beauty, her daughters, and her daughters-in-law are out of sight in the kitchen, making more food. One is on a ladder, picking a cluster of dried red peppers from the roof. "Red pepper is good," she calls to us. "It helps to drive away the coldness and makes the soup taste better."

Another of the women is operating a bellows that blows into the clay stove. In spite of the cold outside, it's hot in the kitchen, and she keeps wiping sweat from her forehead with a towel that's so old I can't tell what its original color was.

A third woman is bending over, dipping water from a large jar on the floor with a half gourd that she uses as a ladle. A fourth stands in front of a hissing frying pan, stirring cabbage and adding green onions, coughing, the tears running down her cheeks. Another brings more food from the family's small reserve in the attic.

In winter peasants often don't have enough to eat, unless

they save food carefully from harvest time. But now these women are using up their precious food reserves for this big lunch, as though it were Spring Festival. I wonder if it's just because Roy and I found them through their city relative, FeiFei.

That's the way Chinese peasants are. If they think you're higher than they are, they'll treat you with great respect, more than they ever show themselves or others of their own kind. They will even belittle themselves. But if they think you're below them, you will get nothing but abuse from them. I saw clan fights and husbands beating wives in Monkey Village. Peasants can be like animals with no mercy.

"This is far too much food for us. I feel guilty," Roy says to me in a low voice. He is moved by the family's generosity and warmth. Doesn't he realize it's all because they think we have a higher status?

The women all stop what they're doing when they notice us at the door. They look curious but friendly.

"Ladies, would you like to join us for lunch?" Roy asks.

"No," says Iron Beauty, waving her hands vigorously. "It's for you. We always eat here in the kitchen."

But Roy insists: "Oh, please. I'll feel honored if I can sit next to you."

Iron Beauty finally gives in.

"Won't the rest of you join us as well?" Roy says to the younger women.

They look at one another shyly and finally choose Little Liu's younger sister National Flower to go as their representative, to eat with the men and their important guests.

Roy offers his seat to Iron Beauty and says, "In America,

the lady of the house customarily sits in the place of honor, not the guest."

Iron Beauty looks at her husband nervously and glances quickly at his friends in silent apology for her intrusion. Old Liu looks at nothing. Iron Beauty doesn't know quite what to do but wants to show Roy her appreciation for his honoring her, so she slowly sits down.

Old Liu doesn't care what Roy's opinions are. He stands up and raises his enamel tea mug, which is brimming with the sorghum spirits his youngest son has brought back. He clears his throat several times to get everyone's attention. When all are quiet, Old Liu starts his welcoming speech:

"First of all, we should thank our Communist Party and the central government for their concern for those of us who are peasants. Thank them for sending two honored guests from Beijing and America to visit our village. Let us drink a toast to the Communist Party."

Old Liu drinks his fill, "bottoms up," proudly showing everyone by his empty mug that he hasn't cheated, and thus encouraging the rest of us to drink as well. His friends all follow his example. Even Naonao, the ten-year-old, dips his chopsticks into the spirits and sucks the ends of them to have a taste of the sorghum wine. Roy, too, has some; Iron Beauty and National Flower have not been offered any.

I'm the only person at the table who doesn't drink. I can't stand the stink of the cheap sorghum wine; the drunkard who raped me in Monkey Village had the same smell in his filthy mouth.

"It's Mrs. Luo-Yi's turn to drink her wine," one of the guests says to me. Others watch and wait for me to drink.

"I can't."

"Of course you can," they say to me.

"I really can't."

"If you don't drink it, we peasants will think you are looking down on us," one guest keeps pressuring me.

I don't know what to do, so I just sit there tapping the side of the mug with my fingers.

"Lili has health problems and is sensitive to alcohol," says Roy.

The health excuse Roy makes up doesn't faze them; the peasants still insist, "She's our honored guest and should drink our spirits."

"Can I help her?" Roy asks.

"No. Substitutes don't count." The peasants won't abandon their customs. They think spirits are no more harmful than soy milk. Drinking spirits and beating their wives are the peasants' favorite pastime.

Young Naonao, urged on by the men, holds a bigger mug to my lips and tries to make me drink. He tilts it and is about to pour it onto my tightly closed lips and down my cheeks when Roy rescues me from this predicament with his magic Polaroid camera. "Comrades," he cuts in, "we should have photos to commemorate this day." He raises his camera and begins shooting.

The men are a little drunk, and the flash of the camera instantly distracts them. To their surprise, pictures begin falling out of the camera instantly. The peasants are awed and delighted when they see themselves in the pictures, talking to one another like monkeys.

For the first time in his life, young Naonao has a photo of himself. He can't believe what he's seeing. "One more! One more!" he begs Roy, as he strikes a refined pose, looking up at the sky like a hero. He pastes the new photo on his chest and walks around triumphantly.

Old Liu feels left out because all the attention has shifted to the pictures and the camera. For a time he just sits there, putting pinches of snuff in his nose. Then he clears his throat several times loudly, as if trying to tell everyone that he is the host, the head of the household, and therefore should be the center of attention.

"Actually, we don't care much for pictures," he says to Roy in a stern and authoritarian tone. "It's good that we can have the pictures as commemorations. But we wouldn't like for you to publish these pictures and create problems for our government."

Roy nods and says, "Sure."

"We're known for our poverty, yet we have a long history of revolution. We have always supported the Communist Party." Old Liu's voice is bloated with drunken pride. Doesn't it ever occur to him to wonder why he and his friends are still so poor and destitute despite all their loyalty to the Party? This old man is pathetic.

Iron Beauty is very pleased with the picture that Roy has taken of her. "Eat more, please do," she keeps saying.

"I'm eating," I assure her.

She says to me shyly, "We don't have much good food to treat you to. I know that our lunch must be very inadequate by your city standards."

"The food is delicious and of excellent quality, even by Beijing standards," I say, not just to flatter her.

Iron Beauty apologizes for not offering us any pork, explaining, "Our household has ten sows, and every year we sell the meat in the town market to get money for the kids' tuition. But we never eat pork from our own pigs. Instead we save other parts for ourselves, such as tripe and intestines, because we can't find anyone to buy those. Today we've made some stir-fried dishes with pig intestines. We all like this a lot. Please try some."

She uses her chopsticks to pick out some of the intestines for us. The chopsticks are still wet with her saliva. I notice Roy looking at the intestines in his bowl with a weak smile.

"Westerners wouldn't understand this warmheartedness," Roy whispers to me.

As we eat, the others watch us, drinking their sorghum wine. I realize that no one is eating except for Roy and me; the others don't even have chopsticks. Later I will remember that in rural villages peasants eat only two meals a day. They skip lunch to save food. I assume that Old Liu's guests have all eaten a big breakfast earlier and so aren't that hungry. They've come came here just to see us and to drink. The huge ten-dish meal is a special offering for Roy and me.

Little Liu's young sister National Flower sits next to me. We have a quiet girl-talk in hushed voices.

"How old are you, National Flower?"

"I'm nineteen."

"What do you do?"

"I stay home, waiting to be married. If I'm lucky, a boy who owns some land may choose me. I don't have to do many chores because Mama has so many daughters-in-law. I read books and listen to the radio every day."

"Do you like reading?"

"Yes. It opens up my eyes. I've always wanted to see the world outside my village, but my family can't afford for me to travel. So I read about the outside world."

"Where do you get books?"

"I save money and buy magazines and books through mail order. My happiest moment is when the mailman comes with his green bike and bags. Sister, do you read books? What type of books do you like? Foreign or Chinese? Do you love romance novels?"

"Do you?"

"I love romance novels. I often cry with the heroines in the books. I especially like romances about city people. I wish I had been born in a city so I could have a *real* life."

"Your life here isn't real?"

"Here I feel like I'm not really alive. My only choice is to get married. I can't save myself. Only a man can save me." National Flower sounds frustrated as she speaks about herself, but then she brightens and asks, "My sister, what do you do in Beijing, where our glorious Chairman Mao once lived?" She looks at me curiously.

I think of telling her that I'm just like her, living at home and doing nothing, but seeing that her eyes so bright and so wide open, I reply, "I play the erhu at a foreign hotel."

"I can't imagine what Beijing, the capital of our motherland, must be like! I wish I could go there someday to see the Gate of Heavenly Peace, and the People's Great Hall, and Chairman Mao's memorial in Tiananmen Square, and the tall buildings, even just once in my life!" She bubbles with excitement.

"It wouldn't be so difficult to make that wish come true."

"Sister, will you help me? Will you take me there? I can be your maid, do the cooking and washing for you."

"What about your folks? What would they think?" I glance at Old Liu and Iron Beauty.

"I'll be a peasant forever if I follow their will. I'll be a peasant's wife, a peasant's mother, and a peasant's grandmother, and never anything better."

"Is that so bad?" I don't want to be cruel, but how can I take responsibility for National Flower's future? My own life is troublesome enough. If she really wants to leave the countryside, she can do it on her own. I did it once. This place is only two hundred kilometers from Beijing.

We are interrupted by one of Iron Beauty's daughters-in-law, who is offering me a big sack. Iron Beauty explains, "Before you and Mr. Luo-Yi leave, I, on behalf of our family, want to thank you for coming. Thank you for taking the time and traveling so far to visit our poor village. Here is a sack full of produce from the village. Please take it with you. It isn't as good as we wish it could be, but we want you to have a token of our high regard for you."

As Iron Beauty talks to us, I steal a look at Old Liu. He is avoiding our eyes, pretending that he has nothing to do with the gift. But I know that all this was his idea. The host can never do it himself. He needs to keep his position. A typical stubborn and proud male peasant from northern China.

The daughter-in-law shows Roy and me the contents of the sack: a basket of eggs, a box of unshelled sunflower seeds, and a bowl of dried dates.

Roy immediately protests, "No, absolutely not. We can't take any more from you. We've already eaten too much food from your reserves."

He doesn't mention that we have also asked them personal questions that made them cry, just to satisfy our own curiosity, or that we haven't done anything for them in return for their hospitality. I'm even worse: I refused to drink their spirits and have ignored their daughter's plea.

But Roy realizes that our host will feel slighted or even lose face if we don't accept the gift. So he finally takes the sack and thanks the family. You have to accept such gifts, just as you have to drink the wine they pour for you.

The Lius are pleased. "It's good to see that you keep our cheap gifts," Iron Beauty says, smiling. "We're glad you don't look down on us."

TWELVE

After spending the night at Little Liu's, the next day, strolling past a row of run-down mud huts, I greet some dry-skinned women doing chores. I see a handsome teenage boy leaning against a wall, carving words into the clay with a small, sharp rock. His bright eyes are unlike the glassy ones of the other peasants; they emit a light of intelligence. He looks at me out of the corner of his eye but doesn't show any curiosity, as others do. Instead he turns his back to me. A little Old Fish-to-Be.

A girl with an oval-shaped face and thick lips comes out of the house and walks over to the boy, pleading, "Please go inside and talk to Papa. You don't want him to beat you again, do you?"

The boy answers, "Haven't I gotten enough? I don't care if he hits me again. Whenever I mention school, he beats me. If he beats me once, I'll run away once. If he beats me twice, I'll run away twice!" Lowering his head, he digs at the clay wall with his fingernails. I see a tear drop to the ground from his face.

"Why does he use my paper as cigarette paper? Why does he treat me like this? Why can't he use just half of the money he wastes on cigarettes for my school fees?" the boy cries bitterly. Reluctantly he follows the girl back into the house.

I don't want to eavesdrop. I laugh to myself that I'm so interested in their problems. Then I turn away. But the girl, who I assume is the boy's sister, looks back and notices me. She invites me into her house: "You must be the lady from Beijing. I'm so glad you're here. Come in and have some tea!"

The boy is in the front yard now, chopping wood. I can still see the traces of tears on his face. He nods and greets me but hides any curiosity he may have about me, this well-dressed visitor from the city.

I know from Little Liu that the boy's name is Military Chen. His father has two eighty-year-old parents to serve and four kids to raise. His wife has lost her ability to speak. His oldest daughter doesn't know how to write anything more than her own name.

Every day Military Chen walks twenty miles to and from school, on rugged mountain paths. His unshod feet hurt and often bleed; his soles are cracked and scarred. Because he is the best student in the school, he has been admitted to the best high school in Hebei Province. But his father won't pay the fees, even after Military Chen's teachers took pity on him and donated half the money. Military Chen's father thinks school is useless. Even worse, to him, is that it causes children to leave home and abandon their parents.

Military Chen's grandma is sitting with his mother on a stool outside the door, each of them holding a baby. His mother has the same thick, dark, weathered lips as his sister. The grandma looks at me with interest and asks, "*Guinu,* are you from a city?"

"Yes," I answer. *Guinu* is a pet name for a girl.

"I went to the next township once, but it was thirty years ago. Girls in the city have it easy. Here we have to work from dawn to dusk and never stop for a moment. My daughter-in-law is a mute, and nobody except me knows how much she has suffered. She had her tubes tied the other day. The government forced her to do it. The Party secretary threatened us, 'If you don't do it, you'll be fined five thousand yuan.'

"We don't have that kind of money, but we didn't want her to do it, so she did nothing. The second time he came, the Party secretary told us that he would have our roof removed if she didn't get the operation right then. The third time he came, he confiscated our rice. So my daughter-in-law had no choice.

"She walked thirty miles on the mountain path to the hospital in our township, all by herself. After they butchered her she came back home on foot, all by herself, without even a sip of chicken broth or anything. The night she returned, we sent Military Chen to the Party secretary's house to beg for a bowl of soup. The next morning my daughter-in-law went back to her duties. She is treated badly, but she works like a cow."

Military Chen's mother begins to sob.

"You'd better shut up," Military Chen cautions hi grandmother.

The walls of their living area are plastered with papers to block the wind. The papers are many copies of the same misprinted page from a dictionary, all of them providing the definitions of the same Chinese character, for *trance*. TRANCE, 1: *A hypnotic or ecstatic state.* 2: *A state of detachment from one's physical surroundings.* 3: *A dazed state.* I look up and look around. The whole room is in a trance.

"In China, you better not be a woman. If you happen to be a woman, don't be a countrywoman. If you're born a countrywoman, don't bear a country girl. It's better not to be born into this world." Military Chen's grandmother keeps talking outside the room. National Flower and Military Chen's sister will repeat their mothers' pattern.

As it begins to get dark, I leave Military Chen's family. On the clay wall I see lines written with a sharp rock:

> Junior high,
> Memories of yesterday
> That I can't avoid
> High school,
> Dreams of tomorrow
> That I can't afford

Military Chen is still chopping wood. I used to dream of school just like this boy. I felt the same despair. I want to do something for him, but what? I can't give him money, as

Roy would. Military Chen is proud and would not accept a handout.

The boy walks toward me and says coldly, "City guest, you've heard and seen enough about our poor life. Won't you just go and leave us alone now?"

"How can you say things like that to our honored guest?" His sister rushes out to scold him. "Sorry," she says to me.

"We aren't her entertainment!" Military Chen says.

"Shut up!" his sister shouts at him.

"It's OK, don't yell at him. I'd better go now." I leave at once.

Military Chen's reaction is like mine toward Uncle Yin: pity and condescension are more insulting than a lack of awareness. I wonder why I am in this village, loitering freely, observing these people's lives and listening to their sad stories. What for? To study them as subjects? I'm no researcher. To gather information? I'm not a writer or a journalist. I am here to walk on my memories.

I return to Little Liu's. Roy looks excited. "I love the Communist Party's idea of *xia jiceng,* being among the proletariat masses! I've learned so much in such a short time."

"What have you learned?"

"A schoolteacher took me to a nearby Christian village this afternoon. And guess what?"

"What?"

"Ninety-five percent of the people there are Christians. Their ancestors were converted by Western missionaries a century ago. They say that in other villages there are even some Jews."

"Really?"

"Yes. The teacher's name is Dada. He's had a sad life. He

had a son who was killed in a fire, and his wife went crazy after that. They live in a barn and sleep on a sack on a platform, above the cows. It's really filthy—there's even dried menstrual blood on their bed sack that they've never cleaned off.

"Despite all that, though, Dada's very dedicated and gives himself to his students and his teaching. I noticed that there was something funny about the hair on his forehead, and I asked him what it was. He told me that when he grades papers, he hunches over so close to the candle that he always singes the hair at the front of his scalp. He doesn't even have a kerosene lamp.

"He gives his students free lessons in their homes, buys books for them, and encourages them to study. He even helps them with their tuition, though he has almost nothing for his own family. Giving is difficult enough; giving when you have almost nothing to give is much harder. Don't you agree?"

"Yes."

"I was really moved when his students told me about all those good deeds he does. Dada looks really shabby, but what touches me most is that he isn't self-righteous. He doesn't try to convert or preach to anyone. He simply, quietly practices what he believes. He's never said that he does all those good things because he's a Christian. I really detest religious fundamentalists and the moralizing Christians in my country who constantly try to tell everyone what's right and what's wrong."

"Maybe Dada is a saint. Or maybe he's a doormat. It depends on how you look at it."

"What do you mean?"

"Well." I sigh. "You see, the government has told the

people to be altruistic. Selflessness and self-sacrifice are said to be graceful and noble, and individualism and self-concern immoral."

"It sounds just like religious preaching."

"By telling the people that selflessness is good, they can take advantage of the stupid ones, like Dada."

"You think he's stupid?"

"Remember how Little Liu's father said that he and his friends have always helped the Communist Party? Well, what about *their* lives? Have they changed much?"

"Probably not."

"I think Dada is dumb. He thinks he's doing something holy, but he can't even take care of his wife and give her a decent life."

"Lili, do you believe in unconditional love?"

I don't say anything. I don't know what I believe in anymore, especially after seeing so much suffering.

"I believe in unconditional love," says Roy. "I think some people are divine and willing to suffer for the welfare of others and the salvation of the world."

"Name them."

"Gautama the Buddha, Mahatma Gandhi, Abraham Lincoln, Martin Luther King, Jr. I think Dada is another, though of course he isn't famous."

"This man makes his wife sleep on a bed sack stained with dried menstrual blood, and you think he's holy? You can't be serious!"

"His love for his students is unconditional."

"But his own wife is being sacrificed!" I snap. During the Cultural Revolution, many people loved the Party and Mao unconditionally, yet numberless families were sacrificed for that love.

"But China needs people like Dada!" Roy insists.

"Roy, do you think you know China well?"

Roy looks up at the gray sky and sighs. "No. But I wonder how much the Chinese themselves know about their country."

"You see the poor peasant life and think it's the real China. But the peasants may assume that the real China is the cities they have never visited, the glorious socialist flags, the grand parades and festivities of Tiananmen Square."

"You're right; it all depends on how we see things. But now, Lili, I have something more important to discuss with you than what the real China is."

"What is that?"

"Can we adopt a little baby girl?"

He must be joking. Roy is always proposing something one minute and then the next minute forgetting all about it. But how can he joke about adopting a baby? It's such a serious thing. So I ask him, "Why?"

"I want to give love to a poor child." Roy seems sincere in this sentiment.

"What baby girl?"

"I met an old couple in the village who found a baby in a wheat field. When they found her, the afterbirth from her mother's womb was still on her, but her mother wasn't anywhere to be seen. It must have been very hard for her to leave her baby there without knowing if anyone would find her, if she'd survive. The old couple can't afford to take care of the child and want to give her away. When they saw me they asked me to take her to America."

"Could you do that?"

"I think I should at least try."

"You know it's very difficult to adopt a baby. You're an

unmarried foreigner, but even if you were married, you'd have to be thirty-five years older than the baby."

"Why?"

"Because the government is afraid that a younger foreigner might later take his adopted Chinese girl as a concubine."

"That's ridiculous."

"Nevertheless, it's the rule."

"I won't give up."

"It's easy for you to say that you want to give love, but do you really know what it means to raise a child?"

"Yes. Especially now that I have you, Lili. I could be a wonderful father. Do you want to be her mother?"

"I'm not a mother," I say tersely.

"You'll learn to be one. I'm sure you'll be a good mother. We three can live as a family," Roy insists.

"But we *aren't* a family."

"We could be one!"

"In Beijing? An American journalist, a Chinese female hooligan, and an adopted baby girl from the country? You must be joking."

"Lili, don't say that. I want to have a family with you. I want us to have many children. I'm serious."

With Roy I live only in the present. I have never thought of our future together. My life has been like a drifting cloud, drifting anywhere my fate takes me. I live with the feeling that one day the two of us will say good-bye and return to our own lives. It shocks me to hear him raise the topic of family between us.

"If you want to adopt the baby, it's your decision. You don't have to ask my opinion."

"Why do you say that?"

"I don't know if I want a family."

"Lili!"

"To me, family is about expectations and disappointment, confrontation and betrayal."

"Family is also about mutual respect, encouragement, harmony, and loyalty. Chinese culture values family for many reasons."

"Roy, can we just drop the subject? If you want to be a father to this child, fine. But I'm not going to be her mother."

"Lili, do you want to be with me, then?" Roy looks intensely at me.

I nod without looking at him.

"I mean forever?"

"We should worry about that later and go see the baby first," I say.

"Then promise me we'll talk more about it later, OK?"

"OK."

"Thanks."

When we return to Little Liu's, I see a baby wrapped in a dirty swaddling blanket, sleeping on the family's *kang*.

Roy says, "Look at her, she's so cute! Her ears are so delicate, and look at her feet—they're so tiny!"

She's a beautiful and healthy-looking baby. Why did her mother abandon her? I say to Little Liu, "Roy told me the story about the baby. But I wonder how a woman in your village could get pregnant and carry the pregnacy all the way to term without it ever being noticed."

Roy agrees: "It does seem hard to believe."

Little Liu sighs and says, "Well, the old couple made up the story. The truth is that their daughter gave birth to the girl."

"You mean the baby is the grandchild of that old man and woman?" Roy asks.

"Yes. The old couple told me the story and wanted me to help them. Their daughter had an affair with a salesman who passed through our village, and got pregnant accidentally. Her parents covered it up by dressing her in bulky clothes after her stomach began to grow. Now they want to give the baby away to avoid a scandal."

"So it is possible to get pregnant and have a baby without being noticed in a village like this," Roy says.

"Yes."

"But can a woman abandon her baby or give it away without being punished?"

"The harshness of life is the biggest penalty for this mother and her parents." Little Liu looks down but doesn't stop talking. "Abandoning a baby isn't something that Chinese parents make a big fuss about. Pregnant women often stand in cold water to force a miscarriage. If they fail, they sometimes try to get rid of the baby as soon as it's born."

He continues, "I remember once, about five years ago, I found a baby on my way to school. She'd been left in a small grove. She still had the umbilical cord attached to her belly, but her whole body had turned purple, like a bruise. She must have frozen to death because there wasn't even a blanket around her. My classmate and I buried her in the woods. I will never forget the color of her body."

Roy frowns, and his voice sharpens. "That sounds like something out of a story by Pearl Buck, about Chinese village life almost a century ago. Is the same thing still going on in your New Republic? I want to adopt this baby and take her to America!" he says.

I look at the baby girl. I think of Math's mother and Military Chen's mother, who work like cows, and Iron Beauty and her daughters-in-law, the servants of their men. If Roy adopts this baby, she will have a different life, a real life—the life of a human being, not an animal. She won't have to use a dirty hole to shit in; she can have a decent pee at places like the KFC in Beijing.

"The baby has a mother and grandparents. I wonder if the government will let you adopt her," I remind Roy.

Roy says, "If I follow the Chinese adoption law and pay dollars to the Chinese government, why wouldn't it let me?"

"What will you tell the government?"

"That I saw this abandoned baby in the countryside. That nobody else wants her except me, and that I love her and have enough money to raise her. That I should be allowed to become her father and take her to America."

"I doubt things will be that simple."

Little Liu interrupts us. "You can ask some of the county officials. The county's foreign-affairs office, which deals with foreign visitors, heard about your visit this morning. Mr. Luo-Yi is the first American journalist to visit the county since nineteen forty-nine. They've invited the two of you to attend a banquet this evening. Maybe you can ask them about adopting the baby."

"Oh." Roy frowns and groans. "I hate official events like that."

I glance at the baby and say, "Well, if you're *really* serious about adopting this baby, you'd better go anyway."

Little Liu echoes my views: "In China, to be able to do something, you have to get the support of the government first."

*   *   *

The banquet is held in the village's public cafeteria. Evidently an American journalist's visit is a big deal for this poor area: county officials, village officials, section chiefs, and Party secretaries all show up. They are seated according to rank. Ten huge, round tables hold twenty people apiece—about two hundred people in all attend the banquet. A middle-aged man with a mustache is the head of the county. He welcomes Roy and me and shakes our hands. And then he gives a formal speech, just as Roy has dreaded. He thinks a formal speech is like the cloth used to bind feet: lengthy, odorous, and destructive.

"We are in a mountain area, an old Communist-liberated area, and a minority area," he says. "One word describes us best—*poor.* We used to be so poor that many bachelors couldn't afford to get married, and this is still so. We were so poor that we had only potatoes on our cutting boards and greasy water in our woks, instead of real soup, and too often this is still so. Why are we so dirt-poor? Because our people lack education!

"Poverty itself isn't our worst problem; our most difficult issue is the ignorance and laziness of our people. Due to both the lack of iodine in our water and intermarriage within clans, too many of our comrades are deaf, dumb, or mentally handicapped. Too many people depend on government aid, which makes them feel that they're failures and that the future is hopeless for their families. So they waste their welfare coupons on spirits and tobacco instead of feeding their children and sending them to school.

"Since the introduction of our Party's open-door policy, the central and provincial governments have given us tremendous financial and political aid. We've been working hard to make our villages better places. Today Mr. Luo-Yi comes to visit us from America. It's our great honor. It's a great thing for our county. Confucius says, 'Isn't it wonderful to have a friend coming from a place far away?' " Looking over at Roy, he concludes, "We're honored that you've come so far to visit us."

Everyone applauds. The next formality is a toast. The determination of who is to give the first toast, and who the next one, has been made according to political rank, just as the order of seating has been decided. Roy, unaware of this protocol, raises his wineglass at the wrong time to the wrong person. I nudge him to indicate that he has to follow the right sequence.

The meal itself is great. We are served deer meat, rabbit ears, bird's-nest soup, soft-shell-turtle soup, frogs' legs, snake meat, eel, and many other big-shot delicacies I can't identify.

The officials are impressed by Roy's command of Chinese. That he knows how to use chopsticks also surprises them. They watch him with fascination, as if he were an alien.

One of the dishes that Roy avoids is sautéed dog meat. "I don't eat my companions," he murmurs, refusing to have even a taste of it. "I'm not a barbarian."

I tell him, "Chinese *are* barbarians. We eat almost anything that flies except airplanes, anything with four legs except tables, and anything that swims except ships. Especially people from Guangdong."

No one here could ever have dreamed that dog meat would offend Roy. They no doubt thought that as long as they offered the best of their food, their guests would be pleased. I don't touch the dog meat, either; I don't eat any red meat.

Roy turns to the county headman and says, "You said in

your speech that your county was very poor. If that's the case, why have you spent so much tax money on a banquet for a simple journalist?"

The man is taken aback. He looks embarrassed and clears his throat several times before replying, "A very good question. But we Chinese have always been well known for our hospitality. We respect our guests and try to treat them as honorably as we can, especially guests like you who come from America, a place so far away."

"Yes, I understand that the Chinese treat their honored guests very well. And I know, certainly, that without the help of my Chinese friends, I could never have seen so many fascinating things. But how can you spend so much money on a guest when it could be so much better used to help children who need to go to school?"

"The expense of a single meal won't solve the problems of our generations of poverty, just as China can't become rich in one day," the county official replies. "A colleague of mine went to America with a Chinese delegation last year, and he says that the host offered the delegation nothing more than pickled vegetables and sausage for dinner. It hurt him deeply because it showed that the host didn't take him and his friendship seriously. We'd never do that!"

The headman speaks with finality: "Our tradition is our tradition. Eating is important, and guests should be honored."

Roy nods without further comment. He wraps a piece of hot and sweet red bean bun in a napkin and asks Little Liu to give it to Math later. Others at our table frown at this gesture. "Don't make them lose face," I whisper to him.

"Sorry, but it's too late now. And anyway, I don't really care," he says. I guess he needs to do what he needs to do.

Toward the end of the banquet, when everyone has had a little taste of the corn spirits, Roy raises the question of his adopting the old couple's grandbaby.

The chief administrator of the county is caught off guard by Roy's request. He pauses at first and then hits upon a suitable tactic: delay.

"Well, first we'll have to confer with various higher officials about the possibility. We'll try our best and let you know of the decision later."

"How long will it take?" Roy asks.

"It depends. But since we don't know who the parents of the baby are, and since you're not a Chinese citizen, it'll probably take a little longer than it normally would."

The county's headman points with his chopsticks to the unfinished dishes and says, "Eat, please eat more!"

"I'm full, thank you. Do you think I have a chance of adopting her?" Roy persists.

"I think you do, but you'll have to be patient. Eat, please. Eat more," he says, without looking at Roy.

Roy asks, "OK, what should I do to get this started?"

"I'll consider it after I return to my office, and we'll let you know later." The administrator makes it clear by his tone that he is finished with this subject, so Roy doesn't push it any further.

After dinner the headman tells Roy that he has arranged lodging for us at the best inn in the township.

"Thank you for your kind offer," Roy says, "but Lili and I would rather remain in the village."

The administrator designates a family with whom we can stay.

"No, that's not necessary. We can camp out or stay at Little Liu's. It's not a big deal," Roy says.

"Once again, we're the hosts here, and you're the guests. We want to give you the best treatment," the administrator says. "You see, you're from the United States. You won't feel comfortable with our poor village's living standard. I need to find a place for you to make sure that you will get a good night's sleep."

"Thank you."

The host family that the administrator chooses has only one son, who is about to be married. The family has just finished building a brand-new room for the new couple, and that is where we will spend the night.

The room is made of red bricks, attached to their old clay house. There are red paper silhouettes of the wedding symbol, for "double happiness," pasted on the new glass windows. It is clean inside. A corner fireplace gives warmth and comfort to the entire room. More double-happiness silhouettes are glued on the dresser mirror, on the walls, on the ceiling—everywhere.

There is a Western-style soft bed rather than an old *kang*. On top of the mattress, folded neatly, are two pink silk quilts with Mandarin duck designs. Everything is untouched.

I know how conventional the peasants are, and I know how important the virtue of "brand-new" is to them. The family and the county official are honoring Roy by inviting him to stay in this wedding chamber; they don't know and could never imagine that he and I are not married.

Since the peasants are treating us like honored guests, I feel we should honor the hosting family, the boy and his bride-to-be. I sit on the edge of the bed while Roy studies the pictures on a calendar hanging on one wall. The calendar features young Chinese actresses wearing bikinis; it is a best-seller in Beijing.

The grandmother of the family enters the room and looks at Roy and me curiously. Roy's back is to her. He is still eyeing the Chinese women in their bikinis. The old woman comes over to me and whispers, in a hushed voice, "He's so tall." She points to Roy's back. "I've never seen such a tall man in my life. He's like a mountain."

I laugh.

Roy hears me and turns around. He greets the old woman in superb Chinese, saying, "Hello, Big Mother!"

The old woman blushes and covers her mouth with her hand. "Oh, my—he—the foreigner—he speaks Chinese!"

"Yes, I do," Roy says, nodding confidently.

The grandmother regains her composure. "Sir, I'm here to tell you that everything in this room is new and clean. We aired the quilts and sheets in the sun just yesterday."

"Thank you very much," Roy says gratefully.

The old woman nods politely and backs out of the room, shutting the door gently after her.

Before we go to bed, Roy decides to go over to Little Liu's to see the baby girl one more time. About half an hour later he comes back into the room, angry and frustrated.

"They've taken my baby! I can't believe it!" Roy says, referring to the county officials. "Little Liu says they're going to send her to the orphanage. They didn't even let me know!"

"At least somebody can take care of her there. And you'll still have a chance to adopt her."

"But why didn't they just tell me that in the first place? If I hadn't told them about the baby, would they have taken her away?"

Before I can answer, someone knocks on the door. It's

the grandmother again, bringing a basin of hot water so we can wash our faces and feet.

Peasants use well water, with nine or ten families sharing each well. It can be a forty-minute trip on mountain paths to fetch a bucket of water. In order to save firewood, peasants rarely use hot water even for cooking, let alone for washing themselves. Hot water is a special consideration. I am ashamed, amazed, to see how they are treating us.

Since shower and bath facilities are rare even in the cities, the Chinese have a tradition of washing their feet at night as a substitute for fully bathing. Soaking one's feet in hot water relaxes one's body, like a foot massage. The old woman puts the basin on the floor and squats down to wash Roy's feet, as a maid would do. Roy blushes and quickly says, "No, please don't, Big Mother!"

"You don't like it?" The old woman dries her wet hands on her apron and leaves quietly.

Roy and I lie on the wedding bed but can't fall asleep. Roy is still angry with the county officials, but he finally calms down. He starts to picture the life the baby girl will have in the United States: "I'll send her to a private school where she can learn English, French, and Chinese. She'll take ballet lessons, go to the movies, swim in the pool in my backyard, and ride her bike in the sun with her girlfriends. She'll go to college and get a good education. My goal is for her to be the American ambassador to China."

"You have high expectations, just like my mother."

"We Jewish parents have ambition in common with Chinese parents."

It is going to be Roy's baby, not mine. If he succeeds in adopting the baby, how will he raise her? Giving love to her sounds so romantic. Life can look so easy through his eyes!

Roy whispers in my ear again as he gently caresses my bare breasts. "Listen to night in the countryside: the songs of night birds, the distant barking of dogs, the soothing sounds of the fields."

I am listening. It is beautiful. His touch is beautiful, too.

"Have you heard of the French painter Gauguin?" Roy asks, his lips pressing on my cheek.

"Yes, I've heard of him," I answer lazily, wondering why Roy wants to talk about a European artist now. I thought the purpose of this trip was to get away from the cultural salons and self-proclaimed artists of Beijing.

"I think I finally understand his breaking away from his solid, middle-class world, why he abandoned Paris and moved to a small Pacific island for the rest of his life."

"Why?"

"So he could live among uncomplicated, innocent people and enjoy the simplicity, serenity, originality, and spontaneity of life. It's a Taoist state of mind, a transcendent form of being." Roy is helplessly romantic, just like his touch.

I don't reply. But I'm learning to like his romanticism. He can see and feel the world in ways I can't. He's able to enjoy a beauty that I can't discover and ignore an ugliness that I can't escape.

"Lili, what are you thinking?" Roy asks, kissing my hair.

I bury myself in his chest. His soft lips and warm body tease me. I have an impulse to shut him up and climb on top of him. Yes, the "originality and spontaneity" of life, show them to me, show them to me. Show me, Roy. But suddenly I remember where we are and cool myself down.

Roy still wants me, though.

"No, I can't do it tonight." I push him away gently.

"Why?"

"It's someone else's wedding chamber, not ours."

"So?"

"You know that purity is important to Chinese brides."

"Yes. Other cultures value it also."

"I think we should honor the bride."

"OK, I agree with you. We should honor the bride."

"What do you think of the notion of purity?" I don't know what makes me ask him this question. Maybe it's being in the country.

"I don't like puritanical stuff. It's all about possession. I don't like possessiveness. I don't think one can ever possess another person totally, own the other person's past. I like the idea of sharing. If I can share things with the person I love, that's enough for me."

"Share the present, you mean?"

"Share the present and the *future,* too. We can't change the past, but we can change the future. Don't you agree?"

"I guess you're right."

"What do *you* think of purity and virginity?"

"I think that impure women often have bad luck."

"What do you mean?"

"Remember my grandma? When her first husband discovered that she wasn't a virgin, he distanced himself from her and went to brothels instead."

"Are Chinese men still like that?"

"Not just the men—Chinese women look down on impure women, too."

I don't say anything more before I finally close my eyes.

The next morning, when I wake up, I can't remember why I'm in a strange room in a remote village. Through the window I see Roy jogging in a field that will be covered with wheat in the summer. Wearing a new pair of jogging shoes, he looks athletic, fresh, and American. The peasants never run around their fields in the morning just to exercise.

The grandmother knocks on the door and says, "Your breakfast is ready." I thank her.

Seeing that Roy isn't around, she speaks to me confidentially: "Hey, your man wears shorts in winter. I've never seen a man wearing shorts in the wintertime! He isn't like our Chinese, is he? You know what I mean?" After that she laughs. I laugh, too. I laugh without any comment.

The grandmother tells me that a jeep and driver have been sent for us by the county government. The driver is waiting in the living room. After Roy comes back, Little Liu comes to see us off, still in his wrinkled, bright yellow suit; his brown face wears a humble expression. Without his help we never would have been able to see so much in such a short time. I feel we are in his debt. I realize I am becoming fond of Little Liu. He could be much more in a city than he is in this poor village.

Children stand at the door of our host's home, looking at us. Math and his unnamed little sister are there, along with Military Chen's sister, and Naonao, and others as well. Each is wearing a small American flag on his or her chest, a souvenir from Roy. They all stand there like toy soldiers, trying not to move, looking at one another, then at Roy and me, all the while suppressing giggles.

Roy and I are taken to the county government's office, where we ask about the process of adopting the baby girl. The chief administrator's secretary gives Roy some forms to fill out and tells us to wait.

"You'll hear from us soon," he says.

*   *   *

Four weeks after we return to Beijing, on a chilly late-winter day, we receive a brief note under the letterhead of the legal department of the county government.

Dear Mr. Luo-Yi and Mrs. Luo-Yi:

We are sorry to inform you that we cannot process your application because the family of the infant has decided to raise her themselves.

Serve the People!

On the same freezing day, in the late afternoon, Little Liu arrives in Beijing and calls from the railway station. "I borrowed money to travel here," he says. "I have something important to tell you." He speaks with a strong twang, as if he were coming down with a cold. Roy goes to pick him up while I prepare a meal at home.

An hour later Little Liu and Roy return just as I'm placing the steaming dishes on the table. Standing in the living room, the two men look numb and strange. They stare at me blankly. They both have red noses and red eyes.

Little Liu greets me with a slight bow.

I bow back to him and say, "Hey, brother, I bet you're cold and hungry. What are you waiting for?"

"I don't want to eat," he says.

"What's wrong?" I turn to Roy.

Roy sits down on the sofa. He looks into my eyes for a second or two. I can't tell what he's thinking. "Lili, I thought I could help. But I *killed* them, that baby and her mother."

Little Liu adds, "They died just yesterday."

I feel dizzy, as if thousands of stars were spinning before my eyes. I have to sit down on the floor. I look at those steaming dishes I've made and smell the aroma of Chinese wine and soy sauce. But I don't feel hungry anymore. I mutter to Little Liu, "You've got to be joking."

"I shouldn't have told you to talk to those officials. It's all my fault!" Little Liu says, casting his eyes downward.

"But you aren't the only one—I told Roy to go, too," I say, sinking back to lie on the floor.

"Look what I've done!" Roy says, his voice trembling. He covers his face with his hands.

Little Liu tells me the entire story.

"When Roy asked to adopt the baby, the county officials got very upset. For them it is a big loss of face that some villager is trying to sell a baby to a foreign visitor. To prevent it from ever happening again, they first found the baby and put her in an orphanage temporarily. Then they sent people to investigate the whole thing. They learned that it was the old couple who had tried to sell the child to cover up their daughter's disgrace. They held a self-criticism meeting at the township to educate the family. Many government officials attended. The family was fined for both abandoning the baby and trying to sell it, illegally, to a foreign national. Finally the government decided to give the baby girl back to the family rather than keeping her in the orphanage.

"Our villagers discovered that the young daughter of the old couple was an unmarried mother. People badmouthed the daughter behind her back. The young woman couldn't stand the humiliation, so yesterday she hanged herself in her backyard. Before committing suicide, she used a pillow to kill her own baby."

The little girl with the delicate ears and feet. The little girl whom Roy wanted to take back to the United States, who he dreamed would one day become the American ambassador to China. She's dead. Her mother, too. Impure women too often have bad luck.

They were both victims of saving face, but the baby's journey in this world was so short that she didn't even have time to open her eyes and learn what a face was.

Roy removes his hands from his face and sobs, "Sometimes I want to offer help, but I only make things worse. I often make the system work against me. Why is China treating me this way?"

Little Liu replies emphatically, his eyes burning with flames of resentment, "Back home, those oldtimers say it's good they're dead. They say that the infant and her mother deserved to die, that only death could redeem the sin of the mother. 'A good death is better than a bad life.' They all repeat a lot of peasant sayings like that, even my own father. I can't stand it anymore. I've finally decided to leave home like my oldest brother did. I won't ever go back to that stupid place."

Roy says to Little Liu, "I went to the country because I thought I wouldn't understand China unless I knew how eight hundred million Chinese lived. But now I'm even more confused. How can China be so promising and so hopeless at the same time?"

"A man can rape and fool around and still get away with it, whereas a woman has to pay with her own life for a single mistake! China *is* hopeless," I say emotionally. Suddenly I'm angry.

"Lili," Roy says, "remember when I gave out money to those beggars in Jianguomenwai? You said I was acting like a savior but I couldn't save China. You were so right. I *can't* save China. I can't even save one Chinese baby girl. I'm too naive; my idealism is nothing more than stupidity."

That Chinese picture of a green rice field and a little boy playing a flute while riding on the back of a water buffalo—it's all simply an illusion. I can't look at Roy. I know he is devastated. When death reveals the truth, it is too often brutal, inhuman.

"Your intentions were good. You have a good heart! It's the ignorance of peasants that is to blame here!" Little Liu tries to comfort him.

None of us can sleep. Roy prays for the baby girl and her mother all night long. I burn some incense and stare dumbly at the ashes.

The next day we buy a tombstone and have the names of the mother and the baby inscribed on it. We hold a funeral for the baby girl in a grove near our apartment. I bury a little sweater and booties I've knitted for her. Roy reads a Jewish prayer. Little Liu places a cup of corn spirits and two bowls of rice in front of the tombstone.

"If they can't eat well on earth, may they have a full meal under the earth," he cries, and then he bows before the tombstone. Roy and I bow as well at the small grave.

The deaths of the baby girl and her mother make me want to scream. I want to let out my anger. I need to talk to someone who can help me understand what I'm feeling. I visit Amei, bringing a kilo of roasted chestnuts with me.

Amei is talking on the phone with her brother, Gang, when I arrive, so I wait for her in the living room. After she hangs up, she joins me, complaining, "Lili, Gang's in trouble again. He was dating a high school girl and got her pregnant. Now the girl's family is furious and plans to sue him for raping a minor. He's scared and doesn't dare tell my folks. He wants me to ask Jun's mother for help, but I told him no way. This should teach the brat a lesson!"

"What about the girl?"

"She had an abortion. He paid money to the family, but her parents said it wasn't enough."

"Will he have to go to jail?"

"He should have been sent there a long time ago! But enough about him. Tell me what's happened to you. You look so tense."

I tell Amei the story about the baby and her mother. As I talk, I find myself unable to control my anger over both Roy's naïveté and the loss of two innocent lives.

"Roy said he wanted to give love to a baby, but what the fuck did he give to that baby? When we were in the country, he gave out things and money as if he were a savior! He's nothing but a savior! He believes things have changed in rural China. But they haven't. I don't understand how he can speak Chinese but still be so fucking naive about China."

"He *is* naive. He doesn't know how the system works here. But most Chinese don't know, either. Lili, did you want to adopt the baby?"

"No, I didn't want to. I'm not a mother."

"Did you argue with him?"

"No."

"Why?"

"He's a foreigner; he has money, freedom, and everything else. He's a winner. What's the point of arguing with him? If he could have taken the baby to the United States, it would have been good for her. How can I explain to him the way I grew up and how difficult it is to bring up a child here?"

"You can't. He wouldn't understand."

"He talked to me about having a family in China and all that bullshit. But how could the three of us have been a family in China? If raising a kid were so easy, why would I have had two abortions already?"

"Life is hard enough without children. That's why I don't want a baby right now, either. But I like my marriage." Amei passes me a cup of green tea and sits cross-legged on the sofa. "Lili, don't you want your own family, a family with a good man like Roy?"

"My own family? What's the point? You have a family with Jun, and everybody envies you. But what *is* your family life? You have to live separately. And look at your parents, my parents, everyone else's—are they emotional, are they intimate? They're more like comrades than spouses. I don't know why they got married in the first place."

"My parents got married because the Party told them to. Their generation married for political reasons or to please their families; they didn't marry for love," Amei replies, cracking a roasted chestnut.

"Like many other women," she continues, "I want security in my life. I want to have a family with a man I love and trust. Even though Jun is far away, I feel safe. A family is a form of protection."

"You think a family can protect you?"

"Yes, I do."

"Amei, you know what?" I look at her round baby face—a lucky face, according to Chinese superstition.

"What?"

"Your parents are Party members. Your in-laws are high-ranking officials. Jun has an important position. Of course your two families can protect you. But my parents aren't Party members, and they have no power. They can't protect *themselves*, let alone their daughter. I don't expect family members to protect me. I once had the protection of a gang leader, but that didn't stop me from getting hurt."

"Lili, I agree with you that I'm more sheltered by my family than you are. But I also had another reason for getting married," Amei says, going to the kitchen to make me some more tea. I look at her from the side. Her figure is buxom and sexy.

"What is that?"

"Very simple: others my age were getting married, so I thought I should do the same. I didn't have the courage to stand alone like you."

"You're protecting your reputation."

"Yes, in a way. People say all kinds of nasty things about you if you don't get married by a certain age."

I laugh bitterly. I don't know what to say. I think of the baby girl's mother, who killed herself, and of my grandma and the worn shoes. Why are we doomed?

After I leave Amei's, I sit down on a bench in a nearby park. Crows fly between naked trees. Retired people practice dancing ballroom dance on a platform to noisy music.

Little Liu stays with Roy and me throughout the winter; I help him find a part-time job at Yuan's travel agency. The season is chilly and gray. The three of us live in the shadow of death. Every evening Roy teaches Little Liu and me English. We don't go out much. We are in hiding.

THIRTEEN

Spring comes late, and when it comes, so does the wind. Girls take off their baggy, quilted coats and begin to wear miniskirts and sandals, exposing their skinny legs. The city government mobilizes citizens to plant and care for trees. Budding flowers and green leaves decorate the otherwise dirty and crowded streets. Roy and I decide to get out from under the shadow of the baby girl.

I continue to play my erhu in the Great Wall Hotel every other night. Roy wants to write down the story of what happened with the baby. I try to help him remember things about the countryside, but my memories are muffled like a *mahua,* the twisted bread in a chef's hand. So much has happened, but at the same time it all seems unreal. It's like a whiff of a fading fragrance, something that you can never grab or see again but that still stimulates your senses. This makes me feel inadequate. I keep asking myself, "Aren't many things just pure imagination, or fantasy, or dreams?"

At night, I stand by the window and look out at the streetlights. I wear the same perfume and the same white silk pajamas, but the darkness of the unknown makes me wonder.

When I take the bus to work, I begin to notice mobs of people in the streets. I start feeling some sort of connection with them, even though they're all strangers to me. I wonder what they're searching for.

I think often of Grandma's word *wu chang,* "impermanence." There is nothing in this world that we can hold on to for too long. Am I following Grandma's path, leading a life without a family?

One day I wake up early from a nightmare. In the dream I had lost my teeth and there was a white-haired sage who pointed at the sky and kept telling me, "It's about time."

Losing teeth is supposed to symbolize losing relatives. I haven't seen my parents for a while. Are they doing well? Are they still mad at me? Without taking a shower or eating anything, I rush out, hail a cab, and give the driver my parents' address. I have no clue what I will do or say.

It's a gray, overcast day. I cover my head with a burgundy scarf, hating the fact that I am trying to disguise myself. The cabdriver is playing Bizet's *L'Arlesienne* on his radio. He brags that he is a big fan of classical music and has hundreds of CDs at home. He goes on to put down those who listen only to Taiwanese and Hong Kong pop songs, saying, "You see, unlike me, most Chinese people have no taste. They're still in their 'primary stage of socialism.' They don't even know who Bizet is."

I smile politely at him and then close my eyes, losing myself in this music that I have heard my parents play so often. The musical notes, polyphonic, precise, and elegant, symbolize everything that my parents admire. An image of Mama's long, skinny fingers gracefully touching the piano keyboard floats through my mind. Those same fingers also mixed manure with hay to make fertilizer in that hideous old Monkey Village.

Through Bizet's music, my days of endless practice on the violin under Mama's rigid supervision come back to me.

When we arrive at the gate of the conservatory compound, the adagietto movement has not yet ended. I want to walk to my parents' home, so I have the cabdriver let me out at the gate. With the music still in my ears, I hand the driver a fifty-yuan bill. It is a crisp, new one—a pleasure to hand out such money. Just this morning Roy casually gave me one hundred of these bills. Did he feel the same pleasure giving them to me as I feel turning over this money so freely now?

The morning breeze blows as, I walk slowly toward the residential area where my parents live. I pass familiar faces. Grandpa Liu is helping a young girl repair her bike. Grandma Wang is practicing fragrance t'ai chi under an old eclipse tree with a group of white-haired old women. She is telling stories as she moves her body, her facial expression still as dramatic as ever. She looks triumphant—she must have discovered some secret about one of her neighbors. Uncle Chang is walking home with a basket of eggs from the morning market. The eggs are probably for his paralyzed wife. He is humming a tune from the Beijing Opera and looks very happy; maybe he has bargained well for those eggs. A man I don't recognize is reading a newspaper in front of the billboard, his hands folded behind his back.

Then I see the familiar back of an old man. It's Papa, walking his bike, which has a bag of rice on its rear rack. He is supporting the bag with one hand and using the other to balance and steer the bicycle. His back is hunched over. He looks like he's having a hard time and seems very lonely. He has to stop and rest from time to time.

Papa, I call him in my heart. I think of going to him and helping him carry the rice. I think of saying something to him, but then I back away. My existence can be nothing but shameful to him, just as the baby girl's was to her mother.

As I struggle with myself, a young boy says, "Grandpa Lin, let me help you carry the rice upstairs." My father nods gratefully and thanks the boy, again and again. I wordlessly watch them enter the door of our old concrete building and disappear into the dark. I can't follow. I can't enter. I stand there unable to move, just looking at the door. I feel that Papa is a stranger to me, that I have never known him.

I remember when I was little, I fantasized that Papa wasn't my biological father. People often say that I don't resemble him. He is small and has round eyes like a cat's and a dark complexion like a fisherman's, whereas I am tall and have almond-shaped eyes and a light complexion. At home Mama always liked to complain about how slow, timid, and clumsy Papa was. She issued all the commands and demands. Papa did the chores quietly. Sometimes Mama would grumble to him, "If I'd come from a better family, I never would have married a blockhead like you."

Once, when I was about five, Papa came to pick me up

somewhere, and the other kids asked me if he was a servant. I said yes. And Mama did treat Papa that way. I also told my little friends that my real father was a tall, handsome, mighty naval officer who'd been assigned to duty overseas. I said the same thing to my classmates in elementary school.

For a while I actually believed my own fabrication. I searched for my parents' marriage certificate, trying to discover their secrets. But I found none.

I never told my parents about the story I made up. But I've always felt somehow alienated from Papa, even though he never pressured me, never pushed me hard. He never yelled at me, was in fact afraid of upsetting me. I just didn't know—still don't know—how to be close to him. He was so quiet that I often forgot he existed. The softness of his voice and the humility of his bearing only made me angry. Maybe my childhood was always colored by Mama's demands, her expectations.

When I was a girl, if I was upset or unhappy, I wouldn't tell Mama or Papa. Instead I would have secret talks with the imaginary naval officer at night. In my mind he was strong, manly, and fatherly. He was my real father, my real hero, my real protector.

Quietly I turn. Grandpa Lin—that was what the boy called my father. He is getting old. An old man now. An old music instructor, I think as I walk to the food stand at the corner of the front gate.

I buy myself a sizzling pancake at the food stand.

"Li-li? I-Is th-that y-you?" The pancake man looks at me with a wondering frown and stutters in a heavy Henan accent. I recognize him—Big Mountain, the Henan peasant. I used to buy a pancake from him every morning. He stutters, and the children in the compound like to make fun of him.

"H-Haven't se-se-seen you f-for ages. Wh-What brings you here? I, I th-thought you, you went to A-America. W-We all did."

"Oh, I left Beijing for a while, but I didn't go abroad," I explain as I taste the pancake. It's hot and spicy.

"I s-see." He nods and wipes his runny nose on one of his coat sleeves. "Is it t-t-true that you h-have a f-f-foreign b-boyfriend?" he asks me curiously as he makes another pancake.

"Yes." I nod and have a big bite of the pancake.

"Oh, you are s-s-s-so lu-lucky! A-All I wish to ha-have is a Beijing g-g-girlfriend. But I c-can't get a-any so far. N-N-not even one f-from He-Henan."

I smile and ask, "How are you?"

"M-Me, you know, l-l-life is not ea-easy n-n-now. Things are getting more ex-expensive and the g-g-government is more c-c-corrupt. I-I ha-have to br-bribe the, the lo-local police and, and, and ta-aax collectors to ke-ke-keep this s-small b-b-business running."

"Did you get a chance to go home and see your folks?"

He sighs. "Some-Sometimes, I, I really wan-want to g-g-go home. I'm a, a r-re-sp-onsible son. Th-There is a say-say-ing, 'If, if p-p-parents are a-a-live, sons and and d-daugh-ters should n-not g-go far-far way.' A-And, w-what's the p-point in b-be-being here in Bei-Beijing, being l-looked down upon and working s-sixteen hours a day?"

He frowns and looks sad. "But, but, my-my f-family and re-re-latives all, all de-depend on the money I, I s-send them e-every month. They s-sell crops to the g-government, but the g-government doesn't g-give them m-money. It g-gives them 'white-white notes,' IOUs."

After my stay in Up Village, I know how hard peasant life can be. Big Mountain isn't joking. I feel sorry for him. But I feel even sorrier for myself. He makes a living with his sweat and hard work. I am just a kept woman, a parasite.

I finish eating the pancake and say good-bye to Big Mountain. I leave the conservatory compound.

I'm feeling bored, so I stop at a teahouse and have a cup of tea. Some performers are doing skits on the stage to entertain the patrons. They're making fun of country hicks. The jokes are getting old, and seeing peasants ridiculed doesn't make me laugh, so I leave quickly.

When I get home, Yuan is waiting for me in the hallway. He looks excited, his glittering eyes sparkling with flames. Even in these boring times, he always has exciting stories to tell. Only Yuan.

No sooner have I greeted him than he bursts out, "Have you heard? Hu Yaobang is dead!" His tone always verges on the melodramatic.

"Oh, really? I haven't heard anything about it." This is big news.

I turn on the radio and quickly check to see if there are any messages on Roy's answering machine. The light is flashing. Roy has left one message: "Lili, do you know that Hu Yaobang died of a heart attack in the hospital? They say he was arguing with . . . when . . ."

Yuan interrupts the message, expressing his grief and shaking his head sadly. "Yaobang is gone. He was only seventy-three; what a premature death for a leader! The wrong person died."

On the radio we hear a very solemn male voice being broadcast from the Central People's Radio Station, which announces the deaths of high-ranking officials.

"Hu Yaobang, a true Communist fighter and great proletarian revolutionary, a great Marxist whose life will forever be glorious for his contributions to economic reform and . . ."

Hu Yaobang, the little man who loved to wear Western suits and use Western knives and forks. Who once said that Lenin and Marx combined couldn't solve China's problems.

He had been removed from office as Party chairman by the same person who once promoted him to that office. Hu Yaobang, supposedly the number-two guy in the whole nation, was suddenly disgraced. We never found out why. But we're all used to the whims of Chinese politicians by now.

Yuan switches off the radio and turns back to me. "So, Lili, what do you think is going to happen now?"

"Wreaths, mourning, eulogies—and then probably no one will care anymore." I shrug it off. I don't know what else can happen.

"Lili, you lack political consciousness. Let me tell you, I foresee a revolution ahead." Yuan speaks with passion and determination.

"That's absolutely right. You do need a change! A big one!" Roy's voice penetrates through the door from outside. He unlocks it and comes in carrying an armful of documents.

Roy gives me a quick kiss on the cheek and goes straight over to Yuan. "I heard you from all the way down the hallway. We need to talk."

Yuan laughs enthusiastically. "You bet! But today I didn't come just to talk; I want to take you and Lili to see something."

"What?" Roy asks, curious.

"Just come with me."

In Roy's jeep we drive through endless zigzag alleys and finally stop in the Eastern City District, in front of a large concrete building. The front door of the ugly Russian-style building is closed, but there are Red Flags parked all along the streets around it. These domestic-built cars are the sedans of high officials. Their chauffeurs are waiting at the sidewalk, smoking and gossiping together.

We sit in the jeep for a while, watching. A number of men, women, and couples come out a side door carrying armloads of shopping bags; they immediately get into their cars and leave.

"This is where the high officials shop. They can buy prawns for the price of cabbage, imported whiskey for the price of soda . . . they can get the best of everything from all over the world. Everything is subsidized," Yuan tells us slowly, with obvious anger and cynicism.

"Officials use their power and their access to import and export licenses to get loans for themselves and their kids and foreign currency at special exchange rates. They can get food and goods almost for free, at cheap prices fixed by the state. The state companies that they set up and hire their children to run make huge profits for their families. They call themselves civil servants, but they aren't civil, and they don't provide service. Instead they just use their positions to suck the blood out of the people."

As Yuan vents his fury about the government, we see more sons, daughters, and other relatives of high-ranking officials leave the unmarked building with bags filled to the brim.

I don't say anything. Politics bore me. But I have been to this building before.

When I went out with Jun, Amei's husband, I often accompanied him here. He would buy imported perfume and other gifts for me with his father's government coupons. My dates with Jun usually started with shopping here, and then the chauffeur would drive us to the Wen Jin Club for dinner and an evening of dancing and cards. Then Jun would take me to a nice hotel room, also provided by the government, where we would watch banned videotapes like *Last Tango in Paris, Lolita, The Scarlet Letter,* and *Lady Chatterly's Lover,* which were internally circulated among the government's elite; Jun rented them in this same bland, concrete building.

I didn't even have to wash my own clothes in those days. Jun's family had the services of a housekeeper and a maid, who did laundry for the whole family, including my dresses and underwear.

FOURTEEN

Several days after the death of Hu Yaobang, Roy calls me from work and tells me excitedly, "A group of students are demonstrating in Tiananmen Square. They've presented a seven-point demand to the government, calling for the rehabilitation of Hu Yaobang, freedom for the independent press, more money for education, and higher salaries for intellectuals."

Roy says he is going over there and asks me to meet him.

On my way to the bus station, I breathe in the crisp morning air. It's a beautiful spring day. White fuzz from the newly budding willow trees that line the streets drifts through the air and floats on the surface of lakes and ponds. The fuzz tickles my face gently, like the touch of a sensual lover, awakening my senses and erotic thoughts.

I board a crowded bus. In Beijing people tend to avoid eye contact. From time to time fights break out just because someone thinks someone else is staring at him strangely. But today the passengers, young and old, men and women, all look intense and curious. They are looking into one another's eyes as though they were listening to one another's mind. Strangers are whispering to one another. There is a sense of excitement, a sense of not knowing what may happen next.

As the bus approaches the downtown area, we can see student demonstrators wearing black armbands and white headbands. They are singing the national anthem, chanting, and waving banners inscribed with slogans like "Long Live Yaobang and Long Live Democracy." The groups of demonstrators come from different schools and have different styles about them. I notice one group of students dressed in the outfits of Beijing's punks. They are all wearing black sunglasses, mimicking the Mafia of Hong Kong. They do not line up. They walk toward the square singing rock songs, not the national anthem. They're students from the Central Drama Academy and the Central Art Academy. I recognize some of them from parties Roy and I have attended. Traffic police at intersections stand dumbstruck, trapped and helpless on their podiums.

Almost all the passengers on the bus get off at Tiananmen Square. I see an ocean of wreaths, banners, and people surrounding the Monument to the People's Heroes, in the middle of the square. The space is huge and crowded. I stand head to head and shoulder to shoulder with student demonstrators and onlookers. There is no way I'll be able to find Roy.

I squeeze into the crowd by the giant monument, where

students are mourning Hu. Here the atmosphere is not sad but rather joyful: students cheer and applaud as a large oil portrait of Hu is placed on the inscribed granite wall of the monument. The portrait is by student artists from the Central Academy of Arts. It is framed in black.

In it Hu Yaobang looks like a bony skeleton, but sad, humble, even pitiful. The humbleness of his face somehow resembles that of my father's. Almost all old Chinese intellectuals wear such an expression on their faces, it seems; I guess it is kind of difficult for them to look cheerful after being treated like shit for so many years. I remember Yuan's once saying to Roy that decades of endless political struggle had destroyed the old Chinese intellectuals' self-assurance and self-confidence.

"Openly Reevaluate Comrade Yaobang's Successes and Mistakes!"

"Those Who Should Have Died Live. Those Who Should Have Lived Are Dead."

"Long Live Democracy! Long Live Freedom! Down with Bureaucracy!"

"A Great Loss for Democracy and Freedom!"

"The Star of Hope Has Fallen!"

"Democracy Now!"

"Guarantee Freedom of Association and Freedom of Speech!"

Most of the slogans praise Hu Yaobang, and some express anger and dissatisfaction toward the government. Mourning for Hu is an excuse for citizens to vent their frustrations against the corrupt leaders who are still in power.

As I copy down the slogans and short poems, a student standing on the monument catches my attention. He gives an extemporaneous speech:

"Comrade Hu Yaobang has passed away. It's a big loss for our country and our intellectuals. He loved and protected us, but he was purged because of this. He wasn't a corrupt official. He had no overseas bank accounts. His children did not climb to high positions because he was the head of the Communist Party. Now his death has awakened us. We should not be silent anymore! We should stand up and run our own country. We want *minzhu*, 'democracy.' What is *minzhu*? *Min* means 'the people.' *Zhu* means 'master.' The people are the master of the country, not the leaders!"

Some give him a round of applause, but others are having their own discussions. I overhear two students talking about something called the "nobility of failure." They speak loudly, seeming not to care whether others are listening.

One of the two, a stout young man with black-framed glasses, asks his friend, "Sea Cloud, why do we Chinese always feel so much sympathy for ill-treated tragic heroes like Xiang Yu, Qu Yuan, Peng Dehuai, and now Hu Yaobang?"

Sea Cloud, the taller of the two, thinks for a short while and then replies, "That's a really good question. I haven't given it any serious thought before. I think maybe it's just because we love the nobility of failure. The good guys don't win sometimes."

"Yes, you're right. The nobility of failure. The whole thing is too familiar. A loyal official, suddenly mistrusted by his superiors, dies much younger than he should have. At the same time, his rivals will live well into their nineties. So he becomes a tragic hero for the ordinary people. They feel sorrow for him and are angry with those who hold the power. It's just a new version of a typical plot for the Beijing Opera."

"You're right. Hu Yaobang is a tragic hero. Nowadays if you follow principles, and have moral values, the best thing you can be is a tragic hero, a noble failure."

"I couldn't agree with you more! Winners know how to break the rules. It's more honorable to fail with dignity."

"But Hu wasn't perfect, either. We should remember that."

"Now that he's dead, though, we should look at his good side."

After they leave, I look around. I see my distorted shadow cast on others' bodies. They are discussing, debating, shouting slogans, venting anger, telling their own stories, or merely observing and then writing down what they see, just like me. Maybe because there are so many of us, everyone seems to have a feeling of safety. They can all let off steam without worrying about getting caught. In the crowd I used to hate, I now have the odd feeling that I am connected with everyone—we share a common spirit. I wander around, letting the warm fingers of the spring breeze run over my body as I savor the flavor of this spring movement and gathering of people.

By the time I get home to the Forbidden Nest, it's late in the evening. Roy has left a note saying that he may stay in his office all night, writing a news story about the demonstrations. I don't eat anything, and I can't fall asleep.

When Yuan told me of Hu's death, all I felt was indifference. People die when they get old—so what? Why is there such intense response to his death? Why am I not as excited as Yuan and all the students? It bothers me that I don't care while others are so passionate. Do I have no feelings at all, or am I just too cynical? What fuels the students' anger?

There are dozens of messages on the answering machine,

229

left by friends eager to exchange gossip and information. I don't reply to any of them. Instead I call Roy's office. I have to do it, even though I don't know what to tell him.

But Roy doesn't answer the phone; it's his coworker Jim on the other end.

"This is Lili," I say.

"Hi, Lili. Do you want to talk to Roy?" Jim greets me like an old friend.

"Uh . . ." I pause. Through the phone I can hear somebody humming songs in the background. It's Roy.

"No," I respond, clearing my throat. "Just tell Roy, uh, I'm thinking of him." I hang up immediately, before Jim can say anything else. I'm surprised by my own craziness, saying something silly like I'm thinking of somebody, but crazy things happen in crazy times.

That night, when Roy is writing his article in his office, I miss him terribly. I'm dying to talk with him.

After that I begin going to Tiananmen Square every day. I like to go simply because I enjoy being with others, seeing colorful banners and wild clothing. People come to make friends, listen to rumors, and share drinks, cigarettes, and the latest news. Some come to the square to feel powerful by breaking the rules, others to feel important by delivering speeches to an eager audience.

Every day there are demonstrations and parades through the streets of Beijing. Some of the marchers obviously have no idea why they're marching; they're just joining in the excitement. Rumors spread from one side of the square to the other in an instant. A sit-in takes place on the steps of the Great Hall of the People. Some students have tried to break in through the New China Gate at the Middle South

Sea Compound, the White House of China. Somebody has written a letter in his own blood. Intellectual leaders are calling for the regime to renounce communism and adopt a multiparty system. A couple decides to get married in the square. Two students kneel on the stairs of the Great Hall of the People to demand a dialogue with the government leaders who have shut themselves up inside. Student leaders press the resignation of high-ranking officials and a boycott of classes at all Beijing universities. Nobody can tell what is going to happen next. Anything can happen at any time.

I don't participate in the activities; I am simply curious. I don't have the political consciousness of Yuan or the college students, nor do I have Roy's journalistic interest. I am just one of the millions of unsure Beijing citizens.

One day, listening to a speech by a Taiwanese pop star near the People's Hall, I meet a funny, big-mouthed street peddler. The peddler stands beside me, bandages covering his left eye, as the rock star talks about the importance of freedom of the press: "The reason corruption is so rampant is that the media do not perform their surveillance function well. Why don't they perform well? Because the media are controlled by the state, by those who abuse their power."

The pop singer says the media should be privatized. I wonder what I will use to get to sleep if there is no more *People's Daily*.

As the rock singer ends his speech, shouting the slogan "Let our cries awaken the young republic," the peddler sticks two fingers into his mouth and whistles loudly.

"Isn't he something!" he exclaims.

The audience disperses after the speech, and lots of girls chase after the pop star to get his autograph. The peddler looks around. His gaze stops at me. Quickly he walks toward me, pats my shoulder, and greets me as if we had known each other for ages. "Hey, girl, come here. I've got something important to tell you," he says, gesturing for me to follow him to a quieter corner.

When we get there, he turns and says, "You won't believe it." He starts in the middle, which confuses me.

"What are you talking about?" I ask him impatiently.

"You see, I'm a good man. I do a little business here and there to make ends meet. I don't rob, steal, or lie. And I'm not a Party member, either. So people have no right to hate me. Don't you agree?"

"Yeah. Whatever."

"But I, Fang the Third, was beaten by the police in broad daylight for no reason at all. Can you believe this happened to me, right here in our new People's Republic? Right here in this square yesterday," he says, his voice rising. His tone attracts the attention of some people who are passing by.

"Yeah, yeah, yeah—that's right, everyone! I, Fang the Third, who have lived on Sesame Alley for twenty years, was nearly beaten to death by the cops for not a single damn reason. Yesterday, right in front of the New China Gate." He raises his voice high, mimicking the rock star's mannerisms.

"Students were rallying and trying to get in the New China Gate. I was minding my own business, selling my tea eggs and Popsicles nearby, watching all the action. Suddenly two men came over, knocked me down, and smashed my cart. I yelled, 'Help! Help!' But they just sneered at me and told me nobody would help. 'Police!' I yelled. They told me they were undercover cops. 'You're the people's police, why are you beating me?' I cried. They said I'd broken Beijing's laws and even threatened to throw me in jail. They took me to an alley and beat the shit out of me. That's how I got this gash over my eye. Look at it, you see it? I'll be a toad's grandson if I'm lying."

"What happened to those students at the gate?" an onlooker asks.

"There were too many of them, and the police didn't dare attack them. Since they couldn't do anything to the kids, they picked on me. Nowadays it's us poor helpless guys they beat up. What can I say? I didn't do anything against our socialism."

"Did you regret being in the wrong place at the wrong time?" someone teases him.

"No, not at all." He shakes his head, like a baby's rattle, and boasts, "I'm a witness. I saw everything. The newspapers aren't going to make me believe their shit. After some of the kids found me all beaten up, they flagged down a taxi and took me to the hospital. They were all strangers, the ones who took care of me. Two girls even gave me a bunch of flowers. I feel like a hero. You know what I mean, a *hero,* like Huang Jiguang or Qiu Shaoyun. I'm a part of something that's a hell of a lot bigger than me."

By now a small crowd has gathered to listen to his story. People applaud, and the peddler nods, grinning from ear to ear while waving his hands in the air to make his audience settle down. Someone shouts, "Tell us another one of your police-brutality stories." But that's Fang's only one, so everyone leaves. They go off to find other stories. He is only a temporary star.

"Part of something that's a lot bigger than me": his words echo in my mind for the rest of the day. He may not have understood the cause or the content of the movement, exactly, but he was excited and touched by something greater than himself. What is it like to be part of something greater than oneself? I wonder.

What *is* it like?

What *is* it like?

I ask myself this on my way home, as I see the crowds filter into the square from different places, with different banners, slogans, and motivations. I ask myself again in the kitchen, when I'm slicing onions for dinner. I ask myself when I'm chewing the ends of my nails, waiting for Roy to come home. I ask myself as I take a shower, letting the water run. I ask myself as I apply lotion to my face, looking at myself in the mirror.

Roy comes home with newspapers, pamphlets, notes, and his constant self-assurance, high energy, and glittering eyes. He hasn't shaved for quite some time and has begun to remind me of the portrait of Karl Marx that hangs in Tiananmen Square.

"Lili! Dinner smells great! I'm starving." He kisses me and starts to eat at the table like a starving dog.

Nibbling on a small bun, I watch him from the other end of the table. In his eyes I see enthusiasm. Eager seeker, I think, where in the world does your passion come from? Will you tell me what "something a hell of a lot bigger than myself" means?

"Lili, I'm so happy for your nation. She's coming alive!"

"Why do you say that?"

"Because people are awakening; they're going into the streets to fight for their rights. That's what democracy is all about."

"What in the world does democracy mean, really?" I have never thought about democracy before, don't understand anything about it. These days, many people speak about it, yet no one ever explains what it really means. Whenever students are asked what they want, they invoke this word as if it were a magical spell. But for me it's like Picasso's paintings: everyone says it's great, but somehow I just can't figure it out.

"What do you think?" Roy looks at me, wanting me to share his excitement.

"For me it's just a word that intellectuals toss around. It makes me think of students, professors, the May Fourth Movement, and America. I don't have any idea what it really means."

Roy puts his chopsticks down and looks at me seriously. He says, "It's not a foreign word, nor a word only for intellectuals. It's about *you*."

"Me?"

"Yes. It's about you, your liberty, your inalienable human rights, and your freedom. Democracy means that you, as a citizen and as an individual, have the right to make decisions about how you're governed; the right to be informed, respected, listened to, and left alone; and the right to express yourself freely and to pursue happiness without persecution. Lili, of course it's all about you."

"So do you think the students have taken to the streets for themselves—for their own liberty, rights, and freedoms?"

"Yes, but they're seeking something much greater than just themselves."

What *is* it? What *is* it? What *is* this something greater than oneself?

Roy's face flushes with passion, just as it does each time we make love.

"What's making you so excited?" I can't help asking him.

"I'm excited because I am a witness to history. I'm excited because the democratic instinct of the Chinese has finally awakened. I'm excited because I'm living in such a momentous time. How can you possibly remain untouched by this, Lili? You can't, can you? Otherwise you wouldn't have been to the square every single day. Am I right?"

Yes, I do have to be in the square every single day. It's magical and I am spellbound. I don't understand democracy or human rights. It feels like a rock concert, where sharing the excitement with others is more important than listening to the performer's lyrics. Everybody is both an observer and a participant. They all come to express themselves, let out their feelings. Is this the *something greater*?

On April 26, 1989, the national newspaper the *People's Daily*, known as the mouthpiece of the Communist Party, publishes an editorial attacking the students. It is headlined "Take a Clear-cut Stand Against the Instigation of Turmoil." This is the first official statement of the government's position. Other newspapers and broadcasters quickly parrot the official line.

Student demonstrators start to criticize the journalists, calling them liars, propagandists, and puppets of the government. But then on the seventieth anniversary of the May Fourth Movement, Chinese journalists from all over Beijing hold a big demonstration of their own to support the students. They carry banners stating, "Newspapers Should Speak the Truth" and "We Don't Want to Lie, Please Don't Force Us To." They go on strike and join the thousands of student demonstrators in the square, chanting and singing revolutionary songs.

People line the streets, cheering and clapping for the

journalists. Only days ago, the journalists were the bad guys, government suckers and parrots. Now they're heroes. Street vendors give them free drinks, Popsicles, and steamed buns. Cab drivers honk horns to show their support. Buses waive the fare for people like me who just want to go to Tiananmen and look around. To my surprise, the police make no effort to stop the protestors; instead they make V-for-victory gestures with their fingers, wordlessly indicating that they're behind them.

The highlight of May 4 is a speech given in the square by one of the student leaders.

The young speaker, a handsome northerner with curly hair, escorted by a group of student bodyguards, begins, "Fellow students, fellow countrymen." He is using a loud-speaker, his voice husky yet hypnotic. The crowds in the square fall silent.

"Seventy years ago, right here in front of the Gate of Heavenly Peace, a large group of students assembled to protest the terms of the Treaty of Versailles, in which the Chinese government agreed to cede the eastern province of Shandong, formerly under German control, to Japan. China was being divided, and the corrupt officials didn't care. Students and young intellectuals felt they must place their lives on the line to awaken the people. They wanted to save the country through democracy and modern science, and to discard oppressive traditions. They came to Tiananmen to protest. Starting that day, a new chapter in the history of China began.

"Today we're once again assembled here, not only to commemorate that monumental day but, more important, to carry on the May Fourth spirit of democracy.

"For more than one hundred years, China's intellectuals

have been searching for a way to modernize our ancient, troubled nation. Waving the banners of science and democracy, they launched the mighty May Fourth Movement. What they meant by science was to adopt new technology from the West to modernize our economy. What they meant by democracy was to end the two thousand years of feudal dictatorship so that the people could govern themselves.

"May Fourth was the first step in the patriotic democracy movement of Chinese students. Due to the social and economic conditions in China, the May Fourth goal of science and democracy has still not been achieved.

"Seventy years of history have taught us that democracy and science cannot be established in one fell swoop. Hard work is needed generation after generation. The previous generations have built a foundation for us, and now it's time for us to do more than we have done.

"While New China has steadily advanced toward its economic modernization, it has greatly neglected building a democracy. Due to the imbalance between its political system and its economic development, our society is plagued by all kinds of social problems, including inflation, nepotism, bloated government bureaucracy, pervasive corruption, and disrespect for intellectual pursuits. People are suffering. They are dissatisfied with and angry at the status quo.

"To carry on the May Fourth spirit, we must hasten the reform of the political system, protect human rights, and strengthen rule by law. These are the most urgent tasks of continuing modernization.

"Fellow students, fellow countrymen, the future and the fate of our nation are intimately linked to each of our hearts. This student movement has but one goal, to facilitate the process of modernization—by raising high the banner of democracy and science, by liberating people from the constraints of feudal ideology, and by promoting freedom, human rights, and rule by law. We are demonstrating, we are protesting, we are fighting, not only for us but for our children. We want our children to be proud of us for what we are doing here today. In one word, we all want a better China! A better China for all!

"Let our cries waken our young republic!"

This eloquent young student leader is a good and powerful talker. His fervor inflames the audience. There is a thunderstorm of applause. Many people have tears in their eyes. Strangers hug me, their tears dampening my cheeks and their hot breath tickling me. It is impossible for me to remain unmoved. I hug them back and feel a sense of camaraderie.

"Democracy now! Democracy now! Democracy now!" the audience chants. I chant with them. I don't know what democracy is, but it's a mantra. The physical vibration of the word can create positive energy.

I wish to ask the student speaker about the meaning of democracy and other things such as feudal dictatorship and modernization, but I can't: he's been swept up by the crowd, is being carried on the shoulders of others. He waves his hands like a movie star. People are screaming "I love you" at him. I know that with so many admirers around, the speaker will have no time to answer my questions. Slowly I walk away, leaving behind the surge of the cry "I love you."

After May 4, with its big demonstration and demand for democracy, the square becomes quieter. The government doesn't take an authoritative stand on this demonstration in which both journalists and students are now involved. The officials don't act or respond. In Tiananmen, citizens come and go. Sometimes they get bored because not much is going on. Students are always surrounding the Monument to the People's Heroes but not necessarily the same groups of students. No one knows what to do or what to expect. Many just hang around and wait.

Buses begin to run on schedule again for the first time since the death of Hu Yaobang. Roy comes home earlier than before. He tells me that some of his colleagues are beginning to think that the student demonstration has run its course. When an event like this drags on for too long, both journalists and their editors back home tend to lose interest.

I'm not a journalist, and I don't care about the news. I still go to the square every day. It has become part of my life. Sometimes I go on my bike so I can offer a ride to some of the protestors. They sit on the rear rack just like I used to do on my father's bicycle when I was a kid. I take them wherever they want to go. I snap photos for couples strolling arm in arm when they ask me to. I tell newcomers where the public restrooms are. I am needed. I am not extraneous.

FIFTEEN

On May 13, having gotten little response from the government, student leaders call a hunger strike. They have two demands. First, the government must promptly meet with the Beijing Students' Dialogue Delegation and recognize as legitimate its call for political reform; a substantive discussion must be held based on the principle of equality. Second, the government must acknowledge the movement as a patriotic initiative, not the "turmoil" defined by the *People's Daily* editorial of April 26.

When I first hear about the hunger strike, I can't take it seriously. It simply sounds too exotic in a culture where people routinely greet each other by asking "Have you eaten yet?"

"How does it work?" I ask Roy.

Roy starts to explain the history of hunger strikes, how Mahatma Gandhi used them as an effective means of protest. He tries to impress upon me the idea that "to fight without fighting is the razor's edge of nonviolence." I'm totally confused.

Maybe because I was born in the year of the Great Famine, I can't imagine how one can achieve anything on an empty stomach. In my mind I see only the convoys of trucks that carry cabbages to Beijing and other northern cities. Citizens store heaps of the cabbages in hallways, on balconies, even in their living rooms. Beijing people save frozen wilted cabbage for winter, just as squirrels save nuts.

I say to Roy, "You see, we Chinese have just begun to have enough to eat after years of buying meat and eggs with ration coupons. And now you're talking about a hunger strike. It's a joke. The Chinese aren't like Muslims, who have a fasting tradition. I don't think the hunger strike will work here."

He shakes his head and disagrees. "Lili, you don't understand politics. Food is something everybody needs, and fasting requires that it be given up. A hunger strike is a means of getting attention, sympathy, and solidarity from others. The student leaders want to pressure the government by winning support from the people."

This still seems foreign to me. "Chinese don't have this 'nonviolent' tradition you speak of. We're taught about class struggle, revolution, and dictatorship of the proletarians. We don't know how to do *nonviolent* things."

"It's true that Mao said, 'Regimes come from the barrel of guns,' and that almost every dynasty in China was established and ended violently. But remember, this is a new era. China is welcoming Western cultures and commodities and ideas, too. Ten years ago, could you have imagined the Chinese loving Kentucky Fried Chicken so much?"

"No."

"So how can you be so sure that the Chinese don't know how to do nonviolent things, if you couldn't foresee the popularity of KFC here? In the West, nonviolent movements are powerful and effective. They can be in China, too."

"What if people die?"

"Risking death is a more heroic and beautiful gesture than actually dying. That is to say, declaring to others that you're willing to sacrifice your own comfort or even your life for your beliefs, showing your determination—that's what the hunger strike is all about," says Roy.

Roy sounds naive.

"Even if some of the students are willing to sacrifice themselves and stop eating, I don't think a nonviolent movement can win in China. During the Great Famine thousands of people, perhaps even more, starved to death. So what? Did the government give a shit?" I ask.

"Lili, I think you're being too pessimistic. We're talking about different regimes. The new regime is much more rational. Although China still has all kinds of problems, it's at least moving in the right direction. You can't compare the past to the present."

Am I being too pessimistic, or is he being too *optimistic*?

"Remember, history repeats itself," I tell him.

"I think the government will go to the square to meet the students if they stop eating and protest in a nonviolent fashion."

"The whole nonviolent thing sounds too elite; I just can't understand it. All I know is that there are millions of poor people in China. All they want is to have enough to eat. If they don't get that, they become violent!"

"But India was poor during Mahatma Gandhi's time, and his nonviolence worked."

"I don't know about other countries. But I know China. Roy, you're optimistic about this country because everyone here is nice to you, a rich foreigner. But you don't know how Chinese people treat one another. When we were in the countryside, you were moved by the peasants' hospitality. You thought they were wonderful people. But didn't you see how the men beat their wives?"

"I still think, despite the violence of the past, China is becoming more civilized and modern. Don't you? Maybe nonviolent demonstration will actually work this time!"

"We'll see," I say, tired of arguing with him. Donkeys' lips just don't match horses' jaws.

Early on Sunday morning, I grab a cold sandwich and bike to the west gate of Beijing University, where the student leaders have their headquarters. This isn't like me, I think—detached Lili who doesn't give a shit about anything.

By the time I get there, hundreds of students have already gathered, wearing white headbands that say the words "Hunger Striker" and "Democracy Warrior."

It's crowded, yet everybody is orderly. Each university has its own group and flag. Two rows of student marshals, wearing red armbands, grasp hands and form a circle around the hunger strikers to protect them.

I park my bicycle and squeeze myself into the hunger-strike crowd. I stand beside a male student wearing a sandwich board that reads, "I Love Life, I Need Food, but I'd

Rather Die than Live Without Democracy." He smiles at me. I smile back.

"You have a beautiful smile," the student says, friendly.

"Thank you," I say, and I look around to see if anyone has spotted me. The student marshals don't seem to notice me among the hunger strikers, an insider now, probably the only spectator inside the ring.

"What's your name?" the young man asks me.

"Lili. And you?"

"Call me Jackson."

"Is that a Chinese name?"

"No, it's an English name."

"Why do you give yourself an English name?"

"My Chinese name doesn't sound good. Michael Jackson is my idol, so I named myself Jackson. All my friends in college call me that."

"Are you ready for the hunger strike, Jackson?"

"I haven't tried before. But why not?"

"It can hurt your body."

"I know."

"You're young."

"Thank you for your concern, but to tell you the truth, I have some backup."

"What do you mean?"

Jackson, seeing that nobody is paying any attention to us, shows me some candies that he's stashed in his pocket. "If I can't hold out, I can always eat these when no one's watching." He speaks in a confidential tone.

"Aren't you going to die for democracy, as you claim?"

"Do *you* want to die?" he asks me in reply.

"But then why did you write on your sign that you'd

rather die than live without democracy?" I ask him, lowering my voice so that only he can hear.

"Girl, it's only a gesture. The government isn't honest with us. Why do we have to be honest with it and risk our lives? We aren't stupid like our fathers, are we? We want to embarrass the government, not die trying."

"I see."

Jackson looks at me and says, "You're really cute—which is why I've told you all this, but please don't repeat it. We still want to win the sympathy of the citizens. Do you hear me?"

"I hear you."

As we're murmuring to each other, a short, plain-looking girl passes by me, and the students applaud and show their admiration for her. Jackson tells me that she is the number-one student leader and has two master's degrees. "The hunger strike was her idea. She has many followers, though some students don't like her because they think she's selfish and manipulative." He adds, "But me, I like her. She's a good speaker, really powerful."

The girl clambers up onto a flatbed tricycle of the sort normally used to transport cabbages and watermelons. The tricycle, her instant stage, is parked on top of some rocks. Balancing herself carefully, she uses a bullhorn to speak so the crowd of students, numbering in the hundreds, can hear.

"In this sunny, brilliant month of May, you are going to go on a hunger strike. Yes, on such a sunny and brilliant day." She has a childlike voice.

"During this most precious moment of youth, you have chosen to put the beauty of life behind you. . . . You love life, and you do not want to die. You're so young and in the prime of your life. There're so many things out there that you would like to explore. You'd like to enjoy your campus life. You'd like to taste the feeling of love. You'd like to be able to see the rest of the world. If you die, you will be leaving behind the country you love, the people you love, and the world you love. Such a wonderful and animated world!"

Then she faces a second group, made up of parents and teachers, standing a little way from the strikers. They are seeing off their kids. The girl addresses them emotionally.

"Listen: we don't want to die. None of us. But, fathers and mothers, when we're leaving, don't be sad, please. Uncles and aunts, when we're enduring hunger, please don't be heartbroken. Brothers and sisters, when we say farewell to life, please don't cry. We have chosen this way because it's the way we can save China, save you, and save ourselves. Remember, remember our wish. We have only one wish, *and that is to allow all of you to lead better lives.* So be happy for us, be happy for our choice, and be happy for the future of China.

"We love this country, this old, backward, and wounded motherland. We love her so deeply, to the point that it hurts. Yes, our love for our motherland hurts us. Love hurts, and we are ready to die for our love. But please don't get us wrong. We are not seeking death. We seek to save lives. We seek a better way of life.

"We all know that sacred word *democracy.* We're calling for democracy in China. We're crying for democracy in China. We're dying for democracy in China.

"But we know, and you also know, democracy isn't the

affair of a few, and it can't be achieved by one generation. And this time, it's our turn. History demands that we fulfill our destiny.

"Farewell, mothers and fathers, take care! Please forgive us, your children who cannot be loyal to their country and their families at the same time! Farewell, people! Please allow us to use this means, however reluctant we are, to demonstrate our loyalty."

The crowd begins to chant with the girl: "Farewell, colleagues, take care! We cannot bear to leave you, yet dictatorship must come to an end. Farewell, our love, take care! I cannot bear to leave you, yet freedom and democracy must begin."

The vows are so loud that I can feel them echoing in the air around the buildings, the trees, and the crowd. I hear Jackson chanting rhythmically beside me. The chant is so solemn, so earnest, that I feel deeply touched. Something that I have tried hard to hide and let go of is rising in me. Watching these parents tearfully see off their kids, I think of my mother and father.

The chant makes me not me anymore. As the students march ahead, I march with them. I am bound to them. They sing the Internationale, their voices resonating with heaviness and tragedy. Even though I have never liked the song, I sing with them. I look up at the sky, the sun and the clouds, and I look ahead at the road, the people, the banners. Whether the hunger strike is real or not, whether it wins or loses—neither of these seems that important anymore. At this moment I am engaged in something larger, and every sense in my body is stirred. How much I wish I could tell Roy, "I've found it, I've found it—the magic of something-greater-than-oneself." Never before have I felt so free, so alive.

As the hunger strikers march along, fellow protesters, supporters, onlookers, and reporters pour into the streets of Beijing to follow the marchers and join them. Factory workers stand on the flatbeds of pickup trucks waving banners, and motorcycles crawl alongside.

Ordinary Beijing citizens who live in the neighborhood put out large pots of tea for the hunger strikers and their supporters; they offer us cups of water, ice cream sticks, and cold drinks and don't ask for money in return. Children scurry back and forth delivering refills of hot water, shouting at the top of their lungs, "Older brothers and sisters, we love you!"

By midday the vast square is scorching hot. Some students, already starving and dehydrated, start to faint. Drenched in sweat, I run around helping them get water, fans, and medicine. More and more students need help. I am so occupied with the work that I forget that I myself haven't eaten anything, either. But I'm not tired. I have become a stranger to myself.

The fading sunlight paints everything gold. The majority of the hunger strikers have settled in for the night. Some students are still singing the national anthem or the Internationale; some are playing cards; some are too weary after their long march to do anything but sleep; and others get sick and are taken to the hospital.

Standing on the stairs of the Monument to the People's Heroes, I stretch and gulp down the leftover cold sandwich I have brought with me. I look around and see immense banners that remind me of celebrations like the National

Day parade. Among the sea of flags, I spot some kites: kids are flying them as if it were a holiday. In the background is a huge black flag raised between two flagpoles, showing the massive Chinese characters for "hunger strike."

I gaze at the Gate of Heavenly Peace. My eyes linger on the gigantic portrait of old Mao, hung at the very center of the dark red gate. Mao is watching the whole scene. I turn away and look toward the south end of the square and Mao's mausoleum, where embalmed remains of the chairman's body are enshrined in a crystal sarcophagus. Mao is physically here in the square; no one can avoid his existence.

Everyone in the city seems to be moving into Tiananmen Square—but in an eerie fashion. They're all appearing like extras on a movie set. The sounds of police and ambulance sirens, blaring loudspeakers, slogans being shouted, and cars honking all suddenly fade away. Movement has slowed down. Everything has become noiseless.

The air turns chilly. Citizens bring umbrellas, quilts, extra clothing, and tents to the hunger strikers.

I roam around greeting the strikers. I don't know if I should stay or go home.

Three female students come up to me, and one says, "Hey, are you looking for a place to sleep?"

"Yes," I say, nodding.

"Do you want to join us?"

I accept their kind offer.

The tent we share is very small for four people, but we're living in the lap of luxury compared to the male students outside, sleeping unsheltered on the concrete slabs.

The girls have two thermos jugs of water and a radio-cassette recorder whose batteries are almost dead. They don't use it to get updates from the Voice of America or the BBC; they use it to listen to love songs by my cousin Johnny. The Chinese-make recorder is a cheap one, with poor audio quality, and the music sounds awful. The girls play Johnny's songs nonstop: "Love Me," "I Cannot Live Without You," "You're My Only Girl," "I Love a Woman Who Doesn't Love Me," "Wanting You Tonight," and on and on. I have no clue why these young college girls are so into Johnny Cardiac's tacky and sloppy songs, in almost every one of which the word *love* is repeated at least ten times. But the girls look so happy as they hum along with Johnny.

White Jade bets that Johnny is going to come to the square and sing for the students. The other two, Little Lotus and Silver Moon, think he's too sweet to be political. But they all hope to be able to see their idol face-to-face. "If he comes, the fast will really have been worth it!" comments Little Lotus, who wears a pair of Coke-bottle glasses.

I am a little surprised. Her statement is so girlish, so unpolitical, so unheroic.

"Hey, you, Lili, do you like Johnny Cardiac?" Silver Moon asks me enthusiastically.

I don't tell them he's my cousin. I just answer plainly, "No, I guess I'm too old for pop stars."

Silver Moon seems disappointed by my indifference. She resumes singing along with the tape. The other two are sharing Johnny gossip.

The girls talk and smoke on and on. Smoking distracts them from their hunger pains. They talk about boyfriends, generation gaps, young mistresses kept by rich old men, hometowns, dorm stories, pop singers, perfume, and ways of cheating on tests. None of their conversation is about the movement, except when they argue about which student leader is cutest. They giggle a lot. They are happy.

I think of the student leader's solemn proclamation at Beijing University that the strikers were prepared to die for democracy. How to reconcile that with these girls' high spirits and lightheadness?

Noticing that I am just listening quietly to their chatter, they start to ask me questions.

"Do you know what the perfume Chanel Number Five smells like? None of us has smelled it before, but we've all heard it's very seductive."

"Do you have a boyfriend?"

"Can you tell me what it feels like to be kissed by a man?"

"You've been on the cover of the magazine *Women's Friends,* haven't you?"

"Are your Reeboks real or counterfeit?"

White Jade names an actress she thinks I resemble. "By the way, she's my favorite. The fire-and-ice type, you know." She winks.

Silver Moon adds, "Lili, don't you want to be a fashion model? It's cool to wear beautiful clothes and walk around showing off your body and making money at the same time."

They seem so carefree and so obsessed with beauty— they're even more superficial than I am. But they are also college students fasting for some kind of ideal that I don't understand.

Being the child of two professors, I grew up in a college compound, but I never attended college myself. I have always thought it didn't matter to me. I had no interest in university students; in my eyes they were spoiled brats, the darlings of society, the chosen ones, living on campuses with high walls, dining in subsidized school cafeterias. But now, listening to these young girls complain about how bored they are by their lecturers, and how run-down their school facilities are, I feel jealous for the first time in my life. I am jealous of their joyfulness, their youth, their innocence, even their plain looks. College students are the pioneers of the movement, heroic and loved by everyone. Historically, students are the backbone of almost every major social movement in modern China. Now they are on hunger strike, in the limelight. Citizens like me are on the fringes: we merely watch, listen, applaud for them, support them, and admire them.

"What do you do in school?" Finally I initiate a question.

"Ha, ha!" Silver Moon laughs. "Love and be loved, I guess," she says lightly.

The other two girls laugh and nod. "She's quite right."

"College is a place to fall in love?"

"Exactly," the three girls chorus unanimously.

My parents met each other in college. I wonder if they fell in love there. My mother used to be her school's *xiaohua,* its most beautiful female student. But none of her classmates except my father, then a timid bookworm, dared to marry a girl like her, who had overseas relatives and a strange mother who smoked pipes and had been married three times. But my father did. He did it in the knowledge that he would have to pay for the marriage with his professional and political future. Shy though he was, he had the guts to do it; it must have been for love. The shy man did a bold thing, maybe the only time in his life. And it almost destroyed him. He couldn't get a good job after he graduated and was labeled a "running-dog lackey for American imperialism" during the Cultural Revolution. He was beaten and sent to work in the countryside. Papa must have done all of it out of love.

My parents don't much like to talk about their past with me, and I've never pressed them. But tonight, as I lie with these three strange college students, I want to know whether my parents really loved each other, or if they just had a passion that faded over time.

Daylight breaks over Tiananmen Square and the hundreds of thousands of students who slept in it last night. Some have set up tents for scant protection against the cold; others lie curled up in sleeping bags or wrapped in blankets. Banners hang limp in the early morning mist. There are piles of garbage frosted with morning dew.

As I'm about to head for the public restroom at the eastern end of the square, I notice a man with his back to me, about ten meters away, looking around and seeming lost. He looks like Roy. I approach him; he turns toward me.

"Lili," Roy calls, charging toward me with a big smile on his face. We hug as if I had come back from a war. I let myself melt into the embrace of his big hands and strong arms, the way the girls who are fasting would want me to.

"Lili, I've been thinking of you all night. I finished my story at four and came here looking for you. The square is so big, but I just followed my instincts. I had a feeling you were somewhere near here. And here you are!"

"Is it ESP, or what?" I laugh.

"Maybe. But you know what? I can smell you. I followed your sweet aroma," Roy says affectionately.

Just then we catch the reeking odor of the public toilet fifty meters away.

"Don't use those toilets. They're overflowing and they stink like hell," Roy says, and he takes me to the nearby Beijing Hotel, where his temporary office is, to use the bathroom and have breakfast.

The hotel is packed with foreign journalists. Roy tells me that they initially flocked into Beijing for Gorbachev's visit but now want to report only on the student demonstrations.

"The story is getting more exciting now." He chuckles. "You see, Tiananmen Square is the official welcoming site for Gorbachev and the other world leaders. If the students are still in the square when he arrives, the government will have to move its military bands, honor guard, and red carpets someplace else. The Chinese officials will lose face. The students see this as a golden opportunity to embarrass the government."

I ask Roy, "You told me you were involved in some anti-war movement in the States when you were in college. Is this movement anything like that one?"

"The passion and the hunger for freedom are very similar."

"What did you feel then?"

"We felt like we could change the government and change the world."

SIXTEEN

It is the third day of the hunger strike. Gorbachev doesn't come to the square; the communist officials welcome him at the airport. I watch the news on TV in a nearby store with a mob of people. Everybody laughs at the government's embarrassment.

I am still staying with the three girls. They have become weaker and weaker, far less talkative. Their lips have turned pale and colorless, their hair is tangled and unkempt, and their bodies reek. Two of them have fainted twice but still refuse to leave. Their radio-cassette player went silent long ago.

Student loudspeakers around the square urge everyone to stand fast: "History demands that we stay!" The girls have little to say in response and just gawk listlessly at the Gate of Heavenly Peace.

Whenever I eat at one of the nearby small restaurants, I think of their cracked lips and weary eyes. It's hard for me to swallow my food.

Government leaders have visited some of the students in the hospital and suggested that they and their fellows return to school and their studies. They say if the students want to talk, they'd be willing to choose some representatives and talk with them. But the student leaders resist leaving the square, saying that to leave would be to betray everything they stand for. "The government first has to acknowledge that we are patriotic and then has to talk with student leaders chosen by us, not by itself," the loudspeaker announces.

Ambulances come every two minutes. I work as a volunteer with medical teams sent by the hospitals, helping to carry away hunger strikers who have collapsed, distribute medicine, and spray antiviral aerosols. The movement has transformed me into a nurse.

On the day of Gorbachev's visit, twelve students refuse to drink water in Tiananmen. They claim to be using the strength of death to fight for life. I recognize one of the water strikers as a student of my mother's from the Music Conservatory. I remember him because he was once almost kicked out of school for stealing library books. But now he is full of determination, sitting cross-legged on the concrete surface of the square, a hero ready to die.

Hearing his name on the news, the boy's devastated father has rushed to the square and to his side. I watch as the dying son stretches his hand to touch his father's weather-beaten face, and then see the silver-haired father collapse on the dirty concrete, wailing shamelessly in public.

Word that some students are close to taking their last breaths brings greater popular support. On May 17 masses of Beijing residents converge from all directions on the Avenue of Eternal Peace, near Tiananmen. The five-kilometer-long road has changed into a ceaseless tidal surge of bodies amid an ocean of banners.

Celebrities come. I see their familiar faces and hear people calling their names. Intellectuals come; some marchers from China's elite intellectual circle wear their names on sashes across their chests for easy identification. They are writers, philosophers, professors, and reformers.

Government employees come. Staff members from the foreign ministry carry banners that say things like "With Corrupt Internal Affairs, How Can We Talk About Foreign Affairs?" Police march with banners reading, "We Are the People's Police! Standing to Protect the People!"

A group of workers from a city nearby have bicycled more than 150 kilometers to join the protest. Peasants from the interior provinces come by train. Military officers and cancer patients in the terminal stages of their illness come. They are here to support the students, but also get support from others.

A peasant nicknamed Iron Egg, from Xianyang in Shaanxi Province, has carried a basket of Shaanxi apples to the square. He tells everyone he meets, "I'm sixty-seven this year. It's a shame that these students must fast; I have come out to tell them we'll have a harvest this year, and there's plenty of food for them to eat." He doesn't have a clue as to what is going on, but he cares about the students.

I spot two members of my old gang, Chou-Chou and

East Wind, riding a tricycle packed with Coke. When Chou-Chou sees me, he says, "Hi, Lili, do you want some Coke? It's free!"

I ask for one can, but they give me a dozen: "Hand them out," they instruct. Before they pedal away again, East Wind tells me, "Hey, do you know that Sweet Grass is reading news for the Autonomous Workers' Union? She works for a textile factory, and her boyfriend is a big shot in the union. She always wanted to be some kind of anchor-woman!"

"What about the others?"

"I bet everyone is somewhere here. Except Spring Ocean." Chou-Chou pauses and looks at me when he mentions the name. "He's still in jail, but he should be out next week!"

"Oh, yes?" I nod, showing no reaction. Spring Ocean has been in jail for ten years now, or maybe more.

"We're going to pick him up next week," East Wind confirms, glancing at me briefly.

"Uh." I nod again.

"Take care. 'Bye now!" They wave their hands and pedal away.

As I sip the Coke they gave me, I see Buddhist monks marching in a line, carrying banners expressing concern for the students. "We Should Love and Support One Another," one banner says.

And then I see, among a group of nuns in saffron robes, my grandma. She is carrying a banner printed with the Buddhist slogan "Put Down the Butcher's Knife; Become Buddha Now." I can't believe my eyes. But it's her—the calm facial expression, the gangly figure! Is this the same person who once expressed no interest in this "sinful world"? The one who told her daughter and granddaughter to go back and "work on their salvation" when they visited her? What kind of power is it that has compelled Grandma finally to get involved? The same unknown force, I suppose, that draws me to the square day after day.

I greet her. She puts her palms together in front of her chest and says *"Omitufu"*—another Buddhist mantra. Her voice is resounding, even musical. I can't tell if she is talking to me or to herself.

"Omitufu!" I repeat, bowing to her slightly. But she has already disappeared into the crowd, leaving me wondering.

Not only do I see my grandma in the square, I also see my cousin Johnny Cardiac. He wears an outfit consisting of a potato sack, a pair of sunglasses, and a white headband marked with the words *Love* and *Freedom*—a hippie wanna-be. He performs for free before the large crowd, though I can't be sure whether it's really in support of the movement. His presence draws a huge crowd of young people to the south side of the square. Before Johnny starts singing, he gives a little speech.

"I was born in the U.S., so I'm an American. But I'm also Chinese, because my father is Chinese. It makes me feel proud to stand here together with my Chinese comrades. I feel so lucky that I'm able to witness and participate in the largest democracy movement probably in all of history. I wish for a better and more democratic China for all of us."

His words provoke a long, delirious roar and applause. Patriotism appeals to everyone! Johnny knows exactly how to follow a trend.

"Cardiac! Cardiac!" people chant his name.

Johnny sings two patriotic songs. The crowd knows

them both by heart. Young people stretch their arms upward, waving them back and forth as they sing with Johnny, "There is a dragon in the ancient East/His name is China/ There is a group of people in the ancient East/They are all the offspring of the dragon."

The faces of the hunger strikers, by now weak from starvation, light up as Johnny sings, their eyes glow. Johnny's songs animate them.

As Johnny sings, his eyes are closed, tears pouring down his cheeks. Maybe the student movement has changed him, or maybe he's just a good faker. But as a pop star, he has a power that most intellectuals lack. I have seen poets, scholars, and professors give speeches in the square, but Johnny unites and mobilizes people—educated and not, young and old—like no one else.

There are many, many Beijing citizens who, like me, come across relatives, friends, and neighbors in Tiananmen Square on May 17. The next day's issue of the *People's Daily* reports that the students' fast has inspired the city's inhabitants to turn out in such force that the demonstration may well be counted the largest for democracy in all of history.

For two days, millions of people come to the square to protest. On the third day Roy, Yuan, and I meet at the Beijing Hotel. I haven't talked with Yuan since the movement began—he's been too busy giving speeches, drafting petitions to the central government, and organizing protests— but I've seen him several times on TV. He has organized a workers' union to back up the students, and written a hundred-thousand-word letter to the Communist Party, demanding political reform. Yuan is the first poet to sign a petition to release political prisoners. This movement has helped make him a household name. Now he is sitting across the table from me, excited and raggedy, as usual.

Our conversation starts with Roy's joking about my doubts that a hunger strike could ever actually happen in China.

"But you see, now it's led to such a grand and spectacular mass movement that *everybody* is involved. It's not like the movements Mao launched, such as the Great Leap Forward or the Cultural Revolution. In those movements people were forced to participate. This movement is completely spontaneous, completely voluntary," Roy says.

Yuan agrees and adds, "The students' hunger strike— our hunger for democracy—has awakened the conscience of the ordinary citizens. When people shout in the square, 'Save the Children!' 'Save Our Country!' those cries are from the bottom of their hearts. You see, Roy and Lili, the Taoist philosophy is that softness that will finally defeat hardness, nonviolence will ultimately overcome force. The whole point of the hunger strike is that it says to your oppressor, 'Even if I cannot hurt *you,* I can hurt myself, and in so doing perhaps win the support of others. And then you will feel great pain and anguish, which is what I want to accomplish.'"

Yuan turns to Roy. "Self-sacrifice is the ideal that we Chinese learn from our revolutionary history. To give you just two examples of our famous patriarchs: Huang Jiguang blocked the muzzle of an American cannon in the Korean War; Qiu Shaoyun made not a single sound after he was burned by a bomb in an ambush attack. We Chinese tend to pay tremendous respect to those of our martyrs who placed the collective interest over their own well-being.

Even younger generations like these hunger strikers are greatly influenced by these values. Their fasting has thus become a symbolic way for them to follow the revolutionary martyrs in their history books."

Roy says, "You're right. Their depth of feeling is almost a religious fervor—only their religion is democracy."

"Yes. But remember, religious passion can be almost impossible to control. I fear that the end of the movement may be as tragic as the endings of many religious martyrs," Yuan says.

"You mean bloodshed?" Roy and I ask at the same time.

"Yes." Yuan nods. "Jesus, in the Christian Bible, sacrifices himself to save all of humanity, shedding his blood on the cross. I'm afraid that some students want the government to change so much that they may even use death as a tool to force that change. They seem willing to sacrifice themselves to this end and may even invite the government to butcher them in order to further their cause of democracy. I wish I could stop the train of these events, but I can't. The movement is escalating so intensely that its own inertia will probably carry it to an inevitable conclusion." Yuan lowers his head.

But Roy disagrees: "The hunger strike may embarrass the government, but it won't shame itself before the whole world by turning guns against defenseless students just because they aren't satisfied with the status quo. I don't think the government leaders are that irrational. It just won't happen."

Yuan responds, "It's hard for any political regime to stay cool in a situation of such growing intensity. The demonstrators are being nonviolent in their protest, but their chants and the slogans on their banners are violent. The students' occupation of the square makes the government look weak. Its embarrassment could easily turn into cruelty."

"It's better to look weak than to look cruel," Roy argues.

Yuan sighs. "I'm afraid you still really don't understand China and our Communist leadership. Showing weakness is more shameful than causing the death of others, because weak leaders can't stay in power for long. Hu Yaobang is a good example."

Roy shrugs his shoulders. He doesn't like Yuan's comments, but he hides his displeasure. He tries to drag me into the argument. "Lili, what do you think?"

My involvement in the movement has been involuntary. At first I simply liked the colorful banners in the square, the atmosphere like a morning bazaar. I liked the fact that the students were thumbing their noses at the people in power. Now I feel I'm needed there. I still don't understand democracy and don't really know what the students want, politically speaking. I am on the outside looking in. I don't even know what *I* want out of this chaos—maybe nothing. But I like this new feeling of being needed by and connected to people. Where I used to worry that things might go wrong because I knew how far the Chinese would go to save face, now I have become fearless: "Whatever the ending is, we citizens aren't afraid," I reply.

Yuan nods. "Lili makes a good point. This movement is a movement of citizens, not of intellectuals or students."

After lunch the three of us walk back to Tiananmen. I feel tired and weak. I realize that I have been living and working in the square for five days straight, with little sleep and no rest. I've been so focused that I have learned to ignore totally the miserable stench and the mess: tattered banners and clothing, broken glass bottles, old plastic wrappers, empty food packages, and leaflets are strewn all over the place.

Walking beside me, Roy notices how weak I am. He insists that I go to his hotel room and rest. But Yuan knows the trouble I would invite by staying in Roy's room, and he tells him, "You know, Chinese don't feel comfortable at fancy hotels."

"Then I'll drive Lili home," Roy says to Yuan. "She looks sick."

"I'm fine, really. I can take a bus home by myself. Actually, I'd rather do that," I say, with what little strength I have.

"Are you sure you can handle it by yourself?" Roy looks at me with concern.

"Sure." I nod and say good-bye to them.

The outbound bus is almost empty since most riders are heading downtown to participate in the grand demonstration. When I arrive at the apartment, my puppy, Liu Ying, welcomes me, licking my hands and face. I give her a kiss and rub her tummy. Our neighbors, a German couple, have been taking care of her. But Liu Ying seems starved for attention; the German couple must be in the square.

The puppy follows me, yapping happily. The Forbidden Nest is still quiet, remote—separated from the outside world. I can see the golden roofs of the Summer Palace from the dining room windows. After being with mobs of people for so many days, I find it a little strange to be by myself, with no one except Liu Ying for company.

I put some music on the stereo, take a shower, have a snack, unplug the phone line, and then fall asleep on the sofa.

I sleep from late afternoon all through the next day,

finally waking up in the evening. When I get up, I feel dizzy and nauseated; I rush to the bathroom and puke in the toilet. Liu Ying barks nervously.

I wobble from the bathroom back to the living room and sink onto the sofa, too weak to do anything else. Liu Ying fetches the remote control for the TV and brings it to me, a trick Roy taught her. I turn on the news.

The anchorman is making an announcement in a very serious voice. From his tone, I can tell that the news is important: "And during the period of martial law, demonstrations, petitions, class boycotts, strikes, and any other activities that would upset the city's normal routine are prohibited. Citizens are forbidden to create and spread rumors or instigate social turmoil in any way, by any means, including community meetings, public speeches, and leaflets. Furthermore, armed police and soldiers of the People's Liberation Army have the right to exercise any force necessary to stop or prevent any violation of these orders."

I switch to the other channels, trying to get more information. Every channel is broadcasting the same thing. I try to call Roy at the hotel, but there's no answer.

I turn off the TV, and the apartment becomes quiet again. It is dead silent. I feel cold, hungry, and helpless; my head hurts. Suddenly someone knocks on the door. The pounding sounds loud, rude. It makes me shiver. Liu Ying yelps fiercely. Roy's and my acquaintances always ring the doorbell. I open the door hesitantly.

Two stern-looking men, each carrying a briefcase, stand in front of me, one tall and big, the other short and wearing large black-framed glasses.

The taller one looks me over coldly from head to toe and

demands in an authoritative voice, "Are you Lili Lin? The daughter of De Lin and Hao Wen?"

I gulp and say, "Yeah," in a small voice. With growing caution, I begin a question, " Are you . . ." But I omit the rest: "some kind of security people?"

"We're from the Ministry of National Security. My name is Li Fong, and this is Wu Han. We have some questions to ask you." The two men show me their ID.

I feel like I'm in a detective movie and wonder if they think I'm one of the bad guys. But I'm not afraid.

I let them in and take a seat in my rocking chair, then begin rocking slowly back and forth. They both stand directly in front of me.

"Lili Lin, we're about to interrogate you. It's in your best interest to be completely honest and to cooperate fully. The Chinese legal system has always been reasonable toward those who cooperate and harsh toward those who don't. You understand us?"

I nod, but I don't really understand. What's is going on here? Am I so sick that I'm going crazy?

"What is your date of birth?" the tall one, Li Fong, demands.

"October nineteenth, nineteen-sixty."

"Where is your hometown?"

"Beijing."

"Where do you live?"

"Here."

"Where did you live before this place?"

"The third Dry Flower Alley, Building Six, Unit Five, Room Two, Western Town District, here in Beijing." As I answer, the shorter one, Wu Han, takes notes.

"Have you ever belonged to any organization or political party?"

"No."

"Have you ever been arrested, convicted, or confined in a prison?"

"Yes, I was in jail for a while," I answer dryly.

"Explain."

"What do you mean?" I shut my eyes.

"Why were you imprisoned?" Li Fong says, raising his voice slightly.

"Hooliganism."

"What did you do, exactly?"

"You can check my old file. All the details are there."

"We want to hear it from you."

I laugh. I can't help it. I just shut my eyes, not bothering to answer or look at them. I do it to save my energy. Shit! I'm sick. I need a rest.

They wait.

I continue my silence. I can hear the tick of the clock's second hand.

Seeing that I am not going to reply, Li Fong asks another question. "What's your occupation?"

After taking a long, deep breath, I open my eyes, stare at my interrogators, and say, "Unemployed."

The men sneer and look knowingly at each other. Then Wu Han whispers to Li Fong, asking for suggestions. They communicate with their eyes. "One of the unstable elements in the society?" Fong nods, and Han writes something down on his notepad. They have placed me in the worst political category.

"If you're unemployed"—Li Fong points at me with a long, fat finger—"how are you able to afford to live in such a luxurious villa as this"—he gestures, waving his arms in the air, and continues—"which, we understand, costs one thousand U.S. dollars a month?"

After finishing this question, Fong begins tapping his foot and cracking his knuckles, a smirk on his face.

He already knows everything about me, even how much the rent is. What does he want?

"Why do you want to know?"

Fong curls his lips into a sour smile. "Why do you ask why we want to know? Why don't you ask *yourself* what you have done?"

I shrug, thinking, Here they go, starting that old dance whose every step I know.

Li Fong begins to get irritated by my indifferent attitude. "What did I tell you when we first came in? The system is reasonable toward those who cooperate, but it's hard on those who resist. Look at you. Do you think you're cooperating with us? Do you want to be thrown in jail again?"

Oh, whatever, I think. A woman like me has nothing more to lose. Dead pigs aren't afraid of boiling water.

"Whom do you live with? What's his name?" Wu Han finally asks a question of his own, tapping his notebook with the end of his pen.

From his question, I suddenly realize that they don't really give a shit about me; they're here to get information about Roy.

"Luo-Yi." I say Roy's name in Chinese.

"Is he Chinese?"

"No."

"What's his nationality, then?"

"He told me that he's an American."

"What's his last name, then?"

"I don't know." I'm telling the truth: I don't remember, and I don't care.

"You live with a man and you don't even know his last name?" Li Fong clucks with disapproval.

"Nowadays girls are so easy," Wu Han adds, shaking his head.

"For your information, his last name is *Gou-Si-Ding*, in English, Goldstein." Fong pronounces the name in Chinese in such a way that it means "mongrel is doomed to die." Roy told me once that Chinese security people particularly hate American journalists, not only because of their highly critical articles but also for their extravagant lifestyle.

"Are the two of you married?"

"Not legally."

"Don't you know what illegal cohabitation means?"

"Yes." I nod without shame.

"Do you know that you can be sentenced to five years in prison for this disgusting misconduct?"

"Yes."

"Do you know that illegal cohabiting with a foreigner can make your case even worse?" Fong asks threateningly.

"Yes."

"OK, then we understand each other, right? We won't have to tell you again to cooperate, will we?"

I nod and think to myself, Nothing new in this game.

"OK, let's try it again. Tell us what he does."

"I don't know exactly."

"Then what the hell *do* you know?"

"Sometimes he take pictures, and he writes articles."

"Do you know that he writes articles denouncing your country and your government? Do you know that what he does has hurt the feelings of your Chinese compatriots and damaged the friendship between the peoples of China and the United States?" With this, Fong gestures to Han, who quickly pulls some American newspapers out of his briefcase.

Fong throws them on the tea table in front of me. It scares Liu Ying, and she barks wildly. I wave to tell her to calm down.

I glance briefly at the newspapers. One of the pages shows several pictures from China. I am in one of them, playing the erhu.

"I'm sorry, but I don't read English," I tell them.

"OK. Here's what it says. In this article you're depicted as a budding artist, not satisfied with the way our great nation is and unhappy about your so-called lack of artistic freedom. So you become 'a freelance musician who does not rely on the iron rice bowl.' Is that true? Are you that good? Are you a budding musician, or just a budding . . . ?"

Fong pauses and laughs sarcastically. "We went to your parents' school and interviewed your neighbors and acquaintances. We also checked your personal file. We know all about you. Confess to us right now about how you hooked up with that foreign devil."

"We want to know who started this hooliganism. Was it you or him?" Han demands.

Facing their suspicious eyes, I remain calm. I don't even feel dizzy anymore. Their interrogation has driven away my headache. If they're trying to humiliate me, they've chosen the wrong person.

Fong clearly isn't expecting me to be so calm. He thinks I'll be hurt and ashamed, and then I'll sob like a guilty schoolgirl. Then remorsefully confess to them. They don't know how I am.

"Say it! Who took the initiative?" Wu Han repeats his question impatiently.

"I don't remember." I look out the window, cool, calm, collected.

"How old are you, girl? Huh? I'm asking you how old you are."

"Twenty-eight." I continue looking out the window, watching the streetlights.

"Have you lost your mind at such an early age?" Fong sneers. "What a pity. How come you can't remember such an important thing? I bet it was unforgettable. You'd better just tell us the truth. Who initiated this illegal relationship between the two of you?"

I look at him. No words. No expression.

Han chimes in, "Say, if he took the initiative, did you resist his seduction at first? Or was he just too smooth for you?"

"No, not that I remember." I think to myself, Why should I have resisted?

"Why didn't you, Comrade Lin?" Fong looks completely serious and upset.

"Is the devil so good at screwing that you lost your class consciousness, or is it that you never *had* any class consciousness?" Han tries.

I ask, "What does my private life have to do with national security?"

"Of course it has to do with our security. Do you know that during World War Two, the German Nazis trained sex spies to seduce allies and discover their secrets? The Japanese did the same thing to our Chinese."

"How many times have you let the foreign devil lie on you? Aren't you ashamed of your unpatriotic behavior?"

Now Han is starting to sound angry, though he also seems rather curious about the details of my sex life.

Why is it patriotic for a Chinese man to sleep with a foreign woman and unpatriotic for a Chinese woman to sleep with a foreign man? What does sex have to do with patriotism? I remember the way Johnny's patriotic songs energized the huge crowd in the square. I think of how the patriotic slogans of the students—for example, "To Love the Motherland Is No Crime"—have mobilized Beijing citizens. Now, because I've had sex with a foreigner, I'm being branded unpatriotic. What the hell is fucking patriotism?

"How many times each week?" Han asks again, peeping at me through his glasses, his eyes looking like two small green beans.

"One more time than you fuck your wife," I answer, softly and calmly.

Han, infuriated, leans forward and points his finger at my face. "You disgusting bitch! How can you be so shameless? You like being fucked by foreign cocks, don't you? You think they are big, don't you? China is corrupted by foreigners' hookers like you. It's obvious that you didn't get enough reeducation the last time you were in prison."

I ignore his comments and demand, "I want to talk to Roy."

Fong snaps, "What makes you think that you can do whatever you want?"

"Do you know where he is?" I pay no attention to his question.

"He's on his way home to America by now."

I gasp. "What? What do you mean? How can that be?"

"Why don't you just go there and climb in his bed and

ask him?" Han says. Seeing me surprised, at last, they smile at each other triumphantly.

Fong explains: "OK, if you want to know what happened, the foreign devil seriously violated the Beijing Martial Law of the People's Republic of China, and we deported him yesterday."

"But he's no threat to China," I stutter, collapsing.

"He may be good in bed—I bet he knows all the tricks!—but look what he did to your compatriots," Han taunts.

Fong waves for Han to shut up and turns to me. Trying a completely different approach, he confides unctuously, "We're here today for your welfare, Lili. We're here to tell you that Luo-yi Gou-Si-Ding, Roy Goldstein, is a class enemy of our nation, and we want to help you get out of this dangerous relationship before it's too late. Gou-Si-Ding has consistently and maliciously demonized and insulted the Chinese people and the Chinese government. You should reject and have nothing more to do with this anti-Chinese devil. An insider should remain inside, and an outsider should remain outside.

"Although you have made mistakes, we welcome your correcting them and becoming a new person. You shouldn't hate us; we're here to help you. We represent your government, which loves you and cares about you. We could easily throw you into jail again, but we aren't going to do that. We understand that you're still young. You don't know how complicated the world is."

He walks around behind me and begins massaging my shoulders, lowering his voice and saying, "Beautiful young women like you are good targets for those vile foreigners, don't you know that?" His hands are fat caterpillars crawling on me. I feel like throwing up again.

"It's very easy for you to be cheated and taken advantage of, Comrade Lin. You should be cautious." Fong keeps caressing me from behind. Yeah, I think, I should be cautious of *you,* grabbing at me like that disgusting old Party secretary in Monkey Village.

"Stop grabbing me." I use the last of my strength to try to get his hands off me. At this moment I am thirsty, hungry, tired, dizzy, and most of all angry.

But Fong totally ignores my request, continuing, "We understand that now it seems fashionable to marry foreigners and go abroad. But many of these men are still our class enemies, and Gou-Si-Ding"—he snarls Roy's Chinese name—"is one of the worst of them. Always remember, insiders are insiders and outsiders are outsiders. No matter how nice they appear, they aren't your people."

I can't take it anymore. I feel hot vomit gushing up in my throat. I pry off his repulsive hand and rush to the bathroom with what little strength I have left. I begin to throw up all over the place. It seems that my whole body wants to spit out all of the filth that Fong and Han have brought into the Forbidden Nest.

I don't know when they leave, or what happens after; maybe I faint, or maybe I just fall asleep. And I don't know when Roy's colleague Jim arrives, but suddenly he's here to take care of me. He collects my stuff and drives me to the hospital.

"Lili, everything will be all right. You're ill. You've been working too hard and resting too little." I hear his voice faintly, but I'm too weak to reply or even open my eyes.

SEVENTEEN

I have a long sleep, a long dream. I open my eyes. I hear a female voice say, "She's awake!" It seems so far away, so familiar. It's Mama's voice, intense and with a trace of worry. I see her face and then, slowly, Papa's. They stand beside me, watching me; their eyes are bloodshot. I'm lying in a hospital bed. Before I can speak, a woman in a white nurse's uniform comes and takes a thermometer from my mouth. After looking at it, she says to my parents, "She's fine now."

I start to think back, hard: Tiananmen, hunger strikes, millions marching, my lunch with Roy and Yuan, feeling tired, going back home, Beijing under martial law, the security people's sudden appearance, the news of Roy's depor-

tation, the interrogation, Fong's nasty hands, my faint-
ing, Roy's friend Jim . . . and now here I am in the hospital.

"What happened to me?"

Before Mama can tell me, the nurse cuts in, "Well,
young woman comrade, you got pregnant, but you didn't
take care of yourself and your baby. You didn't get enough
rest or enough nourishment. Luckily you were brought
here in time; otherwise you could have lost the baby."

I can't believe it: Roy has disappeared, I have no place to
live, and now I have a baby in my womb! *Roy's* baby! I don't
know whether to laugh or cry.

That day in the countryside when Roy told me he
wanted to adopt the baby girl, I said, "I'm not a mother."
I'm not a virtuous, motherly woman like Little Liu's
mother, Iron Beauty. I don't know how to give love. I don't
know how to teach a child. I will not be a good mother.

I had two abortions in my teenage years; I didn't even
know who the fathers were. When Roy said he wanted a
family with me, I didn't want to talk about it. I felt that
sooner or later we would say good-bye and return to our
own old lives. But with this baby in my womb, I realize that
I can never return to my old life. Part of Roy is with me,
inside me.

I thank the nurse.

"Don't thank me," she says. "Thank your parents.
They've been taking care of you for three days straight.
Where is your husband? Is his work very demanding, or is
he in the square every day? He's come here only twice. You
should scold him."

Then she points to some flowers on the nightstand and

says, "Well, maybe he isn't that bad—at least he sent those, and he's handsome. Well, I've got to leave you now, I have others to take care of. Our hospital is packed."

I am totally confused by her words. My husband! Who is acting as my husband? Who's bringing me flowers like Roy used to? My husband! The fact is, I don't *have* a husband, nor do I expect to anytime soon. My baby won't have a father. He or she will be illegitimate and won't be able to get Beijing residency. The poor kid will have the same humiliating existence I have. A Chinese life.

After the nurse leaves, I'm alone with Mama and Papa. The white walls, the ceiling, the blankness. The room looks dull and pale. I feel like a sad bird in the wrong climate. Once again I have to depend on the help of my parents. They come when I'm in need, when I'm devastated.

I remember our last fight. I remember Mama's saying that she no longer had a daughter. I remember leaving their home full of determination, without a backward glance. But despite all that, here my parents are again, for me.

Mama is frowning at me. "You look thinner," she says, half in reprimand, half out of concern. She gently caresses my face, on the verge of tears now. Papa doesn't say anything, just tries to flash me a smile. Mama says to him, "Leave us alone for a while."

"Yes. Yes." Papa nods obediently. "I'll go get the evening paper." Then he smiles at me again and walks out the door. I watched his bony, slightly hunched back until it disappears.

I want to ask Mama why she always orders Papa around. Why can't she just step down a bit and treat him as her equal? But after Papa leaves, Mama bursts into tears and starts to scold me: "Why haven't we heard a single word from you? How could you be so cruel to us? We're old, and we don't have many years left. Your papa thinks of you every day. He has aged since you left. His hair has turned white."

Tears drip down quietly from my eyes, but I say nothing. My eyes automatically fix on Mama's stomach. Twenty-eight years ago I was inside there; now her grandchild is inside me. Mama was the one who always said, "A man lives for his face, and a tree lives for its bark. The most important thing for a woman is to keep a good reputation." For this belief, for years, she has sacrificed her relationships with her own mother and daughter. Will she be willing now to accept an unmarried mother-to-be and a half-breed, fatherless grandchild?

Looking at her salt-and-pepper hair, I want to tell her that I'm sorry, sorry for making her and Papa worry, but I just can't open my mouth. We aren't accustomed to saying "I'm sorry" to each other. Mama has never it sorry to Grandma. We all have the same stubbornness.

I try to change the subject. "Did you go to the square?" I ask.

"Yes." She clears her throat and dabs at her tears with a small handkerchief. "We marched there twice, with our students. In our classes the students talked about political issues instead of music. Every day your papa and I went and read the posters posted on campus."

"You did?" I can't hide the doubt in my voice. My parents are good citizens of Beijing: they're quiet and frugal, they obey the laws, and they take whatever shit is imposed on them. They don't even dare to confront their own daughter when she upsets and embarrasses them. But now they, too, protested in the square! "What made you decide to go?" I ask Mama, as if I were Roy interviewing a Chinese.

"We also want to see changes."

"Aren't you and Papa afraid of what the authorities might do to you?"

"Everyone is in the streets. Can the government punish all of the people? There're so many others like us, why should we be afraid? At the beginning, the students' actions did frighten us. Striking, rallying, displaying huge posters printed with revolutionary slogans—all that reminded us of the Red Guards in the Cultural Revolution. At first we were terrified that another Cultural Revolution was under way. But gradually we realized that the students weren't hurting anyone else—only sacrificing themselves, to make society better. Where the Red Guards hated us intellectuals, the students hate government corruption and unequal distribution. They want the government to raise intellectuals' salaries and provide better school facilities. So we're standing with them."

"What happened after martial law was declared?" I ask, again like Roy.

"Soldiers came, but nothing serious has happened. Don't worry."

I'm waiting for Mama to question me about what I've been doing and how I've spent my time. But she asks nothing. It's unnecessary for her, I guess: she has always anticipated the day when my life would turn upside down. She's known from the very beginning that I was headed straight for the gutter, and that sooner or later I'd get myself into trouble again.

I tell her about seeing Grandma and Cousin Johnny in the square.

Mama tells me that after I moved out, she took Uncle Yin and Aunt Sara to visit my grandma; that was the last time she saw her. Mama says, "That day she was just like she has always been. No words, no emotions. When your uncle Yin got down on his knees in front of her, all she said to us was *'Om mani padme hum.'* I suppose she doesn't want to have anything to do with her family anymore. But"—Mama pauses—"I'm not surprised to hear that she protested in the square. Everyone has his compassion, especially religious folk. When young people are close to death, no one can remain indifferent."

Mama tells me that Uncle Yin and Aunt Sara left China after the government declared martial law. "They think the current situation in China isn't stable, and it's not good for business," she explains.

"But Cousin Johnny performed for the hunger strikers in the square," I say.

Mama smiles at the mention of Johnny's name, but she doesn't comment on him. Instead she returns to the topic of Grandma, asking me about her health: "How does she look?" From her tone I can tell that she's still concerned about her.

I tell her jokingly that Grandma is healthy enough to be a great-grandmother.

Mama's smile fades, and she says, "You need to get some rest. I'll go buy some dinner for you." She pulls the quilt over me to keep me warm and pours some water into a glass for me.

That's Mama. She always refuses to talk about things that she doesn't want to get into. She'd rather be totally silent than talk something out. However beautiful and talented Mama used to be, however many dreams she once had,

Mama has never known happiness. She has an eccentric mother, a timid husband, and a wild daughter. None of us has met her expectations.

As Mama walks toward the door, I call out to her: "Mama!"

"What?" She looks back at me.

"Can I ask you something?"

"Yes. But can it wait till I get back?" Mama says, a bit impatiently.

"No."

"All right." She comes back and sits next to my bed. "What?" She opens her hands and waits.

"What does it feel like to be a mother?"

Mama lowers her eyes and says, "It's hard to describe." She thinks for a moment. "Let me tell you a story. When you were five, your papa and I took you to the North Sea Park. You were very naughty and almost fell into the lake, but your father was quick enough to catch you and save you. On the way home I asked your papa, 'If both Lili and I were in danger, and you could save only one of us, which would it be?' He said he was afraid he would have to choose you, and he asked me the same question."

"What did you say?"

"That I'd choose you, too."

"If someone asked you that now, would you change your answer?"

"No."

"Even knowing that your child had done all kinds of things to upset you?"

"I'd always choose to save my child."

"Why?"

"That's the feeling of being a mother. Your child is

part of you. You care about her as much as you care about yourself."

"But . . ." I want to ask her why she has never shown me any affection, why she makes me feel I have shamed her, but I check myself. Instead I inquire, "Was Grandma close to you when you were little?"

Mama looks out the window and shakes her head. "She was always playing mah-jongg or caught up in her own pain. I was raised by nannies. I've never been close to her. I was always afraid of her."

I feel the same way toward Mama that she felt toward *her* mother. How can I be a good mother?

"Did you hate Grandma?" I ask.

"Yes, I did—I hated her. I hated her family background. She didn't raise me, but her background destroyed me!"

"Is that why you slapped her during the Cultural Revolution?"

She sighs, closes her eyes, and pinches the middle point between her eyebrows. She starts slowly, "Well, you see, I know there's no excuse for what I did. I slapped her because I wanted to protect you and your father. I thought if I drew a clear line between her and me, then my own daughter would not be looked down on. I thought it would keep you from being harassed like I was. And I thought the Red Guards would stop beating your papa."

Mama looks at me solemnly. "The teenage Red Guards were beasts. They beat your papa so badly that he became impotent for several years. He grew quieter after that. I guess I'm neither a good daughter nor a good wife and mother."

"Don't go, please."

"What else do you want to know?"

I bite my lower lip and pause. At last I decide to ask it anyway. "Is Papa my biological father?"

"What? What are you talking about?" She stares at me, annoyed.

"I don't look like him at all."

"You're talking nonsense."

"Tell me the truth, Mama, please."

"Of course he's your biological father. Your papa is my only husband and your only father. How dare you have these thoughts?"

"Do you love him?"

"Why are you talking such nonsense? I think you need some rest."

"Don't go, Mama. I want to know."

"I don't understand you. What are you trying to get out of me? We've been married for more than thirty years and we have you. We're an old couple."

"Did you have boyfriends before Papa?"

"Is that relevant?"

"Yes."

"Why do you care?"

"Tell me if you had boyfriends before, and tell me why you chose him."

Mama studies me for a second or two with surprise in her eyes, and then her gaze passes me and stops elsewhere. She shakes her head impatiently, not looking at me. "Why do you bring this up? What's the point? It's all in the past now. You're tired; better not to talk or think too much."

But I insist, "Mama, I simply want to know."

"You really want to know? You really want to know?"

I nod again and again.

She gives up and starts. "Yes, I had a boyfriend before your father."

"In college?"

"In college. But it didn't work out," she adds.

"Why?"

"His parents didn't want him to marry me, and he was a good son."

"Why didn't they approve of the marriage?"

"Isn't it as clear as a louse on a bald head? Because of your grandma's political background and lifestyle. Who would want to marry a woman like me?"

"Tell me more about the man."

"He studied composition and conducting. We were the two best students in the school. The only difference was that his parents were peasants, and mine were capitalists."

"What does he do now? Where is he?"

Mama sighs and admits, "He's the president of our college."

The president of the conservatory! Everybody knows him. He is a Party veteran, a senior composer—and good-looking, too. Every time his Red Flag car passes by proudly, people in my parents' compound gossip about him. They talk about how lucky his ordinary-looking wife is to have such a good man, how many bedrooms their apartment has, how well their children are doing at their American universities. The man has status, fame, and everything else Mama has always wanted but can never get. I finally understand why she's so unhappy, so dissatisfied. If Papa hadn't married her, what would he be like today? If Mama had been born into a peasant family, would she be the president's wife now? I wonder.

"So in the end you chose Papa?"

"Your papa was an orphan. His mother and father both passed away when he was young. So though he was poor, he had no parents to disapprove of me."

"Do you love him?"

"This sickness has turned you into a fool! Why do you keep asking that stupid question? As I say, we're husband and wife. We've been together for more than thirty years." Mama sounds irritated.

She finally leaves. I am all by myself—fatigued, feeble, and disconnected from the outside world.

Despite all the outrageous things I've done, she and Papa continue to bail me out every time I fuck up. What makes them give a damn?

As I lie on my bed with my baby in my womb, feeling remorseful, there's a knock on the door.

It's Roy's colleague Jim.

"I have a letter here from Roy." Waving an envelope that has U.S. stamps on its upper right corner, he takes a seat next to my bed.

"How is he? Have you talked to him?"

"Yes, I have." Jim nods. "He's very frustrated. You know, among all of us American journalists, he's the one who loves China and cares for her people the most. It's hard for him to accept that he can't come back here for five years. But other than that, he's fine." Jim jiggles his legs as he speaks. His Chinese is colored by a very heavy American accent, but he talks fast.

"Are you getting better now?" he asks.

"I'm fine. It's nothing serious, really."

"Good." He glances at his watch. "So what's your plan?"

"I don't know."

He nods and looks at his watch again. "Lili, I've got to go. I have a deadline to meet. The situation in Tiananmen is getting intense, and I have to get back. Call me if you need any help." He stands up quickly and shakes my hand.

"Are the flowers from you?" I ask him.

"Oh, yes."

"Thanks."

"No problem."

"Please don't tell Roy I'm pregnant," I request.

"But why?" He frowns, pulling his hand slowly from mine.

I don't know how to explain my feelings. I don't respond.

Jim says, "Do you mind my asking you a question?"

"No, I guess not."

"He's the father of your child, isn't he?"

I nod yes. His question doesn't insult or upset me.

"Then he has a right to know." He emphasizes the word *right*. An American word.

"Well, at least don't tell him now. I need some time."

"I don't understand, but OK—I won't say anything."

"Promise me!"

Jim reluctantly says, "I promise," then adds, "I think it would be a good idea for you to leave the country as soon as you can."

He's made this visit out of courtesy and obligation, I can tell. Jim always used to complain that Roy was too attached to his subjects and to his writing, that he was too emotional. Roy said Jim found China dirty and chaotic and saw Chinese women as gold-diggers and easy; he never bothered to learn to speak good Chinese or to make any Chinese friends. Likewise, he preferred Kentucky Fried Chicken to Beijing duck. Nonetheless, I am still grateful to him.

Roy's letter lies in my hand, light and warm; the Chinese characters on the envelope look like lovely chicken scratches. I sit up and lean against my pillow, open the letter and start to read. It's written in Chinese characters and *pinyin*, phonetic symbols.

Lili, my darling,

I'm so sorry that I didn't even get to kiss you good-bye. I'm here on another continent, thinking of you constantly. Tell me why—why are people like me, who care so much for China, kicked out? It seems to me that no matter how hard I try to learn about Chinese culture, I can never completely understand Chinese logic.

I can imagine how difficult it must be for you. I hope you're with your parents now. Don't be distant from them. They love you and care about you. One of the greatest beauties of Asian culture is its strong commitment to family. Tell them that you love them, Lili. Try it, at least once.

I'm back home in California. Everything is the same—the house my parents left me, the food, the streets, the highways, even the corner grocery store. I'm the only thing that's changed. I feel like a foreigner in my own land. Something important is missing. Just think, on the other side of the globe students are demonstrating for democracy and being confronted by armed PLA soldiers, and here I am, sitting in my comfortable living room, surfing the TV channels! But what the hell, at least I can enjoy the free flow of information and see what's going on in China on TV!

I've been asked to give interviews about why I was

deported. The media want me to predict what will happen in China. For now, I've said no; I need to sit down and gather my thoughts about it all.

This morning I mowed the lawn and fixed the roof—a lot of work. This is a big house compared to the Forbidden Nest. Standing under a palm tree, working in my backyard, I kept asking myself, Where's Lili? She's supposed to be right here with me.

Lili, Jim tells me you've been sick. I'm very worried about you. You worked too hard to help the hunger strikers. I'm proud of you for getting involved in the movement. Not only do you have a lovely face and body, you also have a good heart and a beautiful soul! I know it—I've known it since the first time we met.

Lili, I can't live without you, just like I can't live in the United States without thinking of China. Remember how, in our first conversation, I told you that I'd come to China to seek a yin and yang balance, to discover the Eastern side of myself? Well, I found you, sweetheart. You're my Eastern side. You know it as well as I do, don't you?

Sweetie, why don't you come to the States? I want you to be my wife. We can have a Chinese wedding and a Jewish wedding. I want us to be a family and to have children. Our children will speak both Chinese and English perfectly. You can teach them to play the erhu, and I can teach them to play the trumpet. They'll have the freedom to travel back and forth between China and the United States. Say yes, Lili, please.

Oh Lili, my love, every morning when I wake up and every night before I go to bed, I think of your sadness. You know, sometimes you look sad. You once told me that you didn't let things worry you, but somehow I feel that your sadness has something to do with the lack of space in your culture. You *don't have space enough to breathe the air that will allow your spirit to grow. I sense this so profoundly—that something in your culture deeply troubles you, even though you have never admitted it. You just continue to fight in your own way.*

Sometimes you pretend not to care, but I know you really do. Sometimes you say you have no opinions, but I know you have many. I know you have the desire to explore more of the world. You have experienced so much sadness in your life (what you have told me is probably just the tip of the iceberg). It's time for you to make a change; to finally have joy and happiness. I remember how much you loved the Beach Boys' song "California Dreamin'," so popular in every karaoke bar in Beijing. Haven't you ever thought of visiting California? Our California sunshine and nice beaches will recharge you, free you, and cheer you. You deserve to have a peaceful, normal, healthy life filled with love. California extends her warm arms to welcome you.

I know I've argued that Chinese should stay in China to change their country. I still believe that. But because I can't be there with you, I'm asking you to come to here to join me. We'll never put China behind us; we can do a lot of work here to help bring democracy to your country.

I want to end this letter with my endless love for you. I wish I could tell you face-to-face how very much I love you, and love our wondrous China. Lili, I will love you until I die. Even my ashes will love you after I die. I'm right here waiting for you, Lili. Please come soon! I'm anxious to hear from you.

Yours always,

Roy

The letter makes me realize that in all my twenty-eight years of life, I have never before been respected. At the same time I myself have refused to respect anyone—my parents, my neighbors, even myself. A country of courtesy, that is how the Chinese describe China, but Chinese life is full of disrespect and humiliation.

This American man, with his penetrating eyes, his insight, and his generous *love* and respect, has become the person closest to me in the world. I carefully fold the letter and put it under my pillow. I lie down and shut my eyes. Roy's magnifying face is all over me. I will keep his baby, and I will be a mother, I'm determined this time. "From now on I won't let you down. I promise," I swear to him quietly.

Amei comes to visit. I have not seen her since the death of Hu Yaobang. She looks fresh, young, and high-spirited; she wears her hair in braids like an American Indian's in a Hollywood movie, a long skirt in a sunflower pattern, and stylish colored string sandals. She presents me with two bags of fruit and a bunch of flowers. She brings the wonderful outdoor summer into this plain and sterile ward.

Amei hugs me. "They told me everything," she says. Her voice is soothing; an old friend is an old friend. "It'll be OK. Everything will be OK." She sits on the edge of my bed with her arm around me, patting my shoulder to comfort me.

I look at her and say, "Do you know I'm pregnant?"

"Yes, I heard that, too."

"You have ears everywhere."

"I'm well informed. Are you planning to keep the baby?" Amei asks, stating to peel an apple for me.

"Yes." I nod.

"You've decided to be a mother?"

"Yes," I say, twirling my hair with my right forefinger.

"I'm surprised."

"Read this." I hand her Roy's letter.

When Amei has finished reading, she looks at me. "You really love him, don't you?"

"Amei, please don't use that big word. My vocabulary isn't sophisticated enough for me to understand it. All I know is that he doesn't treat me like a female monkey; he treats me like a woman. I want to be a woman, a woman who can give birth to his child."

"You should marry him and leave China as soon as possible."

"I don't want to do that."

"No one knows what we're going to get out of this movement. Maybe bloodshed, maybe civil war, maybe years of suppression. You never know."

"Are things so bad that people are trying to get out?" I ask.

"It's a stalemate. People are confused; soldiers are everywhere. Who knows what's going to happen? Have you heard anything from your friend Yuan?"

"No, why? What's happened to him?"

"He disappeared all of a sudden. He may be in jail or under house arrest. No one knows."

"I don't want to leave China," I say to Amei.

"It's not a matter of what *you* want; it's a matter of what's best for the baby. A child needs a father and an entire family. You should think of your baby's future."

I insist, "I want my baby to be born and grow up under the Chinese sky. Not in a life of exile."

Instead of answering me, Amei asks, "Why have our Chinese people tried for a hundred and fifty years to leave

China? Huh? Why? Can you give the baby a better future than Roy can? Maybe you can endure the shame of being an unmarried single mother, but do you really want your baby to suffer the humiliation that will entail? He or she will be labeled a half-breed and a bastard, won't have Beijing residency, and won't be allowed to go to high school here. Your child's life will be worse than yours was!"

"So what? The humiliation will teach him or her to fight back. Hardship makes children tough and strong."

"A baby needs a father as well as a mother."

"Do you think we'd be an entire family in America? No, Amei. I know it; I know too well that the story of Roy and me can happen only in the setting of China. Anywhere else it would die."

"How can you say that after reading Roy's letter? This man wants you to be his wife. He wants to start a family with you."

"But I don't want to be his wife in California."

"What *do* you want? To be an unemployed single mother, raising your child here?"

"Maybe." I nod, chewing on my lower lip.

"You don't feel secure about his love for you." Amei shakes her head, looking at me with a piercing gaze.

"Who do you think I am, Amei? Look at me. I'm unemployed, uncultured, and uneducated. Why should I go abroad? I'm a failure even in my own country. Look at those students in Tiananmen: they know the values of the West, and they speak English. It makes sense for them to go to America, but not me."

"Lili, can't you just stop? I'm sick and tired of your self-contempt. Why do you always play the victim? Why do you act like everyone owes you something? *Everybody* is a victim. You aren't the only one who feels pain. Come on; wake up and grow up. Why are you always so negative about yourself? You can pursue happiness if you want. You're entitled to have happiness, just like anyone else."

I'm entitled to happiness? Ha! Amei sounds like one of those self-appointed lecturers in the square, talking about rights and entitlement. I retort, "I feel contempt for myself, and I'm not a victim. Nobody owes me anything. And don't flatter me: I don't *have* any pain. I'm not that *deep*!"

"Stop lying to yourself. Roy sees through you. I see through you. And so do your parents."

"Well," I say stubbornly, "I have no desire to go elsewhere, and I want my baby to be born in China."

"Why? Who told me before that she wanted to live in a open space without so many nosy, prying people? Who said she wanted to be independent from her parents? Who said she had some small dreams that she wanted to fulfill?"

"Well, I do. But so what?"

"If you go to America, you can make those small dreams come true. Don't you know why so many Chinese women dream of emigrating there? Don't you know why so many high-ranking officials want their grandchildren to be born there? America's an escape from the chains of China's old system. Lili, you're dying for a change, aren't you? Otherwise you wouldn't have been so enthusiastic about staying in that dirty, filthy square, would you? You were there to fight for your small dreams.

"In America you can have a completely new beginning. You can live with a nice man who loves you and doesn't judge you: you can raise children together in clean air, in your very own home; you can study English, play music, learn to drive and have your own car, travel freely wherever you want without worrying about government officials, and say whatever you want to say. You're still young and beautiful. You deserve a better life."

With the fervor of Tiananmen, everybody has become eloquent. Even the quiet ones like Amei. Yes, I long for a change, but can the California sunshine burn away the darkness in my heart? Will I be able to lead a healthy and normal life there as Roy's wife? What the hell is the meaning of a wife anyway? America is a dream, but it's probably for the dreamers. And China, what about China? What about those students in Tiananmen? If they choose to stay here, why should I escape?

"China is my *home*," I say.

"This isn't just about China or the United States. We're talking about love."

"Not that word, please."

"I want to use that word. I love to use the word *love;* you can't stop me. Lili, I've told you before, love is about trust. I know you love Roy. Don't deny it anymore. You should join him. Trust him and trust yourself, for once."

"Am I trustworthy?"

"Of course you are. You're very loyal."

"But I betrayed Little Rock, I betrayed Jun, I betrayed my parents. I don't want to be a traitor anymore."

"Lili, love is about trust, but that doesn't mean no one ever gets hurt. You'll get hurt again, and those who love you will get hurt again. But don't dodge love anymore."

I touch my stomach and wish my baby could tell me whether he or she wants an American life or a Chinese one.

When my parents come back with the takeout they have bought for me, Amei greets them, then leans over and kisses me good-bye lightly on the cheek.

By the next morning I'm ready to go home. My parents come early to help me pack. For the first time in many years I say thank you to them. I also thank the doctors and the nurses in the hospital.

When Jim comes to pick us up, the nurses say I am a lucky woman to be married to a man with a white Cadillac. One nurse tells Mama that my baby should be born in this same hospital, saying the staff would like to see a mixed-race infant. "Mixed kids are all good-looking and smart," she confides.

Jim doesn't bother to set the nurses straight, nor do my parents. We wave good-bye and get into the Cadillac. I ask Jim if he'll take us to see Tiananmen Square. He drives very slowly through a corridor of human beings. We pass military trucks packed with soldiers who wear helmets and carry guns. The vehicles are blocked by citizens, some of whom are lying down in front of their wheels. Others offer the young soldiers fruit and cucumbers and try to talk to them. But the soldiers just lower their heads, making no response. They look tired.

Jim tells me, "Once Gorbachev left, the soldiers came to enforce martial law, but the Goddess of Democracy had already been born." He suggests that my parents and I go have a look at the Goddess in the square before the military gets rid of her.

He parks his Cadillac behind the Noon Gate, inside the Gate of Heavenly Peace, and we all walk to the square together. It's dirtier than before. Groups of students still occupy the core of the square, around the Monument to the People's Heroes. From the back we can see the Goddess of Democracy standing in the center of the vast space, holding her torch in a faceoff with Chairman Mao.

The statue is surrounded by people. They are admiring her, taking pictures of her, or just plain staring at her— a strange thing for the Chinese. When we get close, Jim volunteers to take a picture of my parents and me with the Goddess in the background. The three of us stand together, me in the middle, right in front of my parents— the same pose we struck many years ago, not far from here. This is the first time in fifteen years that we have had our picture taken together.

After the picture-taking, we walk around. By now many of the students in the area are from outside Beijing; their camps are identified by banners bearing the names of their universities. The hunger strike ended before the declaration of martial law. Now the demonstration is confined to sit-ins and be-ins.

The square reeks, and there are piles of filth, rotten food, plastic and glass containers, and all types of trash everywhere. Little children pee freely on the ground. But despite the foul smell, the square is still magical. Once you're there, you don't want to leave. You feel a desire either to witness things or to be a part of them. Gossips run about, spreading the latest rumors. They say that Beijing's jails have been emptied in preparation for mass arrests. The Flying Tigers, a group of motorcyclists, drive through the square reporting to the students the troops' whereabouts. Foreign TV crews interview people and broadcast their comments right on the spot.

I am still weak, and my parents suggest that we leave. As we head back to Jim's white car, we see military helicopters whirling over Tiananmen.

Once again I am living with my parents in their small, familiar apartment. It's awkward because we've hurt each other so much. But we are trying to talk, though not about my unborn baby, not about Roy, not about whether passionate love fades over time, not about us—instead, we spend most of our time together sharing opinions and information about the political situation. The progress and the uncertainty of the movement excite and animate us. We check the conservatory's bulletin board and read big-charactered newspapers together. Tiananmen has become our common ground, a connection among the three of us.

The neighbors are a bit surprised to see me. They all thought I had gone abroad. But they don't bother us; they have lost interest in me. They, too, have their new priority, the movement. They are too busy listening to the Voice of America to wonder about me. Sometimes they knock on our door, and we all listen to the Voice of America or the BBC together.

One day I go to the bulletin board myself to check the news. A newly posted item catches my attention. Although the author hasn't signed his name, I recognize my father's handwriting.

Intellectuals and Osteomalacia: An Old Teacher's Proclamation

I'm a small man, not a Party member, just an old music teacher. I don't raise my voice when I speak to my students, and I don't make trouble. But today I want to howl, and I

want everyone to hear me: "I can't keep silent as a lamb
anymore!" The scholar Wen Yiduo says we either die in the
silence or explode in the silence. I want to explode!

I don't know when it started, maybe a long time ago, but
since the feudal times we intellectuals have been hated and
mistrusted by the country's rulers. Our physical bodies have
been tortured, our honor has been insulted, our talents have
been manipulated, and our integrity has been doubted. For
thousands of years we have been no more than an appendage
to society. To survive we have bent our backs as if we had
osteomalacia, a softening of the bones—kowtowing like slaves.

In past movements, including the Antirighteous Movement,
the Cultural Revolution, and the Anti–Spiritual Pollution
Campaign, we intellectuals were always the targets and
enemies. This student democracy movement is for us. It's our
chance to end our kowtowing and stand up! My fellow
intellectuals, stand up for yourselves and for China, stand up
in front of armed soldiers!

A professor
An intellectual
A small man

I don't know how many times I read the proclamation. It
says so much about Papa and his sense of defeat. He always
followed rules and taught me to follow them, even after he
himself became the victim of those fucking rules. He
worked damned hard to build up socialism but got nothing
in return. Still, he never complained. Mama calls him stupid and stubborn. When he was young, he must have been
an idealistic, romantic intellectual, something like Roy, but
he was flattened, his idealism was castrated over the years.

This political movement has awakened him. He vents his dissatisfaction and anger in this proclamation. But can a silent lamb howl?

At home, Papa is cooking. Mama isn't home yet.

"Can I help you, Papa?" I ask.

"If you like. I'm making dumplings." He's wearing his apron, making wraps, the same him.

I help him cut vegetables. "Papa?"

"Yes?"

"Can I ask you something?"

"Sure."

"Do you want to be a Party member?"

"No."

"Why?"

"I'm not interested in politics."

"Do you think politics are dirty?"

"No. But I just want to be a teacher, nothing more."

"But you know that Party members have power, right?"

"I'm not interested in power."

"Mama wanted to be a Party member badly when she was young, didn't she?"

"Yes, she wanted to devote her life to communism."

"Papa?"

"Yes?"

"What do you like about Mama?"

Papa smiles shyly. "Her energy. She's always alive."

"Are you afraid of Mama?"

"She's my wife. Why would I be afraid of my wife?" Papa says, looking at me as if he didn't understand my question.

"You never say no to her."

"Well"—Papa raises one eyebrow—"we always have the same opinions. So why should I say no to her?"

"You yield to her. Why?"

"Lili, unlike you, your mother grew up without a father. Although we're the same age, to her I'm not only a husband but a father figure."

"If you're not afraid of her, what *are* you afraid of?"

Papa narrows his eyes behind his glasses and thinks for a second or two. "Any danger to my family."

"What do you mean?"

"Lili, your papa grew up an orphan. My parents died in an accident when your uncle Hua and I were young. Over the years, especially during the Cultural Revolution, I've seen so many families broken up and so many innocent people killed. My greatest wish is that everyone in our family be safe." His voice is low and soft.

"Papa, why don't you ever raise your voice when you speak?"

"I'm not a tenor like Pavarotti, I'm an instrumentalist. I don't have to raise my voice."

"But *can* you speak in a louder voice?"

"I'm a small man with a small voice." He smiles.

"Papa, does the movement excite you?" I ask, but then I realize the answer is obvious.

"It's our opportunity to speak up."

"You mean the intellectuals?"

"Yes, and other citizens, too."

"Will it win?"

"It's already won! It's won the heart of everyone!"

That evening my parents and I have a good dinner. The dumplings are tasty. After dinner we play violin together.

Nobody mentions anything about the poster pinned on the school's bulletin board.

On the night of June 3, the neighbors in the compound, young and old, men and women, gather in the courtyard to share news of Tiananmen. Troops are moving downtown, and tanks are rolling in to clear out the square. The community leaders try to come up a plan to help the students. They are afraid that the troops may throw smoke bombs at the crowd. The women start to prepare damp towels; the men are to give them to the demonstrators to use against the smoke bombs. Many go out to set up barricades to stop the military vehicles. They take along their quilts because somebody says these can screw up the tanks' caterpillar tracks.

I listen to the radio at home. The anchorman's voice is stern: "Martial law units will take all necessary measures. Those who incite opposition must suffer the consequences." The radio also repeatedly warns people not to go out on the streets; those who do will "bear the responsibility for their own fates."

I really want to go to the square, but Mama and Papa plead with me to stay home, for the sake of their unborn grandchild if not for myself. "You're our only daughter, and your child will be our only grandchild. How can we survive without the two of you? You can't take any risks, I beg you!" She has never spoken to me this way before. She used to always command Papa and me at home. But now she's tender, like a mother.

Someone is knocking on the door. Little China and Chou-Chou, from the old gang, drop by. They're wearing headbands, and their pockets are filled with rocks. They tell us that the troops are starting to fire real bullets at citizens. "Fuck, those bastards have gone crazy! We Beijingers have to protect those kids in the square!"

When my parents go into the kitchen to make tea for all of us, Chou-Chou tells me that some of the old gang have formed a dare-to-die squad, with Spring Ocean as their leader.

"Spring Ocean?" I'm surprised.

"He was released from jail last week. You've got to see him, he's much older now," says Chou-Chou.

Little China puts in, "We have steel sticks, clubs, and incendiary bombs made out of beer bottles."

"But the students wanted this to be a nonviolent movement," I say, thinking of what Roy explained to me.

Chou-Chou says impatiently, "Fuck! Don't you know that the soldiers are armed with tanks, assault rifles, and machine guns?"

Little China adds, "We have seen with our own eyes students being gunned down!"

Steel sticks, clubs, and incendiary bombs can't compete with machine guns. I know I have to go to Tiananmen. I belonged to the gang once; this time the gang is greater. I tell Chou-Chou to meet me at Mu Xudi, near the square. He and Little China leave.

I sneak out while my parents are washing up. Carrying my weapons—Papa's Seagull camera and Panda tape recorder—I jump on my Flying Dove bicycle. I pass student propaganda buses. The blare from the buses' loudspeakers urges the workers and citizens of Beijing to go to the square, where "the democracy movement has reached a critical moment. Students and their supporters are in danger. We call on the workers and citizens to go out. Go to Tiananmen Square to uphold justice! To defend our square!" I see people on their way there on foot, on bikes.

"Lili, my child," someone is calling my name. A man is riding his bike beside me. In the dim light from the street, I can't see his face clearly, only his glasses reflecting the streetlights. But I recognize the voice. It's my father.

I'm surprised, but I say to him immediately and firmly, "I'm not going back home with you!"

"I'm not asking you to."

"Why have you come, then? Go home!"

"I'm going to Tiananmen with you."

"What?"

"I want to protect my child and grandchild, and the children and grandchildren of other parents."

"Papa—"

"You can't stop me. Nothing can stop me tonight!" Papa sounds determined. I have never understood him. I used to think he was, like many Chinese intellectuals, servile and gutless. He was beaten into impotence for years and forced to do hard labor in the countryside during the last political upheaval. He has suffered, but his passion isn't dead.

He is the same soft-spoken, short, and timid Papa, but now he is standing up for himself and for China.

"Let us three generations go to the square together!" Papa cries.

"Yes, three generations!"

I become more and more excited, fearless, just as I was when I was in those gang fights so long ago. The air is filled with gunpowder. Bombs explode in the dark sky like beautiful firecrackers. It's almost hypnotic. I think of my endless days of playing musical instruments, the wolves that followed me that starry night, Little Rock's scars and wolf eyes, Grandma's flute piece, Domestic Love's curse at Republican Village, Cousin Johnny's tears when he sang for the students, Math's retarded mother, the little feet of the dead baby girl, the chanting in White Cloud Temple, Mama's words to me in the hospital, and Roy's glittering eyes. I am pedaling ahead in a nameless, timeless, ageless city. A city of revelation.

As I move forward, I feel Roy in me. I start to think as he would and to look around with his eyes. I have to participate; I have to find the truth; I have to document it; I have to bear witness.

When my father and I get to Mu Xudi, we see soldiers in helmets sitting on the ground, holding guns. Citizens are condemning them to their faces: "How dare you turn your guns against your own people? Where are your hearts and your consciences?" The soldiers listen silently.

Some citizens are throwing small rocks at the soldiers. Although their targets are wearing helmets, some may get hit, I think.

I look for Chou-Chou and the others. Suddenly a big whistle sounds. The soldiers stand up. They start to shoot.

"They're firing their guns!"

"Fascists!"

"I've been shot!"

Screams sound here and there. People flood back. Some tough ones throw rocks and glass bottles at the soldiers. Papa urges me to pedal away as fast as I can. He's pedaling close behind me.

The gunfire eases. I look around for my old gang members, but it's too dark to recognize anyone. People are running around like ghosts. In front of me someone is pedaling a tricycle with a flatbed. On the flatbed is a wounded man.

"Hi! Can I help?" I catch up with the driver and ask.

He turns around—it's Little China!

"Lili," Little China cries out, "I'm glad to see you're still alive! Brother Spring Ocean has been shot!" He points at the man lying on the flatbed, his shirt soaked with blood.

"Spring Ocean!" I scream, abandoning my bike and jumping onto the flatbed.

Still pedaling, Little China cries, "He was hit by a bullet aftre we threw rocks at those bastards. Fuck, why didn't the bullet hit me instead? Our brother just got out of prison!"

Spring Ocean's eyes are closed; I hardly recognize him. He used to be such a handsome, attractive boy, but now his face is wrinkled, his hair salt-and-pepper, his body puffy. Life in jail has turned him into a middle-aged man! I take off my jacket and use it to cover his chest; there's a small hole there that's gushing blood. Spring Ocean extends his hand, searching for me, and I grab it.

"Lili, is that you?" he speaks weakly.

"Yes. I'm here beside you."

"Long time no see."

"Please don't talk, just save your energy."

"I want to talk. I'm going to die, aren't I?"

"No. We're taking you to a hospital. You'll be fine."

"Lili, you don't know how much I missed you when I was in jail."

"I know."

"You know, all men want to be heroes."

"Yes." I place my free hand on his chest and feel warm

blood run over it. My other hand is gripping his, cold and weak now.

Papa is pedaling along beside the flatbed still.

"You know what?" Spring Ocean says. "Little Rock died like a man, a hero. I want to die like him, die like a hero. I thought I could be a hero tonight, but I was shot so soon, before I could do anything. . . ."

"You're *my* hero tonight! I'm here with my hero!" Tears blur my vision, and I can't see him clearly.

"Lili." His voice is getting weaker and weaker. I lay my face on his chest like I used to, my face now stained with tears and blood.

"Lili, don't cry. It's my retribution."

"Spring Ocean, you'll be fine! You'll be fine!"

"Lili, I'm not a good man. Will you forgive me?"

"I forgive you! Spring Ocean, I forgive you!" I shout, but he can no longer hear me.

I survived the crackdown.

My life changed forever the night tanks rolled into my hometown.

The Lili of Beijing died that night, but a new Lili was born somewhere else. Somewhere where freedom and respect blossom.

ACKNOWLEDGMENTS

I never realised how beautiful, sexy and difficult English was until I started to write *Lili*. From age 16 to 26, it took me ten years to finish it. *Lili* to me is a manifestation of my youthful rebellion. It records the growth in my understanding of humanity, politics, culture (both Chinese and Western) and the English language. Writing *Lili* was a lonely, painstaking, sometimes abusive process. I suffered from two years of depression, perhaps due to the forced recollection of the undeniable memories associated with tragedy and the hopeless obsession with metaphysics. But it was also a hilarious experience. It is while writing *Lili* that I learned how much love, compassion, pride and confidence my friends (so many good friends all over the world) and my family have had in me. Without their encouragement and support, the task of writing *Lili* in English would have been impossible. I am also grateful to my agent, editors and those who show so much enthusiasm for *Lili*. I look back and want to bow to everyone. You have done me proud, making me feel spoiled as a writer, strong as a woman, lucky as a free thinker.